The Life We Almost Had

LAURA MILLER

This book is a work of fiction. Names, characters, businesses, places and incidents are the product of the author's imagination or are used fictitiously. Any resemblance to actual events, locales or persons, living or dead, is coincidental.

Copyright © 2017 by Laura Miller.

LauraMillerBooks.com
The Life We Almost Had

All rights reserved. Except as permitted under the U.S. Copyright Act of 1976, no part of this publication may be reproduced, distributed or transmitted in any form or by any means or stored in a database or retrieval system.

ISBN-13: 978-1544651279
ISBN-10: 1544651279

Printed in the United States of America.

Cover design by Laura Miller.
Cover photo, title page photo (rose petals) © janonkas.
Second title page photo; quote pages photo; contents page photo; chapter headings photo; dedication page photo; and acknowledgments page photo (jar) © derbisheva.
The End page photo, quote page photo (flower) © okalinichenko.
Flower photo design by Laura Miller.
Author photo © Neville Miller.

*To the Keeper of our days,
For a love that lasts a lifetime.*

*And to my mom,
For teaching me to dream.*

Thank you, Mom.

*And to my dad,
Who taught me how to drive a tractor, fix the sink, cut wood and change the oil. And for everything else, there's duct tape.*

Thank you, Dad.

CONTENTS

Prologue 1
Chapter One: Just Promise Me 6
Chapter Two: The Color of Rain 11
Chapter Three: I Didn't 17
Chapter Four: Did You See? 32
Chapter Five: Miss America 39
Chapter Six: Does She Know? 54
Chapter Seven: Berlin's the Boy 62
Chapter Eight: You 68
Chapter Nine: Don't Call Me Baby 74
Chapter Ten: It's the Long Hair 105
Chapter Eleven: That First Cut 114
Chapter Twelve: Angel's Tree House 125
Chapter Thirteen: Like the Boy 130
Chapter Fourteen: He's Wrong 143
Chapter Fifteen: Your Place 152
Chapter Sixteen: One Hundred 165
Chapter Seventeen: Stay Broken 171
Chapter Eighteen: I Can Do This 180
Chapter Nineteen: You're Home 189
Chapter Twenty: I Saw Your Name 208
Chapter Twenty-One: So Lucky 220
Chapter Twenty-Two: You Need to Go 227
Chapter Twenty-Three: The Time in Between 236
Chapter Twenty-Four: You Have a Tattoo 244
Chapter Twenty-Five: Did You Love Her? 254
Chapter Twenty-Six: Saturday 262
Epilogue 268

I take her in.
She is the breath, warming my soul.
I taste her on my lips.
She is the salt, consuming my tears.
I feel her in my bones.
She is the ache my heart craves.
I repeat her name.
Hers is the name forever on my tongue.

She began as a dream.

She ended at sunrise.

The Life We Almost Had

LAURA MILLER

*When our minds cannot,
our hearts remember.*

Prologue

My mother always said that a memory can get you through the rest of your life. So, that's why I don't know where to begin. Do I start at the beginning of my life or at the memory—where I believe my life might have actually begun?

It's been years, but I still think of him—just like I still think of that sleepy, little ghost town we both call home. But just like a memory, I guess, both that little town and that boy are now really more like a dream— one that disappears as soon as the morning sun comes slithering through the blinds. But true to a dream, I suppose, it always leaves something behind. And this dream always leaves behind a longing—for Sweet Home, but mostly, for him.

I grew up in Sweet Home, Missouri. I don't know if I'd call it sweet, necessarily, but it is home, to me. Today, it looks different than it used to. Today, grass grows up out of the cracks in the brittle sidewalks that line Market Street. A short twelve years ago, I used to wheel a roller dog my grandpa gave me down those same concrete walks with ease. And it's not just the sidewalks. Tall water hemp covers the bases on the baseball diamond in the park. And now, nearly all the storefront windows have plywood boards covering up dark and dusty, empty rooms. And if that's not enough, where there once were people from birth to ninety-nine spilling out of the old United Church of Christ every Sunday morning, now there's a *no trespassing* sign on God's big, wooden door.

But back in its namesake years, Sweet Home was pretty sweet, I think. I've seen old pictures. And people lived in Sweet Home at one time. Happy people. Proud people. There were cars at the filling station and women buying yards of fabric in the general store. There were men along the street, laughing next to big cars and holding wide-eyed toddlers. Every little front yard had bright green grass that was meticulously cut. And all that green grass was fenced in with wrought iron, all the way down the street, each yard just like the last. And every little home along Market had an American flag that jutted out from some part of the house. And every other house had a rocking chair on a little front porch. And in every rocking chair on Sunday, just when the sun was sinking back into the earth, there would be an old man smoking a corncob pipe or a young woman rocking a baby.

But I'm not too familiar with the Sweet Home of then or the one of today, really. The Sweet Home I knew wasn't booming, but it wasn't abandoned quite yet, either. The Sweet Home I knew was about the size of a tire valve cap, and all the people who lived inside that cap could be counted on three sets of fingers and toes. But people were happy, and the buildings still held some life.

When I lived there, there was a bar and a post office and a fire station that we'd take cookies to every Christmas Eve. And there were still lights that lined the streets. Some perpetually flickered, but there were lights, all the same. Nearly every summer night we would dance on the asphalt under their light shows and pretend we were rich Hollywood stars.

There weren't many babies or kids, though. And except for me and the girl who lived across the street, there was no one else my age. The girl's parents owned the only watering hole in town. She was quiet, and she mostly kept to herself, but we got along just fine. Her name was Angel. And I always thought it was a funny name. Angels glowed and wore halos. Angel did neither. But then there came a day when I changed my mind about that. Angel really was an angel—sent straight down from heaven above to save me—not once, but twice.

The first time was around the year that we both turned eleven. Angel and I were playing hopscotch outside her parents' bar, and a dirty old Nova pulled up to us and asked for directions to the nearest grocery store. Angel was her usual self and didn't say a word, so I decided I'd have to tell him myself. He had long, scraggly hair and a crooked nose, but his eyes were kind. I told him how to get to the IGA, but he craned his neck and said he couldn't hear a word I was saying. He said I'd have to come closer. So, I took a step toward his car, and that's when Angel grabbed my arm and screamed louder than I've ever heard anybody scream before. I flinched, and my ears cracked. Angel had never spoken more than maybe ten soft words at a time in front of me, and here she was screaming loud enough to shatter that old bar's glass windows. Within seconds, her momma came running out, and the car with the man in it sped away. And all that remained from that quick moment was the red imprint of Angel's fingers on my forearm.

Two days later, we heard through the grapevine that a guy in a dirty old Nova had tried to pull a young girl into his car in the next town over. She had managed to slink out of his grip—just about the same time that the man had slipped into the grip of the girl's daddy. And that's where that story ended—although, there are quite a few rumors that circulated, none of which ended too well for the man ... or his Nova.

I never thanked Angel for saving me. I never really had the chance. The bar closed down the next day, and Angel and her family moved somewhere far away from Sweet Home.

And that was not too long before the rest of the town left, too. Some said it was just time—time for everybody to go. But most said it was because the old hat factory had closed in Holstein, just east of town. It employed most of the people who were left in Sweet Home—those who didn't make a living plowing dirt, like my daddy did.

As for me and my momma and daddy, we stayed, though. We stayed in our little ghost town, where daddy drove back and forth all day in the fields, planting money, as he called it. And momma kept working part-time collecting antiques and selling them in a little booth down the road.

And life was quiet—just like Angel had been—until the day that he showed up. And that's actually the second time that Angel saved me. She moved out of that little house across the street, and he moved in. So, the way I see it, Angel gave me him.

From that day and for a while after that, you couldn't hear the sound of the water dripping in the kitchen sink or the branches scraping across the tin roof above my room anymore. Those sounds were all drowned out by the crack of Clearly Canadian caps hitting the concrete and his laugh and the high-pitched hum of an engine, as his dirt bike made little circles in the bottom land.

That was all I heard, anyway.

But eventually, he left, too. Everyone always left. And we—we just stayed. And in time, it got quiet again—just like Angel. But I still remember that little piece of moonlight he brought into my life. And that's where I really feel as if my story begins. It begins with that boy I fell in love with, nearly seven years ago, back in Sweet Home, Missouri.

Chapter One
Just Promise Me

Present
Berlin

"**B**erlin, remember you're picking up Oliver from basketball practice tonight."

I nod my head and push in the chair so she doesn't plow into it on her way to the door.

"That's still all right, right?" she asks, turning back to look at me.

"Yeah, I've got him," I say, my mouth full of buttered toast.

"Good. And tomorrow, if you still can, Madeline needs help with her tornado project. And for some reason, no one can help her but you."

Still chewing, I lean back against the kitchen counter and fold my arms against my chest. "Because no one can make tornados like Uncle Berlin."

She stops shoving groceries into the pantry and glances up at me. Her look is thankful. I get that look a lot from her.

"I'll be here," I assure her.

"Thank you." She says the words with a tired smile.

"You don't have to thank me, Elin. I'm your brother. Plus, I'm still just makin' up for that time I superglued all your curling irons together ... and that one time I scrubbed the toilet with your toothbrush."

Her eyes cut to mine. "You didn't."

I laugh out loud. "I didn't," I say, taking a seat in a kitchen chair. "I swear. I thought about it. But I didn't do it."

She throws her hand to her hip but keeps her eyes trained on me. I don't know if she believes me. But after a moment, her expression grows soft, and an audible sigh escapes her lips. "I just can't imagine doing all this without you. Where would I be?"

I shrug. "Well ..."

"Don't say it," she warns, giving me a stern look.

Elin married one of my good friends, who turned out to be a better friend than he was a husband. So, technically, without me, she probably wouldn't have gotten so close to him. They've been divorced for two years now. They're civil toward one another, and he's still around—just not as much as I am, I guess. In all fairness, though, I did warn her. I told her not to date my friends. I even threatened her, but what I hadn't quite figured out back then was that the moment something became off limits to Elin, that was the very moment she wanted it.

Other than that, I can't complain. I got it pretty easy in the sister department. She's three years older than me, so for most of my life, she was too cool for school ... and me. But I did have friends, and she would let us play war games in the backyard when Mom and Dad made her babysit. And occasionally, when we were stuck in the house because of rain, she would stay up all night with me and play Battleship. And on rare occasions, she was good for throwing a baseball because she's an Elliot, and Elliots are strong. So, in the end, I never really missed having a brother.

"I know you think about her."

"What?" I look up to Elin staring at me.

"Nah," I say. "That's not what I was thinking about."

"That would be a first."

I chuckle to myself. "I have no idea what you're talking about."

"But you do," she says, kneeling down to pour some food into the dog's bowl.

"No, it's not like that. I don't think about her anymore."

She gives me a disbelieving look. I ignore it. "I don't," I lie.

"Okay, then." She stands up from her kneeling position and smoothes out the wrinkles in her sundress. "Then, I have this girl I want you to meet."

"No."

"Berlin, I really think you'd like her."

I shake my head.

"You didn't even give her a chance"

"Still, no," I say.

"I knew it." She sits down in one of the chairs across from me and crosses her arms.

"What?" I ask.

"That's how I know you still think about her. You haven't taken one girl seriously since her."

I meet her challenging gaze. "Oh, really?"

She cocks her head to the side—the way she does when she thinks she's right.

"Maybe it's just your selection of girls," I say.

She rolls her eyes, but I keep going.

"Last spring. The cat lady," I remind her.

"You like cats."

"I've liked two cats," I say. "Just two. That's it."

She takes a long breath and then pushes out a sigh.

"Or what about the girl who told me that I'd be hotter if I were a felon?" I ask her. "Or what about Justine?"

"No." She wags her finger at me. "Justine was not my fault. That was Natalie's idea."

I rest my elbows on the table and cup my face into my hands.

"Besides, how were we supposed to know she liked women?" she asks.

"Well, her Facebook, for one." I sit up and refit my cap over my head. "No one thought to look at her damn profile first?"

"Well, you could have as well, mister."

"Well, that just goes to show how much I trust-ed you two."

She playfully rolls her eyes once more before standing and pushing in her chair. "It would also help if your name wasn't a girl's name."

A laugh gets stuck in my throat. "Yeah," I say, nodding. "That might have helped, too. But you've gotta take that up with Mom."

She fights back a smile but keeps her hooded stare

on me. I know she's thinking up something. She's got that look on her face again.

"Just promise me," she begs. "Promise me you'll stop living in the past, Berlin. You were young. She was young. We were all young. But you don't know where she is. And it's not like she's just gonna come walking up to you one day. And even if she did, she's going to be a grown woman, who's made choices ... that didn't involve a little boy who she used to know for a little while ... a long time ago."

I let her words sink in for a good minute. They hurt going in one ear, almost as much as they hurt going out the other. But I nod my head, like any good brother would do.

"It's the weekend. Go and have a little fun tonight. Okay?" she says.

I meet her pleading, gray eyes.

"Can you do that, for your big sis?"

I can't help but smile—even if it is hidden behind the bill of my cap. "I can do that ... but only for you."

She shakes her head in a scolding kind of way. "Thank you," she says, placing her hand on my shoulder before walking out of the room.

Chapter Two

The Color of Rain

Present
Berlin

I throw a hammer onto the truck bed and slam the tailgate shut.

"What are you building now, Elliot?" Doug asks, pulling out his handkerchief. He's standing under a big sign that reads: *Channing, Kansas' Number One Source for Lumber*.

It's the only source for lumber, but who's counting, I guess.

I rest my stare on the two-by-fours he just helped me load into my truck.

"Swing set ... for Elin's kids."

The Life We Almost Had

"Man, you spoil those kids rotten."

A crooked grin edges across my face. "They're not quite rotten, yet, so I've got a little bit more time."

Doug chuckles to himself. "Hey, when do I get to ride in your car?"

"Never," I say, squinting one eye at him.

He makes some kind of snarling sound, and then he points a finger in my direction. "One of these days, I'm gonna ride in that car."

"I wouldn't go bettin' my last dollar on that," I say.

He laughs once more, and then he slowly saunters back into the lumber yard building.

"Hey."

I hear the soft voice behind me. I don't know if it's directed at me, but I turn, all the same. And when I get all the way around, I stop, and I meet her gaze. And immediately, my heart slams against my chest.

She smiles, and her eyes instantly falter to the dirt gathered around her short cowboy boots.

A wave of panic surges through my veins. I attempt to speak, but the words don't come. So, I clear my throat and try again.

"Hi," I say.

I try to lean back against the tailgate, but I'm a little farther away from it than I thought, and I fall against it instead.

Her smile deepens, while I steady myself, and this time, I simply concentrate on blocking out the sun from my eyes and staring back at her. I figure I can't screw that up.

She's gorgeous, and she sure doesn't look as if she fits into this little town. In fact, she looks as if she just walked right off of a billboard. She's wearing a dress that moves with the breeze. And her hair is long and in waves, while her body curves in all the right places, but right now, I can't leave her smile.

She lowers her face, and my mind floats back down to the dirt and dusty gravel we're standing on.

"Um ... how ... uh," I start to say, but then I realize I'm just rambling, so I stop.

I watch her tuck a strand of her dark blond hair behind her ear. If I didn't know better, I'd say she was nervous, too.

"Do you know Natalie Cueto?" she asks.

I nod and grab the back of my neck. "Yeah," I say. "Yeah, I do."

She shrugs her narrow shoulders, but she holds her pretty gaze in mine. There's a pair of big sunglasses on her head. I'm thankful they're not covering up her eyes.

"Well, I know her, too," she says.

I know I can't hide the little lines on my forehead, giving away my confusion.

She takes a long, steady breath in, and then she carefully lets it go. "We're cousins," she says.

I keep my eyes on her. I'm trying to figure out if she's telling me the truth. But then, why would she lie about that? I just can't believe it. How have I never seen this girl here before? Beauty doesn't hide too well around here.

"Cousins?" I say.

She bobs her head.

"No shit," I mumble, rocking back on my heels.

She laughs a little and then bites the side of her bottom lip. And with that action, my heart surges in my chest.

God, if I'm dreaming ...

"Iva." Natalie yells from across the street, and our attention shifts to the voice.

Iva. Iva. Iva. I echo her name in my mind. And before I know it, Natalie is planting her feet right between me and her, not even paying any attention to me.

"I was wondering where you wandered off to," she says to Iva.

I suck in some air and fiddle with the bill of my cap, trying not to look too nervous.

"Oh," Natalie says, noticing me, right before she sets her sights back on the beautiful blonde. "You've met Berlin."

"Uh, yeah, I have," Iva says, smiling back at me.

I brace myself better against the tailgate; I'm starting to feel lightheaded.

"Well, you ready?" Natalie asks her.

Iva's smile trails off, along with her gaze, for just a brief moment.

"It was nice seeing you, Berlin," she says. Her voice is sober, all of a sudden. "Just don't go getting yourself into any trouble with that hammer."

Immediately, I find her blue-gray eyes, and I feel my head slightly cocking to the side.

"You remember?" I ask.

Natalie looks at me, as if she's lost ... or as if she thinks I am. And I can tell Iva wants to say something. Her pink lips part, but the words never come.

The moment starts to get awkward, and Natalie hasn't stopped staring at me as if I have rats in the attic. I stand up straighter. "Uh, my name," I clarify. "You remember my name."

Iva gives me a satisfied smile. "Of course."

I feel my own grin slowly start to turn up.

"It's a pretty extraordinary name," she adds.

My eyes go to my shoes, as I nod. "Yeah."

She's quiet then, and I take the moment to glance up at her. She's looking down at the toes of her cowboy boots now.

"What's wrong with you?" Natalie asks, jolting me out of my stare and giving me a weird look. "I said your name, like, two seconds ago. She's not an idiot. She's gonna remember your name from two seconds ago."

I laugh and bob my head. "Yeah, you're right."

In the meantime, Iva's gaze has found mine. *Those eyes—the color of rain.* "It's nice seeing you too, Iva," I say. "And I won't get into any trouble." I gesture back toward the hammer on my truck. "I'll be careful."

Her knife-like stare cuts into mine almost as if she's tattooing her name onto the whites of my eyes.

"You remember, too," she says.

It's not a question. And somehow, I know it's not about her name.

"Well, you've got a pretty extraordinary name, yourself," I say.

And that's when I lose some time. Maybe just a couple seconds. Maybe longer. All I know is that there were thoughts—a lot of them. *What am I supposed to do now? I feel like kissing her. Would it be completely crazy if I were to just kiss her, right here? What is she thinking?*

Damn, she's beautiful.
I want her.
I want all of her.

"Ugh. What is wrong with you two?" Natalie looks at me and rolls her eyes. "Berlin, she's off limits. You hear me?"

Iva seems as if she tries to hold back a rebellious grin.

"Come on, Iva. Jenny's waiting."

"Wait, how long are you in town?" I ask.

Iva turns back toward me. "A week."

"A week," I repeat, trying not to show how happy I am to hear that.

"Well, what are you doing tonight?" I ask.

She shrugs her shoulders.

"We're going to Chester's," Natalie calls out over her shoulder. "And I guess we'll be seeing you there then, too?"

I try unsuccessfully to keep my wild smirk at bay. "Yeah. Yeah, you just might."

"Yeah, well, just keep your paws off my beautiful cousin, Elliot. I'm warning you." Natalie gives me a devilish look before pulling on Iva's arm.

Iva's lips edge up once more before she turns to leave. And my sister's nagging voice rings in my head, telling me not to look at her ass. But I quickly shake that off, and I look at her ass. Then I force out a long, slow breath and sit back against the bumper of my truck.

"You okay?"

I look up, and Doug's on the loading dock, standing behind a cart full of lumber.

"Yeah," I say, quickly straightening up. "Yeah, I'm fine."

He lifts an eyebrow. "You look like you've just seen a ghost."

I think about it, and then I nod once. "Yeah," I say. "Something like that."

And without another word exchanged between us, I climb into my truck. "She sure isn't an angel," I mumble under my breath, smiling to myself.

Chapter Three
I Didn't
Present
Berlin

"Why are we here again?"

"I don't know," I say. "For something different, I guess."

I don't look at Isaac, but I know he's staring at me funny. "Something different?"

I take a drink of my beer.

"More like *something underage*," he says, leaning his back against the wood paneling that makes up the wall. "I haven't been here in years."

His eyes skirt around the little room. It's a restaurant during the day, but at night, it's more of a

The Life We Almost Had

hangout for anybody in Channing who's under the age of twenty-one. They're known to serve alcohol to minors here. The owners' kids sneak it to their friends and then their friends sneak it to their friends; it's that kind of thing. And since nothing's really come of it, everybody just turns a blind eye. The big assumption is that all the adults would rather the kids be here than in the next town over, getting into even bigger trouble.

"Who is she?"

I stop scanning the room and force my attention to him. Isaac and I have been friends since I moved here about five years ago. I guess you could say he's my best friend—since my other good friend had to go and marry my sister and then break her heart. Isaac's crazy, too, though. But, I guess, who isn't? And he might have the sense of a rabid squirrel at times, but he does have a good heart, and anyway, he might as well be family now; we've been through a lot together.

"Who?" I finally ask.

"The girl you're looking for. The reason why we're here."

My glance turns down to the scuffed wood floor. "Who says I've gotta be looking for a girl?"

"Well, are you looking for a guy then?"

I hold back a smile, as I take another swig of my beer and swallow it down. "Fine. I'm looking for a girl."

"Who is she?"

"You don't know her."

"Of course I do. I know everybody here."

"No, you *know* every girl here."

He tilts his head to the side. "That ain't a lie."

He keeps looking at me after that, so I feel the need to say something—just to get him to stop looking at me. "It's Natalie's cousin."

"Iva?"

My eyes dart to his.

"Easy, buddy, I've just heard about her," he says, lifting his hands in defense. "I don't *know her* know her, if that's what's got your nuts in a bunch."

I let go of an unsteady breath.

"Everybody's been talking about her; that's all."

"Like who?"

"Like, Russell, up at the machine shed. Jim, Nick, Darrell ..."

"Okay, okay," I say, shaking my head, "you can stop."

"What? I'm just sayin'. She's quite the talk of the town." He takes a swig of his own beer and then sets it down onto a ledge on the wall. "I mean, come on. A pretty girl we ain't never seen before walks into town. I'm just sayin', you probably need to get in line."

I'm about to open my mouth, but then I see her.

She's with Natalie, at the door. She walks in with a smile on her face—as if she's not at all uncomfortable—as if she belongs here or something. I notice her little, red dress first. It's short and tight. And I don't know what I want to do more—put my arms around her or find some kind of coat or something to cover her up with. I can feel all the lustful looks from here. I know exactly what all these minors in here are thinking, and it's making my blood boil.

"Earth to Ber-lin ..."

"Yeah, what?" I try to look at Isaac, but I can't tear my stare away from her.

"Now that she's here, can we just get 'em and go? This place makes me feel like I'm in a daycare. I don't even feel right talkin' to anybody in here. Plus, everybody keeps staring at us, and it's freaking me out."

I briefly look at Isaac; there's a question hanging in my eyes.

"They are," he says. "Look for yourself." He gestures toward the rest of the room.

I look up, and several gazes quickly cast down to the floor.

"And anyway, what if she's thirteen or somethin'?" he asks, going back to his original point. He's suspiciously eyeing a girl now.

"Like that one," he says, flippantly pointing toward a brunette in the corner of the room. "That girl ain't eighteen. Nope. That's it." He takes a drink and then sets his bottle down. "I've gotta get out of here before I get into some kind of unwanted trouble." He takes a hurried step toward the door. "I'll take the *wanted* kind, but I don't do the *unwanted* kind, if you know what I mean," he says, looking back at me.

I watch him breeze right by Natalie and walk out the door. And with that, I set my bottle down on the ledge next to his and make my way to the two girls.

"Berlin," Natalie says. She wears a big smile as she says my name. I can tell she's already had a drink ... or two. "You're here. You weren't lying."

"No," I say, as she gives me a quick hug. And as soon as I can, I look to Iva. Her eyes are already on me, and I damn near lose my words.

"Hi, again."

"Hi," she says.

"Did I just see Isaac run out of here just now?" Natalie asks.

"Uh, yeah, he's, um, just having a hard time with some math, that's all."

Both girls look at me as if I'm talking gibberish, but I expected that.

"So, I know you guys just got here, but would you maybe want to try something else tonight?" I ask.

"Like what?" Natalie chimes in. She's got a curious look in her big, round eyes.

"Well, I was just thinking about opening up the shed tonight."

"Really?" Natalie exclaims. She claps her hands together.

"Yeah, I thought it might be a good night."

"But it's not Saturday," she says.

I shake my head. "But Friday's just as good a reason as Saturday, I guess."

Natalie turns to Iva. "Do you mind? I promise you'll have more fun there than here."

Iva shrugs and then smiles. "Yeah, why not?"

Natalie squeals and then pulls Iva's arm back toward the door. And I follow them out.

Outside, Isaac is talking to a girl. He was right to leave. This place is trouble for him.

I walk behind him and whisper a number.

He looks at me, then at the girl and then back at me.

"Sixteen?" he shouts in my direction.

I nod as I'm walking away.

"No way!" he yells back.

"Way," I say, still following after the two girls.

"Are you sixteen?" I hear him ask the girl.

I don't hear what she says, but fifteen seconds later, his shoes are leaving prints in the dirt behind ours.

I eye him up once he's shoulder to shoulder with me.

"Sixteen," he says, lowering his head in defeat.

I don't say anything. I know I don't have to.

"Natalie, why can't I tell how old they are?" he asks

The Life We Almost Had

her.

"It is hard, Ize," Natalie says. "I can see how her conversations about curfews and cliques can get you all confused. I mean, maybe she spent some time in a Kansas state prison, right? How could you know?"

Iva laughs, and I laugh, too.

"She could have," Isaac says. "You never know."

I like Natalie. Natalie's sharp. But Isaac has been dating her off and on since the sixth grade, so she's always been off limits. And I'm okay with that. She's good for Isaac, even though they happen to be *off* now. But then, I don't know the difference between *off* and *on* anymore—and I don't think they know, either. It all just kind of blends together after a while. I think everybody, including me, just considers them a couple.

"So, Iva, right?" Isaac asks.

"Right," she says, in her sure, smooth voice.

"How you likin' corntown?"

Her lips curve into a sweet smile. "It's nice."

"Where are you from, anyway?" he asks her.

Before Iva can get a word out, Natalie's speaking for her. "She goes to school in Kansas City. She's not used to backwoods parties like this, so just ... try to act normal tonight, okay Isaac?"

Isaac flashes Natalie a challenging look, while Iva and I trade amused glances.

"So, Iva," Isaac says, changing the subject, "I have a hunch that you're the reason why Berlin and I are here tonight." He plops his hand down hard onto my shoulder.

Iva shifts her curious stare in my direction.

I really try hard not to turn red.

"Well, how you likin' him?" he asks her.

"Isaac," I bark.

"What? It was just a question. I didn't mean any harm by it."

"He's not so bad, either," Iva says, glancing up at me through her long eyelashes.

That's it. I lose my damn mind with that. Her look is like that look somebody gets right before you dare them to do something, and they're just about to do it.

"Wow." Isaac sounds surprised. "Well, there you go." He pats me on the shoulder again and then drops a not-so-subtle whisper near my ear: "Looks like you just got promoted to the front of the line."

I try not to grin like a five-year-old kid opening his first slot car racetrack, even though I want to and even though my heart is about to race out of my damn chest.

"Where are we going anyway?" Isaac asks.

"I'm opening the shed tonight," I say.

"You are?"

"Yeah."

"I didn't know that."

"Yeah, well, it seems like a good night for it," I say, trying to make eye contact with him, so he shuts up. It doesn't work, though. He never looks up at me.

"Well, nobody's gonna be there," he says. "You didn't tell anybody. People know the shed's gonna be open on Saturday. Nobody knows it's gonna be open tonight."

"They'll be there," I say, stopping at my truck.

He stops, too, and rests his hand on his belt, like he's thinking. "Okay, okay," he finally says, pulling out his phone, as if he's just solved world hunger or something. "I guess I'll send out a mass text, and we'll see who shows up."

At that, my attention falls back to the girls. Secretly, I don't give a damn who shows up, if anyone.

The only person I wanted to see tonight is already standing right in front of me.

"So, you guys want to ride with me?" I ask.

"Yeah, can we?" Natalie shoots me an excited look.

"Sure, we can all fit," I say.

Isaac opens the passenger door and gestures for Iva to get in. She does, and I watch her scoot to the center. I pray a silent prayer that there's not enough room and she has to squeeze next to me.

"All right," Isaac says, climbing into the truck next.

Natalie gives him a funny look. "So, I get the window then?"

"No, we both get the window," Isaac says, patting his thigh. "Come on, there's not enough room."

"Well, I can scoot over some more," Iva says, scooting more toward the driver's seat. And with that, I send a silent *thank you* up to the good Lord above.

"Nope, nope, still not enough," Isaac says, not even bothering to move an inch. "Climb on in, Natalie Jo."

Natalie cocks her head to the side and looks up at Isaac with a pair of reprimanding eyes.

"Come on, Natalie Jo," Iva chides, through soft laughter.

"Yeah, Natalie Jo, time's a wastin'," I say, as I make my way to the driver's side.

"Fine." I hear Natalie huff as she climbs on top of Isaac's lap.

I get in last and turn the key in the ignition. Immediately, I feel the warmth of Iva's skin against my arm. And for a split second, I forget how to put the truck into gear.

"First, I believe it is," she quietly says.

I stifle a nervous laugh under my breath. Natalie and Isaac are too busy giggling about something that they don't even notice us anymore. I let the air in my lungs funnel past my lips, not really knowing if I should feel excited that she talked to me—the hum of her voice sends chills down my spine—or embarrassed that she noticed I was momentarily frozen.

I move my hand to the stick shift, and at the same time, I unintentionally brush my fingers against her bare leg. An unsteady breath follows—from each of us.

"You drive a truck," she says.

Both the truck and my mind shift gears.

"Yeah," I say. "Yeah, I do."

"I prefer fast cars," she whispers near my ear, leaving a trail of heat on my neck.

My eyes drop to her mouth and to her pretty smile, and then I look back at the road, nodding. "I bet you do."

We go about a mile without saying anything after that. The highway is dark, and the radio is down low. In between Natalie and Isaac's incessant chatting and giggling, I can hear a soft mumbling sifting through the speakers. But to be honest, neither is loud enough to drown out the rhythmic purr of her breaths and the voice in my own head that keeps telling me I'm dreaming.

"So, this, um, place we're going ... it's a shed?" she asks, plucking me right out of my dream.

I clear my throat. "Well, it's more like a big barn, I guess. It's on my parents' farm. We just go there to hang out every once in a while."

I take my eyes off the road for an instant to glance at her. She meets my gaze, then quickly drops her eyes.

I swear my heart is going a mile a minute. And if

that's not enough, my palms are sticking to the steering wheel, and I can't seem to swallow down the lump that keeps rising up in my throat. And meanwhile, every time I have to shift, my fingers brush against her leg. And every time, I know she notices, which makes my heart race just a little more.

"Your parents have a farm?"

I nod. "They do. It was my grandparents'."

"Oh."

I can almost see her mind trying to connect all the dots.

"This is it," I say.

I pull onto the gravel path and up to a dark patch of rocks. And I stop the truck.

"Isaac, if you touch my butt one more time," Natalie scolds, throwing open the door.

"I would never," Isaac says. I hear a fake shock in his voice.

I get out, and Iva slides my way. She's calculated with her actions—as if she's carefully planning her next move. But then again, she's also smooth and adult-like, as if she's lived a thousand lives before my one. I think I'm just in awe—of her.

She plants her feet on the ground, then stops and looks up at the sky above us. It's a new moon, so you can see the stars especially good tonight.

I watch her fingers delicately play with the little gold necklace around her neck. *What is she thinking? Is she as nervous as I am?*

Her eyes gradually land on the old, wooden barn in front of us.

"This isn't where nightmares start or anything," I assure her, through a thin smile. "I promise."

Her gaze quickly finds mine, and she searches my

eyes, as if she's looking for something there.

"I was thinking it was more like where dreams are born."

There's this twinkle in her eyes that I can't quite figure out, but I want to. Everything about her is so foreign, but then again, it's not at all.

I lower my gaze and nod my head before looking back up at her again. "Yeah," I say. "You could say that."

I watch her lips edge up just a little more, and I'm damn sure mine do, too.

"Berlin, you gonna get this thing open? I can't see a damn thing," Isaac yells out into the night.

I look up toward the voice and then back at Iva.

"Here," I say, holding out my hand.

She looks at me and then at my hand.

"It's dark," I say.

She gives me that look that says she knows it's not *that* dark. But in the next moment, I feel her hand in mine.

Her fingers gently weave a soft web, making it hard to know where her hand stops and mine begins. And with it, comes so many emotions I haven't felt in a really long time.

I swallow hard, and she must notice because immediately, her eyes find mine.

"Damn it, Berlin, hurry it up!" Isaac shouts.

I ignore Isaac, taking my time. This girl's hand is in mine, and I'm in no hurry to speed up time.

As we walk, I take a deep breath and then force it out. And then I try to say something, but it doesn't come out, so I just retire to the comfortable silence between us.

Every once in a while, our eyes meet, and we both

just smile. But that's the extent of our conversation, until we make it to the big door of the barn, and I pull out my keys and search for the right one—all the while, holding her hand.

Within a few moments, the padlock clicks, freeing the door. And Isaac is there to slide it open.

He charges right in after that and flips the light switches. There's a half-second delay, and then the barn lights up in a soft, yellow glow, making the pitchforks hanging on the wall look more like a scene out of the Christmas story than one out of *The Texas Chainsaw Massacre*.

"I've got the music," he says, plopping down on a straw bale. He sticks a phone cord into a set of dusty speakers and fidgets with his phone.

"Isaac, we're not listening to that stuff you call music," Natalie says, making her way toward him.

My eyes get caught on the two of them for a moment. I'm thinking I've already had enough of both the music and the party—neither of which has even started yet. I'm thinking I need some Iva time—just me and her and the moon, for a little while.

"Can I show you something?" I turn to her, and this time, my eyes get stuck on our hands, interwoven together.

"Okay," I hear her softly say.

My eyes flick up to hers, and I lose some time in her blue gaze before I come to and remember what I'm doing. In the meantime, she just smiles.

I clear my throat and run my hand through my hair. "Okay," I say.

I lead her out a door near the back of the barn. I don't think Isaac or Natalie even notice us leaving.

We get outside, and instantly, I'm blinded by the

black outside. I stop for a second to let my vision catch up.

"They'll all show up soon," I say, squeezing my eyes shut a couple times.

"Who?"

I shrug my shoulders. "Anyone who wants to. Mostly people I went to high school with. A few other stragglers. All decent people. But everybody will stay in the barn. They don't know about this place."

"The place we're going?"

I look at her. I can just barely make out the soft features on her face now. "Yeah," I say.

We walk in silence for about a dozen more steps. If I were to say there were a thousand things running wild through my mind right now, I'd be lying. There's a million. But honestly, there's only one thing I'm really concerned about—and it's her.

We get to the base of a little, wooden ladder, and I stop.

"Is this a tree house?" she asks. I can hear a smile in her voice.

"Yeah, it was my dad's when he was little."

And without me saying another word, she starts toeing off her boots and making her way up the tree. I let go of a wild grin and then follow after her.

"Doesn't a house usually have a roof?" she asks, looking up at the sky, once we've both made it up the tree.

"That it does," I say. "But Grandpa had this thing about the stars."

Her face instantly turns my way, and our eyes lock for a few heartbeats.

But right before I fall completely apart, her gaze leaves mine, and she rakes her fingers through her long

The Life We Almost Had

hair.

I let an uneven breath go and watch her as she finds a spot along the floorboards and leans her back against the wood railings that make up the wall.

My first instinct is to sit right next to her, but I decide against it. Instead, I sit with my back against the opposite wall. Our legs are outstretched and crossed in front of us. They're not touching, but they're so close, they could be. She eyes me up and down. I watch her in the little natural light there is mixed with the glow from the barn. *I wonder what she thinks of me.*

I feel her shameless stare crawl up my skin, leaving a trail of fire in its wake. Adrenaline is pumping through my veins; I can't even think straight. My own eyes start at her red-painted toes and travel up her long, tan legs to where that short, little dress starts. I follow a path from her wrists to her bare shoulders and then to her neck and that little, gold necklace. It's as if I'm seeing every inch of her for the first time. And then suddenly, I get stuck in that ocean in her eyes and stay there, while the silence deepens, and my breathing quickens.

Then, without so much as a warning, she parts her red lips, and my eyes drop to her mouth. And that's when the silence is broken—like a tiny needle to a big balloon.

"How did you get over me?"

I hear her words, and everything just falls away—the soft breeze, the echoes from the barn, time. It all just disappears into the quiet space between us, while the sea in her eyes rests its heavy weight in mine.

"Berlin Elliot?"

So delicate and innocent, and yet somehow, her voice cuts just like a carving knife.

I clear my throat and then try to swallow down all

the uncertainty and anxiousness swirling around us.

"I didn't," I manage to say in my next breath.

And as if the earth suddenly shakes and causes her expression to shift, a small smile slowly claws its way back to her pretty face.

"I didn't," I repeat, with more conviction, this time.

Chapter Four

Did You See?

Twelve Years Old
Iva

"*Daddy, I have this weather project I have to do for school. Can you help me with it?*"

"*Sure, honey. What do you gotta know?*"

I shrug my shoulders. "Well, I'm doing this paper on how we need rain to grow crops to make money."

He laughs. "All right. So, maybe we can look up the years we had good rain and compare those to the years we had good yields."

I nod. "Yeah, that sounds good."

Daddy smiles at me and then goes back to his supper.

"Did you see who moved into the Gunners'?" Momma asks, looking up from her plate. Her question is

directed at Daddy.

He nods once and then goes back to stabbing his peas with his fork.

I stop chewing and look at Momma. "Who?"

Momma's scolding eyes scrape a jagged trail into the supper table's surface and meet mine. "Not with your mouth full."

I swallow and try again. "Who moved in?"

"Um, a family, I think." *Her words come out softer, this time, as she pushes her long, brown hair behind her ear.*

"Awesome! How old are they?"

I watch Momma shrug her shoulders and look at Daddy. Daddy meets Momma's gaze for a second before going back to his plate. I hate when they do that. It's as if they have this secret eye language, where they can just glance at each other and have an entire conversation. And it's impossible to decode. I've tried.

"I don't know," *Momma says.* "There was a girl, who looked like she might be in high school. And there was a boy—maybe around your age."

"A boy?" *I ask.*

"No," *Daddy says, shaking his head.* "No boys."

I imagine my face scrunching into an awkward question mark. I'm appalled he would think I would like some boy in this town.

"I mean, he's probably too old for you to play with anyway," *he says, almost scrambling for words.*

Instantly, I feel a whole different kind of offended. Play? *First, he's talking to me as if I'm an adult. Now, he's acting as if I'm a little, helpless baby.*

"I don't need someone to plaaayyy with, Daddy." *I draw out the word* play, *just to make it clear.* "I'm not six."

He doesn't even look my way again. Instead, he trades cryptic glances with Momma.

The Life We Almost Had

"Well, do they look normal, at least?" I ask, ignoring their secret conversation.

Another cryptic glance shoots between the two of them. Why are they being so weird?

I chew on a piece of pork chop, as my question falls to the empty mashed potato bowl, unanswered.

Ugh. They're so weird. I probably have the weirdest parents on the planet. They're, like, from 1952 or something. We eat supper at exactly seven every night, except during harvest time, when Daddy's in the field until nine. And it's always either beef or pork. If it's not a part from a cow or a hog ... or a potato—potatoes are okay— we don't eat it. We've never ordered a pizza. I don't exactly know where we would order it from, but still. Lillian's family, who lives on the other side of the county, has pizza night once a month. And Austin gets to have tacos and sushi. My momma has never made tacos—ever. And I don't even know what sushi is.

And I can even overlook my lack of culinary choices, but there are other things, too. Like, we've never owned a car. Instead, we have two one-ton pickup trucks, three tractors and one combine. And before you go thinking that's not so bad, picture my daddy driving, me in the middle and my momma by the window, our heads bobbing up and down in unison to the holes in the road. And if that's not enough, it's really hard to look cool when you pull up to the cute, high school bank teller, and you're just stuck there—in between your momma and daddy, like you're five or something. And don't even get me started about the time Daddy took me to the snow route bus pickup across town in the tractor.

Sometimes, I just wish we had a normal car, like a van or something—like Kyle and Melissa. And more than that, I wish we went on vacations like they do. While all the kids in my class come back from summer break with stories about how the salt water fried their perms or how sticky Florida got at night, I'm just sitting there wondering if finding a new route to the abandoned house in the bottoms was really the coolest thing I did all summer. I barely made it outside of Missouri once, much less to Florida. One time, about three years ago, we got lost in St. Louis and accidently crossed over to Illinois. Daddy was frustrated and mad, but I was happy. Though, I have to say, Illinois didn't really look that much different from Missouri. If the river hadn't been there, I wouldn't even have noticed I had been in another state at all.

But anyway, Florida and the ocean seem more like dreams to me. Since cows can't feed themselves and crops can't just jump out of the field and into a grain bin, I'm stuck within this forty-mile radius—at least until I'm eighteen.

So, yeah, this is my weird life.

"*Can I be excused?" I ask, balling up my napkin and tossing it onto the bone of my eaten pork chop.*

Momma looks at my plate and then nods. "Yes, you may be excused."

I push my chair back and take my dishes to the sink. I'm trying to do everything as I would normally do it, so they don't catch on that I'm on a mission. I've got to find out more about these new people.

"*Do you have homework?" I hear Momma's words right as my foot hits the first stair.*

"*Yeah, on my way to do it," I call back, without stopping.*

That's all I hear from either of them before I get to my bedroom and shut the door. My window looks right at the house across the street that Angel used to live in. There's a moving truck in the driveway. I got right off the bus earlier this afternoon and didn't even think to look in that direction.

Angel's house has been vacant for months now. I was beginning to think that was just the way it was always going to be.

There's a light on in the kitchen. I picture the inside of the house looking just like it did when Angel lived there. I'm imaging the old, oak table in the dining room that my momma helped Angel's momma find at an estate sale. I imagine the dog's food and water dish by the door and that silly, old decorative bird cage that hung in the hallway. It was booty from my momma and Angel's momma's first antique extravaganza. The bird cage was ugly, and it wasn't even meant to hold a real bird, so I never understood the point of it.

Suddenly, a light turns on in the bedroom across the street. I freeze, and without even thinking, I drop to the floor, as if I'm in some kind of spy movie.

The room used to be Angel's. We would sometimes make funny faces at each other using flashlights after our parents had sent us to bed.

I breathe several breaths into the old wood floor before I count to three and then slowly lift myself up again.

When I can just barely see out the window, I peek over the sill. The pale blue curtains that used to cover the window of Angel's room are gone now, so it's easier to see right into the room.

A shadow crosses in front of the window, and I quickly hide behind the wall this time. I probably should feel guilty for spying, but I don't feel anything but this crazy, new energy shooting through my muscles.

I count to three again and then slowly peer around the window frame. And just when my eyes get focused, I see a dark figure staring back at me. I jump and then quickly drop to the floor.

I feel my heart pounding in my chest. For a second, I think I might be having a heart attack. I roll over onto my back and stare up at the neon stars glued to the ceiling. Then I press my hand to my heart and slowly breathe in and out. I'd rather not go out like this—especially over a boy.

After a few, long seconds, my heart starts to slow. I don't think I'm dying. I flip back around, so that my belly is pressed against the hard floorboards again. And I feel this sudden desire to pop up. And I even start to lift my chest back off the floor, but then I stop. Lately, I have been getting this annoying urge to rethink everything I do before I do it. I used to do just about everything that ever popped into my head. Consequences were inconsequential—until one day, they just weren't. Now, I can't do anything without this little, dumb voice in my head playing it all out first. "What would he think?" the dumb voice asks. "Wouldn't you look stupid? Like a creeper? Like a stalker? And what on earth are you wearing? Didn't your grandma give you that tee shirt for your tenth birthday? For the sake of all things cool, you're wearing a darn Winnie the Pooh *shirt? What are you thinking?"*

Momma told me the dumb, little voice was called my conscious. I called it a waste of time. Then she said that all adults have one. And it made me give it a little more consideration. I want to be grown up. And I guess if this is part of it, then I've just got to accept this little, nagging friend that keeps hanging around. But, that doesn't mean I've got to like it—or listen to it all *the time.*

I force another breath into the old floorboards, and then slowly, I start to push myself up. Everything in me is telling me to close the curtains and just let it go; I can find out more about these people in the morning. But I'm not very good at listening to the little voice, yet, so instead, I crawl to the door, turn off the lights and then scurry back over to the window. At least, now, he can't see me.

I peek out the window for the third time. And this time, there's no figure in the window staring back at me. This time, I see a bed and a dresser and someone moving things from the bed to different parts of the room. It's a boy, and he does look as if he's my age, maybe. He looks taller than me. He has long hair—for a boy. And he's kind of stringy, like those shoestring potato straws my grandma always let me get at the dime store when I was younger.

Just then, he stops in front of the window and looks in my direction. I gasp before I realize that he can't see me.

I stay frozen, as I watch him. It looks as if he scans the whole house and then stops back at my window. And after a moment, he smiles. He smiles. And for a few more seconds, he just stares at my window. And then eventually, he goes back to moving things again.

What a weirdo. What was he smiling at?

I shut the curtains and then jump onto my bed and switch on the lamp on the nightstand. I've had enough of the weird boy across the street for tonight. No wonder Momma and Daddy were acting strange. His whole family is probably weird. They probably have dead bodies in their basement and eat kittens for breakfast. I'm going to do everything I can to stay away from that boy, even if he is the only other kid in this whole town and even if he does have a cool, older sister. I have a subscription to Seventeen *magazine that Angel's momma secretly bought me just months before they left town. I'll figure out one way or another how to be a cool teenager someday. I don't need any strange neighbor's help. And I'll even be fine if I have to spend the rest of my adolescence alone in this town. I've got my sketch pad and charcoal, and I've also grown quite good at entertaining myself, so I'll be fine. I'll be just fine.*

Chapter Five

Miss America

Twelve Years Old
Iva

I spot a little rock at my feet. I kick it to the left with one foot and then I kick it back to the right with the other. This keeps me busy for maybe a minute, and then I'm bored again. I would wait inside if it weren't for last winter, when I missed the bus. I didn't even hear it pull up. I waited until eight for it. And when I didn't see it, I figured maybe they canceled school, so I stayed in my room drawing pictures of the ocean all day. But when my momma got home and found out what I had done, she was furious, for one, that I had missed the bus in the first place and for two, that I didn't call her. I didn't bring up the fact that I wouldn't even know who to call to find her. How was

The Life We Almost Had

I supposed to know if she was at the craft store or Grandma's or some salvage sale? It's not like she has a phone taped to her Jordache jeans. And I wasn't about to go calling every Tom, Dick and Harry looking for her.

And I would dread today more if it weren't Friday and if summer weren't almost here. I dread every morning I have to go to school. I don't hate school, necessarily. But I do hate the dumb, long bus ride. It's an hour and fifteen minutes of driving around the county, picking up all the weird kids that live around here.

I seriously can't wait until I get my license.

I'm about ready to find a new activity to help pass the time, when a rock shoots across the street and lands at my feet. Instantly, my gaze travels upward and to a long-limbed boy staring back at me.

My body freezes—kind of like it did last night when I thought he almost saw me through the window. He's cute—cuter than I thought he was, which makes me feel embarrassed for spying on him last night.

"You waiting for the bus?"

I feel my eyes narrow, and that little voice tells me to just say yes.

"No," I say, dryly. "I'm waiting for the aliens. This is their beam-up location."

He eyes me suspiciously—as if he's trying to figure out whether or not I'm crazy. I don't care. Let him think I'm crazy. Then, maybe he'll just automatically stay away from me, and I won't have to waste my time trying to avoid him at every turn.

"Why the backpack then?"

I pull the strap of my bag up to its place on my shoulder. "It's full of foil—for the radioactive waves."

Another suspicious look, followed by a slow-crawling smile, sweeps across his face.

"Well, I think you missed 'em."

"What?"

"They came last night. You missed 'em."
I narrow my eyes even more.
"They took my sister." He shrugs. "But then, they gave her back because they figured out what a pain in the ass she is."

I keep a watchful eye on him, while I try really hard not to laugh. He, on the other hand, just squares his feet in my direction and stands there, in his place across the street—not saying a word.

I don't know what to think of him. The little voice is telling me that he seems kind of interesting, not to mention, cute, and that I should be nice to him. But then, there's another voice yelling that I don't know him and that every boy I've ever known has been stupid or weird or has thought that girls can't do anything.

"Hey, it's kind of like last night," he says.
I snap out of my thoughts.
"What are you talking about?" I keep my eyes on him for only a second before I feel them awkwardly shifting toward my momma's yellow roses along the sidewalk.

"Us," he says. "Us, staring at each other from our rooms across the street."

I shove my hands into my jacket pockets. "I wasn't staring at you."

He shoots me a disbelieving look and then pulls his own backpack strap higher up his shoulder. "Okay."

My gaze falls to my pink and gray sneakers. I'm wishing now I would have worn some nicer shoes today. I'm pretty sure I wore these to the farm last weekend, and that means there's probably cow shit stuck to the bottom.

Why does he have to be sort of cute? And why does him being cute even have to matter? I'm okay with him thinking I'm crazy. But I can't have him thinking I can't dress myself—or that I'm okay with cow shit on my shoes, which, I guess, technically, I am.

"And I wasn't smiling at you, either, then," he says,

The Life We Almost Had

regaining my attention.

I look up at him from underneath my eyelashes, as if my eyelashes are some kind of protective shield, and I watch his grin stretch wide across his face.

Heat rushes to my cheeks. I'm mortified. He definitely saw me last night.

I sigh inwardly. Fridays used to be good days.

I hear the sound of the bus's loud engine even before I see its big, yellow self barreling down the street. Thank you, God.

It stops right in front of my house, and I hurry on.

A few seconds later, I try to act as if I don't notice that he gets on, too. I watch him from the corner of my eye scan the ugly, brown seats. We're one of the first ones on the route, so no one is on the bus, except for Blueberry Ben. He's in first grade and lives on the other side of town. I don't know what his first name really is, but he always smells like blueberries, and Ben *goes pretty well with* blueberry, *so ...*

The bus starts moving before new, weird boy can pick a seat. There's a gazillion seats to choose from; I don't know what's taking him so long.

I force my stare to the window. The last thing I want is for him to catch wind that I'm staring at him. I focus on his house, instead. There's an old dirt bike propped up against the faded, red brick. I've never known anyone who's owned one. Daddy and I went to the county fair last year and watched the motocross race. Ever since then, I've been wondering what it would be like to ride one. I'd ask Daddy if I could have one if I didn't already know what he would say. He has a weird definition of danger. Like, last weekend, he said I couldn't go to the movies with Melissa because her older sister was going to drive us. Yet, just yesterday, I was helping him fix the roof of a grain bin thirty feet in the air. And when I slipped once on the slick, tin surface, he took a rope, tied it around my waist and

42

*then tied the other end to the top of the bin. And no joke—
he looked at me, smiled and said:* Now if you fall, I can
just pull you back up, and we can get right back to
work.

Falling thirty feet: Simple work hazard.
Melissa's sister: Danger.

*Out of nowhere, a girl shoots from the neighbor's
front door, leaving the screen door to slam behind her. She
looks older than me. She's pretty, with blond hair and big
boobs and cool clothes. Within seconds, the bus comes to
an overly dramatic halt, sending me and Blueberry Ben
face-first into the stiff vinyl.*

*I peel my cheek from the seat in front of me and
notice the girl again. She runs across the lawn and in front
of the bus, as the doors open and the* STOP *sign
mechanically flaps into position. The boy isn't seated yet,
but that doesn't stop her. She just pushes her way right
past him, giving him a shove as she moves to the back of
the bus. And for a split second, I meet eyes with the boy,
and I feel sorry for him. But I quickly remind myself that
he was staring at me last night and that worse, he knows I
was staring at him. I turn my attention back to the window.
But it's not even two seconds later that I feel the seat puff
up beneath me.*

*I look over, and he's sitting right next to me—in my
seat.*

*I study him. He doesn't look at me. He just stares
straight ahead into the aisle.*

"*You had every seat to choose from," I say.*

*His eyes meet mine. They're brown—just like the
seats. But I have to admit, I guess, the brown looks better
on him.*

"*I wanted this one."*

*I'm never without words, so I can't quite say I'm
speechless, but I'm close—maybe the closest I've ever
been.*

"But this is my seat," I say.

"And that's why I picked it."

His eyes tunnel into mine. I didn't even know eyes could do that. And for some reason, it makes me feel awkward. And suddenly, all I want to do is turn into vinyl and melt into this ugly seat. And all I can think is that Seventeen *magazine has failed me. It's the first moment in my entire life that I actually need to be cool, and I'm clueless.* Completely clueless. *I want to smile. But I don't. And I'm not sure what's going on with my stomach, but something's wrong. I don't feel sick, but I don't feel right, either. I press my lips together and force my stare to the window again. Old farmhouse after old farmhouse flies by as the bus hightails it down the road. There won't be a stop for another five miles, so for five miles there won't be anyone else to distract us. For five miles, it's only me and him.*

I take in a healthy breath and then slowly force it out. I have to say something. I can't stand the dumb silence any longer.

"Are you in the habit of calling other people's things yours?" I ask, sharpening my gaze on him.

I watch him shake his head. "No, just your things."

I feel my forehead scrunching up, as I pull my backpack closer to my chest. There's a battle raging in my head. I feel as if I could really get along with this kid. He's funny. And he seems nice, I think. And on a scale from that big guy on The Goonies *to Justin Timberlake, he's definitely closer to Justin. But that being said, there's also a very high likelihood that he eats kittens. I look at him kind of like I look at Joseph Gordon-Levitt from* 3rd Rock from the Sun—*nearly perfect, except he's an alien.*

My gaze accidently crosses paths with his, and he smiles. I roll my eyes and try my best to fight back a rogue smile of my own. This boy is crazy, with a capital C. But I'm not altogether sure I don't like it.

I didn't talk to the boy the rest of the ride to school. It was weird, but then again, it kind of wasn't. Every once in a while, I would look his way, and our eyes would meet. And each time, he would smile, and I would try not to, as I quickly forced my stare back out the window.

I didn't see him at school the entire day, either. The teacher announced that we were getting a new student but that he would be in the office all day doing new-student stuff.

Hearing that he was in my class kind of made me a little giddy, but it also kind of made me a little nervous, too. I usually know how to act around people. But in front of him, I just turn into a bumbling, blue elephant.

I get on the bus after school and sit in my regular seat. The bus fills up fast, just like it always does in the afternoon. And just like always, no one sits by me because no one my age lives in Sweet Home.

The boy gets on last. I keep my eyes trained out the window, but for a split second, I steal a quick glance at him. He's scanning the seats, as if he's looking for something ... or someone. I quickly look back out the window. One part of me is hoping he walks on by my seat and picks another one, while the other part is hoping he plants himself right next to me—just like he did this morning.

I take a deep breath in and then let it go. Seconds crawl by as if it's the week of my birthday. And then, I feel it—the rise of the air in the seat as someone sits next to me. I wait a second, and then I turn my head.

He's smiling when our eyes accidently meet.

"Were you waiting too long?"

I narrow my gaze.

"I wasn't waiting for you."

He doesn't say anything. He just keeps grinning.

I try to ignore his grin.

"Where are you from, anyway?" I ask.

"Sulfur."

"Is that a name of a town?"

"Unfortunately."

I push my lips to one side, weighing his answer. "Where is it?"

"Three hours south of here."

Again, I take a few moments to weigh his words. I've been south of here. I went with my daddy to a livestock auction in southern Missouri just last fall. There was nothing there. Then again, there's nothing here, either.

"Well, why did you move here?"

"My dad. He's the new manager at the bottling company."

"Oh," I say. People around here respect the bottling company. It means jobs and money and happy people.

"How old are you?" he asks.

I contemplate adding a couple years to my age because it might make me look cooler, but he's in my class, and he would figure it out Monday. And then it would just look as if I had flunked or something.

"Twelve," I say.

"Really?"

"Yeah, why?"

He shrugs. "I don't know. You seem older."

"Really?" I don't even try to hide my pride, as I sit up a little taller in the seat.

He's still looking my way a few seconds later.

"If I can guess what grade you're in, will you let me

ride that dirt bike that's sitting outside your house?" I ask.

He doesn't say anything at first, and it makes me regret the deal I've just made. What if he thinks I like him now ... or that I'm desperate? Seventeen *magazine says that acting desperate is the worst.*

"All right," he says, "what grade am I in?"

My fears all scurry away, and I silently breathe a sigh of relief. "Seventh," I say, boldly.

He starts to smile.

"I'm right, aren't I?"

"Yep. You win."

He gives me an approving look.

"What grade are you in?" he asks.

"Seventh," I say.

He nods. And then, it gets quiet. I turn my attention to the passing trees outside our little, rectangular window. I have this new desire rising up in me to know everything about this boy. I've never cared to know anything about any boy that wasn't already on some poster in my room.

"Wait," I say, looking over at him. I've just realized that I have no idea what to call him. "What's your name, anyway?"

"Berlin. Berlin Elliot."

I weigh whether I want to say my thought out loud. But before I get to any conclusion, I just blurt it out. "My daddy says you shouldn't trust anybody with two first names."

He smiles. "He's right."

I stare at him, apprehensively.

"My mom says a name should be as ordinary as the person who owns it," he adds.

I take a second to think about what he just said. "So, does that make you extraordinary or just really abnormal?"

He laughs. And for the first time since I met him, I kind of feel a sense of pride for making him laugh.

The Life We Almost Had

"Probably a little bit of both," he answers.

The bus comes to a careening halt, and we both thrust our hands to the seatback in front of us to prevent our bodies from slamming into it.

"I didn't see you there, John," Carla, the bus driver, calls out. I can see her big, blue eyes and gray hair in the long mirror over her head. "You got your walkin' shoes on today?"

Berlin and I watch the second-grader as he makes his way down the aisle, toward the bus door. "Yes, Ms. Carla," he says, in a defeated, monotone voice.

"Good," Carla says, pushing up her big glasses. "It's only about a hundred feet to your driveway; I think you can manage that."

John nods and then disappears down the bus steps. And a second later, we're barreling down the county road again—just like that part in Ghost Dad, *right before the taxi flies off the bridge.*

And D.A.R.E. is worried about drugs killing us.

Berlin suddenly turns to me.

"What?" I ask.

"See," he says. "Ordinary-name almost got a one-way ticket to Carla's house tonight."

I surprise myself and laugh out loud.

"And what if he didn't wear his walkin' shoes today?" he asks.

I squeeze my eyes shut and force my hand to my mouth, trying to hide my giggles. Meanwhile, he just smiles at me.

"What's yours?" he asks.

"My what?"

"Your name?"

"Guess."

He chuckles, and for a moment, I think how I kind of like his laugh. It's relaxed and cool, and afterward, it sort of hangs on his lips—as if he's trying to soak up all its magic.

"You do know there are, like, a million names out there?"

I nod. "Yep."

"Okay, fine," he says. "What do I get if I guess it?"

I think long and hard about it. I've always liked guessing games, and part of the fun of the game is the prize, I suppose.

"If you guess it by tonight, I'll let you sit with me on the bus Monday."

He nods, as if considering it. "Okay, deal."

I smile, and when it gets awkward, I toss my stare outside the window.

"Do you have any brothers or sisters?" he asks.

I shake my head. "No." I say it kind of sadly, but I don't know why I do. I've never really cared about not having any siblings. I get by okay on my own, and anyway, Angel was always kind of like a sister.

"You're not missing much," he says.

"Is that your sister?" I ask, gesturing toward the back of the bus.

"Elin?"

I just stare back at him. How am I supposed to know her name?

"Yeah," he says. "She thinks she's Miss America."

I smile at that. She probably could be Miss America.

"She's all right," he goes on. "But just wait until you catch her on a bad hair day or on one of those nights that her boyfriend doesn't call her. You'll be happy you're an only child."

I watch his mouth as he talks. I wonder if he's ever kissed a girl before. I realize it's a silly thought. Who thinks about that?

I bet he has.

"Well?" I hear him say.

I jump and quickly force my eyes from his lips to the

window.

"Hmm?" I ask.

He laughs to himself. "I said: What's this town like ... that we live in?"

That we live in. I like how that sounds.

"Oh, it's fine, I guess," I say, shrugging one shoulder. "There's not much to do sometimes, but it's all right."

He looks satisfied enough with that answer.

"Was the town you came from bigger than this one?" I ask.

"Yeah, but it wasn't too big."

I look down at the legs of his jeans. His clothes are different than the clothes most people wear around here. Most guys just put on normal blue jeans and a collared shirt and call it a day. But Berlin's jeans are black, and his tee shirt is black, too. And he's wearing a leather jacket, and it's also black. When I saw him this morning, my first thought was Johnny Cash—like the Johnny Cash on all my daddy's old record covers. But then, my second thought was: licorice—long, skinny, weird-tasting black licorice. But in the end, I settled on Johnny Cash because he reminded me more of the guys on my band posters above my bed than food.

Another screeching halt, and my hand is yet again pressing into the seatback in front of me.

"I think this is our stop," he says.

I look out the window and notice Angel's—his—house across the street, and it startles me. We're already here? That was the fastest bus ride ever.

I look over at him, and he's already standing.

"Come on," he says, gesturing toward the aisle. "I've had enough of this spaceship for one day."

I look at him and smile to myself, right before I slide out of the seat and follow him off the bus.

I walked right to my front door, once I got off the bus. He said he would see me tomorrow. I said: Yep. *And that was it.*

It's been five hours since then, and I'm now in my room working on a drawing of the yellow roses that line the little, iron fence out front.

My momma planted the roses all around the house when I was little. They're her favorite. She never said exactly why she likes them so much, but I'm pretty sure I know why. She told me a bedtime story once when I was really young. She probably doesn't even think that I remember it. But I do. It was about a boy who liked a girl. And every day, that boy would give her a yellow rose because, to that boy, the girl was the color of happy. The story ended there, and when I looked up at my momma, there were tears in her eyes. I didn't know why, and I was too afraid to ask. It wasn't until years later that I reasoned that the girl in the story was my momma. Though, I never did find out who the boy was. I know it's not my daddy. He has an aversion to flowers.

Suddenly, a noise pulls my attention from the roses on my sketch pad to the window.

Across the street and in his room is Berlin. His hair, which is a little shorter than shoulder-length, is pulled back into a ponytail now. And I can see, as clear as day through the glass, that he's holding up a piece of paper.

In big, black letters is my name, IVA SCOTT, *sprawling across the page.*

I look down at the sketch pad in front of me and tear off a page near the back. And with my charcoal pencil, I write in big letters: How? *And then I hold it up in front of the window.*

I watch him. He goes to his desk and hovers over it

for a few seconds before returning to the window. And then he holds up another piece of paper. This time, it simply says: tree house.

Tree house?

And then I remember. Years ago, Angel and I had carved our names into the old tree house in her backyard.

I go back to my sketch pad and pull out another piece of paper.

I write: How do you know it's not Angel?

Then, I hold it up in the window.

He squints, as if he's trying to read all the letters. Then he goes back to his desk.

I wait a couple seconds, and then he holds up a piece of paper that reads: I figured you weren't an angel.

I let go of a sideways smirk. And then he goes back to the paper and scribbles something else down. After a moment, he holds it up, and I read: Plus, your mailbox says *Scott*.

He's a crafty, little one.

He bends down and writes something else. I wait until he holds it up, and then I read: You can't trust anybody with two first names, Iva Scott.

I roll my eyes after I finish reading his chicken-scratch words. And I hope he sees me doing it, too.

Before I can do anything else, he goes back to his desk, hovers over it and then comes back to the window and holds up another page. And this time, it only says one word: Extraordinary.

I try really hard not to smile.

He scribbles something else under the word. I squint to read it: Goodnight, Iva.

I shake my head and mouth the words: Goodnight, Berlin. *And for a moment after that, we just stand there. It would be weird if I said I felt good to stand there with him, who's practically a stranger, smiling back at me. So, I won't. I won't say there were butterflies in my stomach. I*

Laura Miller

won't say that I liked how my heart raced. I won't say that I liked his smile or his stupid, leather jacket or his seat-colored brown eyes. And no one—especially him—will ever know that for a tiny, little flash of a second, I thought of him as Johnny Cash—and me as June.

Chapter Six

Does She Know?

Present
Iva

"**H**ow have you been?" I ask him.
His eyes travel over the old, wood two-by-fours of the little tree house. Then slowly, they rake their way up my body and to my gaze.

"Okay," he says. His voice is barely over a raspy whisper. "And you?"

I nod once. "Okay."

Silence immediately sneaks into our conversation. It's almost as if we're both afraid of saying too much.

I study him. I watch his eyes drift from mine to the place where my hand rests on the floorboards. I wonder what he's thinking. I feel as if I'm in a different world. This is all so strange, and yet, so familiar. It doesn't feel as if any time has passed, but then again, it also feels as if a thousand years have come and gone. I want to know everything. I want to know what led him here and how long he's been here and how the last seven years of his life have been. But it's just too much for the moment; it's just too heavy. Right now, all I really want to do is feel what it's like to simply breathe in and breathe out in his presence.

"So, here we are," I say.

He nods. "Here we are."

I lower my head and try to fight back a smile.

"Sooo," he says, drawing out the word. "Natalie's your cousin?"

"Yeah." My eyes gradually wander back up to his.

"Does she ..." He stops and starts over. "Does she know about us?"

I shake my head. "She knows about a boy I used to know back in Sweet Home. She doesn't know that boy is you."

"You told her about me?" He peeks up at me through his long eyelashes.

I smile, remembering briefly the effect his eyes used to have on me. Some things never change. "In hindsight, it would have been nice if I had mentioned your name."

He gives me a curt nod. "In hindsight ... that might have been nice."

And with that, my smile grows a little wider. "I'm guessing your friend has no idea, either?"

"Isaac?"

"Mm-hmm," I hum.

He moves his head back and forth. "No."

I watch him slide his foot against the boards so that one knee is bent.

"It was hard to talk about you ..."

He stops, and silence fills every crevasse and crack in the wood surrounding us. On some level, I understand. On another, I don't. I'm not the reason we haven't seen each other in seven years.

I watch his gaze wander off into the distance—somewhere opposite the barn.

"How was life for you ... after you left Sweet Home?" I ask. "I mean, how was the rest of high school and ...?" I don't finish the sentence because his eyes return. They wander slowly up my legs and eventually to my eyes and stay there. His slow, deliberate act causes me to lose my words.

"It was okay," he says, bobbing his head. "It turned out all right, I guess."

I take in a deep breath, mostly because I feel nervous all of a sudden, and I don't know what else to do.

"And you?" he asks. "It looks as if life's been treating you pretty well."

Instantly, I feel my cheeks grow hot. I lower my head to hide them before I catch sight of a spot in the corner of the tree house. There's a piece of wood that has something etched into it, but I can't tell what it is.

"What?" he asks.

He looks over at the piece of wood, and then back at me.

"Nothing. It's just ... This is kind of ..."

"Crazy," he says, finishing my sentence.

I nod. "Yeah. Something like that."

Our eyes meet again, and I feel it—that dark blanket of comfort his look always gave me.

I drop my gaze and try to shake off the thought.

There's a hushed calm for a couple heartbeats, and in that time, I notice the muffled voices from the barn for the first time, and I think about Natalie. She's probably wondering where I am. Though, she seemed pretty cozy with Berlin's friend; it could be that she doesn't even notice that I'm gone.

"It's just a girl I used to date," he says.

My eyes quickly find his. "What?"

"The name ... in the wood, it's just an ex-girlfriend."

"Oh, I ..." I hadn't even realized that my eyes had meandered back to the carving in the wood.

"No, it's fine," he explains. "I just noticed you were looking at it."

I smile, despite the unsettled feeling in the pit of my stomach.

"She put it there," he adds.

I nod, but I'm strangely glad he felt the need to clarify that.

He laughs to himself and lowers his head.

"What?" I ask.

"Oh, it's just ... Your smile is nice. I just remembered that; that's all."

I press my lips together, trying my hardest to hide my grin—though, I'm not exactly sure why.

Suddenly, someone yells in the distance, and I jump.

"They get a little rowdy sometimes," he says. He winks at me. And if you didn't know Berlin Elliot, you'd think he was flirting. But to the Berlin Elliot I know, he's just having a normal conversation. See, that's the thing with him. He'll make you forget your own last name, and then in an effort to help, he'll offer you his.

And after the fact, he has no idea how he's just stolen your heart.

And with that one flutter of his eye, I swear, every emotion I've ever felt for this boy comes rushing back to me. Happiness, pain, anger, love—it's all there.

"How did we get here?" I ask.

"Well, I think the question is: *How did we* not *get here sooner?"*

I can't help but smile at that, as I clear my throat and habitually tuck a piece of my hair behind my ear. "You said that's your ex-girlfriend." I gesture with my eyes toward the name in the wood. "Where's the current one?"

He shakes his head. "There isn't one. We broke up a few months ago."

"Oh." My eyes immediately find his. "I'm sorry."

He watches me, as if he's judging my sincerity, considering it carefully. "Nah," he finally says, "it's fine." His eyes trail off to that corner and to her name. "After that first cut, it's not so bad anymore."

I would try to avoid his eyes if mine hadn't already gone and got stuck in that light, sticky honey that swirls around his. He's beautiful. But then, of course, I can't remember thinking anything different—even when he was just arms and legs. On that very first day I saw him when I was just twelve years old, I was drawn to him. But he's grown up now. His eyes are the same, but they're filled up—as if he's got more words behind them than he knows what to do with. And he cut his hair—that long, wild hair that probably made my daddy write him off at first sight. And gone is that shoestring-potato-straw profile, and in its place is an athlete's body with large biceps and forearms. And on the surface of his tanned skin, it's almost as if time itself is written.

Calluses mark his hands, and scars, both new and old, carve thin lines into his arms. He's the same boy from my past, but he's also a very different man—who I'm not even going to pretend to know anymore.

"I just can't believe you're here," he says.

I sink my teeth into my bottom lip.

"And I can't believe Natalie's your cousin," he adds. "Do you know I've known her for ..." He stops, as if to add up the time. "For nearly five years now? How have we never crossed paths?"

I shake my head. "I have no idea. I've been here once before in the last several years, but I stayed mostly around her and her family." My gaze wanders off to a corner of the tree house before returning to him. "I've mostly been busy with school, I guess."

"Where do you go?" he asks.

"Weston University. It's a little fine arts school in Kansas City."

A slow, gradual grin finds his face. "You graduate soon?"

"In May," I say.

"You got some famous artist job lined up?"

"Minus the *famous* part, yes, I do."

He nods, as if he suspected my answer.

"What about you?" I ask. "School? Job?"

"No school. But I do have a job, and it suits me."

"What do you do?"

He smiles again but then quickly drops his gaze. "How about I show you later?"

My lips go to form a word, but I stop and softly laugh, instead. "Okay then."

"Well, what are you doing all week?" he asks, smoothly moving the conversation away from himself.

I tilt my head back and look up into the dark sky

above us. There are so many stars; it reminds me of a different time. "I don't know, really. I think we're just hanging out. It's spring break, and it might be a little while before I see Natalie again, so ... Yeah," I say, my eyes roaming back to his, "we're just hanging out."

"She working?"

"Natalie?"

"Yeah," he says. "Is she working tomorrow?"

"Um, actually, she is, I think."

He stares back at me with a little smirk playing on his face.

"Why?" I ask.

"Well, turns out, I'm not up to too much this week myself, and ... I could entertain you while she's working."

"Could you, now?" I ask.

"Yeah, I think I could manage."

I keep my eyes on him for a good, couple seconds. If I say *yes*, I just know I'll be jumping right down the rabbit hole. Berlin Elliot is all sorts of madness.

I think about it. I think about the first day I met him. I think about all those nights in between then and the day he left—all those nights we spent wrapped up in each other's arms. And then I think about all the nights after that when he didn't call, and my heart aches. But somehow, I never even contemplate *no*.

"Okay," I whisper.

He just nods his head and smiles.

"One week," he says to no one in particular. "One week with Iva. It's got a nice ring to it, don't you think?"

I roll my eyes and shake my head slowly back and forth.

"What kind of trouble do you think we can get into

in a week?" he asks, still entertaining that devilish, though ever-charming grin on his lips.

"Berlin Elliot, I should have listened to my daddy and never peeked through that window that first night."

"Oh," he says, sitting back against the boards, "but aren't we both so glad you did?"

Chapter Seven

Berlin's the Boy

Present

Iva

"Iva, why are you so quiet over there? Did you not have fun?"

I look over at Natalie. Natalie's pretty. And she seems happy tonight. She and I didn't hang out much when we were kids because she lived so far away. But after I graduated high school and went to college, we reconnected. She goes to school at a small college in Kansas near here, which is only a couple hours from my school, so we've spent the last four years, mostly at each other's schools, making up for lost time.

"No," I say, answering her question. "I had fun." I

look over at her. "I had a lot of fun, actually."

She glances at me suspiciously before returning her eyes to the road. "Oh, my gosh, Iva. Were you with Berlin all night? Is that where you were?"

I just smile.

"He got to you, didn't he?"

I start to laugh.

"Iva, he is ...," she starts.

It seems as though she's really being careful with her next words. And it makes me pause.

"He's what?" I ask.

"Oh ..." She glances over at me, and then quickly plants her eyes back on the road. "No, he's great. He loves his family. God knows he's gorgeous. It's just ... He's ... um ..."

"What?"

I don't know why exactly, but I feel my heart sink a little in my chest. What on earth is this girl trying to say?

"He's risky," she says.

"Risky?" I look over at her.

"Yeah, risky."

My laugh fills the inside of her little sedan.

"Why is that funny?" she asks.

"I don't know." I lift my shoulders and then let them fall. "I didn't know that driving too fast was a red flag when it came to spending time with somebody."

She takes her eyes off the road for a second to look my way. "Oh, he got you with that?"

"With what?"

"The whole *I drive fast cars* spiel." She playfully rolls her eyes.

"What? No, I just ..."

"He's in love with someone else, you know?" she interjects.

My smile quickly dissolves. "What?"

"Berlin," she says, "he's in love with this girl he used to know."

I sink into my seat. I'm a little surprised. I'm a little surprised that I feel this way. I shouldn't. It's been too long. And it's definitely too late.

"Is it his ex-girlfriend?"

"What? Who?"

"Kayla or Kylie?" I say.

She looks at me with a puzzled face. "Kalen?"

I shrug. "Yeah, maybe."

"What?" she says. "How do you even know about her?"

"I don't know. I saw a name carved into the tree house behind the barn."

"You were in a tree house all night?"

I smile for the first time in what feels like a little while.

"You know," she sighs, waving her hand in the air, "I don't even want to know."

"It's not what you're thinking," I say.

She narrows her eyes at me.

"Natalie," I scold.

"You like him, don't you?" she asks.

I feel my top teeth press hard into my bottom lip. I'm trying to think of how to say my next words.

"Do you remember the boy from Sweet Home who I told you about a while ago?"

She's quiet for several heartbeats. I can tell she's thinking, though the whole time, I don't look her way.

"Yeah," she finally says, "I do."

"Well ...," I say, drawing out the word.

"Well, what?"

I look at her, as I chew away the nervous seconds

on the inside of my cheek. She glances over at me a couple times. But then, each time, she returns her eyes to the road, without incident.

"Wait!" she suddenly shouts.

The car comes to a dramatic halt. My hands fly to the hard dashboard, and I feel my seatbelt tighten against my chest.

"Geez, Nat! What are you doing?" I pat my chest to make sure my boobs are still there.

She ignores my question. "Are you telling me Berlin's the boy?"

I suck in a breath, partly because I'm thankful I'm still alive and partly because I'm also still trying to wrap my head around this night, too. "Yeah," I breathe out.

"No," she says, shaking her head. "No." She looks straight out the windshield in front of her now, as if I'm not even in the car. Then, she puts the car in park—right in the middle of the road—and sits back in her seat. "Are you sure?"

I look behind us. There are no car lights for miles, so I guess it's okay to have this conversation while parked in the middle of the highway.

I turn my body so that I'm facing her. "I'm sure."

"But Berlin is from some little town in western Missouri. Sweet Home's not in western Missouri."

"No, he moved to western Missouri after he left Sweet Home. He must have only been there for a short time before he came here."

"Oh," she says, as if she's slowly absorbing every detail.

"Does he remember you?"

I nod. "He does."

"Wait, so when you two were talking to each other in town earlier today ... you already knew each other?"

I nod.

"Wow," she exclaims.

I can just see the understanding sinking into her bones.

"Well, shit," she breathes out.

"I know, right?"

"So, let me get this straight," she says. "He showed up across the street one day when you were like, twelve, and then he was gone? And then that was it? And this whole time, it was Berlin—the guy I know ... the guy I've known since high school?"

"Yeah." I force out a puff of air. "I guess so."

"You really can't make this shit up."

"No," I agree, "you can't."

She looks straight ahead; her mouth agape.

"Wow, Iva. I love Berlin like a brother. He's Isaac's best friend. I mean, I know Isaac and I aren't a thing right now, but I don't know, we're always a thing, really. But that's a different story. And anyway, it's just ..."

She takes a breath before going on.

"It's just that ... Does he know about ..."

"No," I say, looking down at the floor. "And anyway, you're getting way ahead of yourself. He's only a boy I used to know a long time ago. That hardly means anything now."

She's staring at me with a strange look on her face. "Are you trying to convince me ... or yourself of that? Because I remember the way you looked when you told me about him."

My eyes are planted on her, as I try not to smile.

"Oh, come on!" she nearly yells. "He's *THE* boy, Iva. *The boy.* You found *the* boy. You found him before it was too late. That's gotta count for something."

I laugh. "You're crazy, Nat."

She gives me one of her big, mischievous grins. "Am I?"

I don't say anything after that. I just gaze out at the dark world outside my window and think about how insane this night has been.

"Well, listen," she says, "I can keep you away from Berlin for the rest of the week. This place is small, but there are ways to avoid people you don't want to see. But ... I don't know if I can keep him away from you." She looks over at me and gives me a small, roguish smirk. "But I'm not so sure you want me to, either."

Natalie puts the car in drive. I quickly make sure my seatbelt is secure.

And for the rest of the drive to her house, I just stare out that window and at the black night as it lulls me into a series of my own thoughts.

Berlin.

When he left our hometown, I knew he had gone to that little town in western Missouri. I even knew the name, though that's evidently not where he stayed. But none of that mattered. When he stopped calling, I stopped caring. At least, that's what I've told myself almost every day these last seven years.

I feel a shot of adrenaline jet through my veins, and it forces my lips to turn up. I untuck my hair from behind my ear and let the strands fall against my cheek, so Natalie doesn't see my giddy grin.

I did find *the* boy—the elusive boy from Sweet Home.

Chapter Eight
You
Twelve Years Old
Iva

"**O**kay, first things first; this is the clutch." He squeezes the little lever on the handlebar. "And this is the throttle."

"The throttle?"

"Yeah," he says, "it's what makes you go." He turns the opposite handle. "And these are the front brakes and the back brakes. And this is how you shift gears." He points to a little peddle by my foot.

"Okay," I say, trying really hard to concentrate on everything he just told me.

"You want to start in neutral."

"Neutral, got it."

"Okay, rock it back and forth."

I rock the bike forward and backward. It takes almost all my strength to get it rocking.

"You see how it moves?"

"Yeah," I say.

"That's how you know it's in neutral."

"Okay," I say, bobbing my head. I'm wearing his helmet. It's hot, but it fits fine.

"Okay, so now push down hard on the starter." He points to a piece of metal near the back of the bike.

"All right." I take my heel and push down on the peddle, but nothing happens.

"You gotta push hard," he says.

I try it again, and this time, it's like magic; the bike starts. I'm one-part nervous and one-part so excited I can't even take it.

"Okay, now hold down the clutch, and we're going to put it into first."

"Okay," I say.

"Now, you want to let out the clutch slowly, and at the same time, give it some gas."

I fill my lungs with a deep breath, and then I nod.

He steps back, and I do what he told me to do.

Instantly, the bike lunges forward, and then just as quickly, it dies.

Berlin laughs. "It's fine." There's patience in his voice, and it makes me feel better. "You'll get the hang of it. Here, try it again."

I try again, and this time, the bike moves forward without stopping right away. I go in a straight line until I hear the engine starting to work. I know I'm supposed to shift, but I've forgotten how, so I just brake, instead.

"That was great," Berlin says, running up behind me. "You're better than I was when I started." He rests his hand on the small of my back, and little pieces of energy radiate from that spot where he's touching me. "Of

course, I was seven when I first learned, but still."

I laugh, as I take off the helmet and run my fingers through my matted-down hair. But soon, I feel the strangely welcomed weight of his stare.

"You know," he says, "I would have let you ride it even if you didn't guess the right grade."

I immediately scrunch up my nose. "You wanna know a little secret?" I ask.

"What?"

"I cheated."

He tilts his head to one side, but then a big smile sneaks back to his face.

"What?" I ask, trying to figure out why he's smiling that goofy grin.

"I know."

"What? How do you know?"

"They said they were going to tell the class about me—being new and all."

I force my eyes to the bike's seat. "So, you knew I was going to win?"

He nods. "I had spent all night trying to figure out how to get you on my bike. It was like an answer to my prayers."

I shake my head. "You're so dumb."

"Apparently not that dumb. I got you over here, didn't I?"

I roll my eyes and playfully shove the helmet into his chest. And at the same time, I tell myself that I don't like him—that I'm not in any trouble whatsoever of falling for this boy. But then I hear that little voice rising up in the back of my mind. It's soft, but it's immediate. It echoes back at me, almost as if it's a taunt: You're sunk. You're so sunk, Iva.

We walk back across the railroad tracks after we're done with my lesson. And when we get home, we prop the bike up against his garage.

"It's almost seven," *I say.*

"Okay, what's at seven?"

"Supper," *I say, feeling stupid now that I had said it that way.*

"Okay, well, I'll see you tomorrow, I'm sure."

I nod and smile. "Okay."

I make my way across the street. I want to look back at him, but that just seems weird, so I don't. And as soon as I make it inside, I round the corner to the kitchen, and I spot Momma and Daddy. They're sitting in two chairs, glaring at me with a pair of ominous stares.

"What's wrong?" *I ask.*

The last time they looked like this they were about to tell me that Spike, our Great Pyrenees, had died.

"Where were you, young lady?" *my momma asks.*

"I was with Berlin. I ... I told you I was gonna go hang out with him."

"What were you doing with Berlin?" *Daddy chimes in.*

My eyes turn downward. "We were riding his dirt bike," *I mumble into the floor. I purposefully didn't tell them that part, but I didn't really think it would be* this *big of a deal, either.*

"That's dangerous," *Momma says.*

"I don't want you hanging around that boy anymore," *Daddy growls. He's quick to add that part.*

"What?" *Just like that, I sound outraged. And I am.* "I can drive tractors, but I can't ride a dirt bike?"

"Tractors are different," *Daddy says.* "Tractors are safer."

I swallow down my anger. I don't believe tractors are safer. Tractors are bigger. You get in a fight with a tractor, the tractor wins—every time. And who are they to tell me that I can't hang out with Berlin?

"It wasn't his fault," I protest.

"No, it was yours. You're smarter than that," Daddy says.

My momma gives my daddy a conspicuous look. He counters by crossing his arms in front of him.

"You can hang out with him," my momma says, "as long as you tell us exactly what you're doing."

"Fine," I say. Momma has always been the more reasonable one.

"For now," Daddy adds, gruffly.

I look at him and then at my momma. I want to smile because I'm happy I still get to hang out with Berlin, but at the same time, I don't want them getting the idea that I'm okay with this conversation.

"I have homework," I lie.

I charge up to my room, taking two steps at a time.

"Supper will be ready in ten minutes," I hear Momma call out behind me.

I get to my room, switch on the light and close the door. When it comes to the big picture, I'm still a prisoner, in a way. Everything I do in this town somehow gets back to my parents—even before I do. And now, they're just going to be ten times more likely to question every little thing I do. So, that's great. But then again, if you look at it with one of those big magnifying glasses—like the one they use in Where in the World is Carmen Sandiego?*—it's not really that bad, I guess. I actually had fun today, and I still get to hang out with Berlin tomorrow. So, yeah, that's pretty cool.*

I pump both my fists in the air and scream silently into the ceiling. And about halfway into my dance, I freeze. And my blood runs ice-cold.

Berlin is standing in his window across the street—staring straight at me.

I'm mortified. Frozen—and mortified.

He laughs and shakes his head. Then, he slowly goes to his desk. I watch him, but I can't see what he's doing. His back is toward me. I'm too curious and too much in shock to run away and hide, even though that's exactly what I feel like doing.

It's only a few seconds, and he comes back to the window and holds up a piece of paper that reads: Why are you so happy?

My mind scrambles up words to say. I go to my desk and find a black marker, and then I write: You. *But then I scratch it out and write instead:* I like dirt bikes.

I hold it up to my window and watch him strain to see it. And then after a few seconds, I see him smile.

My gaze follows him back to his desk. His back is to me for a brief moment, and then he turns and holds up another piece of paper. This time, it reads: I liked your first answer better.

And before I can even respond, he turns out his light.

The blood is fleeing my head in waves, running straight down to my feet, but yet, my heart is doing this weird, wild dance.

I glance down at the piece of paper in my hand. Then, slowly, I hold it up to the light. And there it is, underneath the black scratches, in plain view: You.

Chapter Nine

Don't Call Me Baby

Present
Iva

I hear the doorbell ring, and my heart nearly jumps out of my chest. I could barely sleep last night. The boy who haunted my dreams for most of my life suddenly shows back up in my life, and sleeping—or dreaming—no longer seems necessary.

Another chime rings through the hallway. There's glass on either side of the front door, but the glass is covered by a curtain. I pull the curtain back and see that it's Berlin. Then I suck in a deep breath and pull open the door.

"Hi," he says. He looks rested ... and happy.

"Hi."

I notice his eyes roam down to my chest. "I remember when I was a Terrapin."

I look down and see the big turtle stretched across my tee shirt. Above the turtle are the words: *Franklin County High.*

"Anyway, these are for you," he says.

He holds out a bouquet of roses.

"Yellow roses," he says, "like the ones from your house in ..."

"In Sweet Home," I finish the sentence for him, remembering the flowers that lined the little iron fence.

I take the bouquet. I can't say I'm surprised he remembered them. The Berlin Elliot I knew was nothing if not observant. But the fact that he thought to bring them to me makes my heart melt a little.

I breathe in their soft, flowery scent, and it instantly brings me home. I almost forget that there's a part of me that still hates this man. Though, it's funny how the years have somehow all but erased that hurt. It's still there. It's still there, as much as a knife would be if you just kept it festering in your flesh. But I think I also just kind of got used to it being there. And now, it's more a part of me than I would like to admit. I hate him, but I also love him because the fact remains: I can't unlove him.

"Thank you," I say.

"Well, you're welcome." He bobs his head once. "Every time I see yellow roses, I think of you."

I steadily inhale. There are a million questions in that one breath—a million questions that I'll have to wait to get answered ... for now.

"You look the same," he says, regaining my attention. "I mean, grown up, but the same."

The Life We Almost Had

I drop my eyes to the old, hardwood floor at my feet. This moment is weird. I never imagined I would see him again, much less be standing in the same room with him—getting ready to spend an afternoon *with him.*

"Is that a good thing?" I ask, peeking back up.

He nods.

I smile and then open the door wider.

"You can come in. I just have to get my shoes from upstairs."

He steps inside, and when I leave for the stairs, he makes his way to the kitchen. I stop and watch him. I'm a little taken aback by how comfortable he seems.

"Natalie or Susan here?" he asks.

"No, they're both at work."

He stops and looks back at me.

"What?" he asks. He must notice my curious look.

I shrug. "It's just, you know my aunt on a first-name basis."

A crooked grin slides up his face. "Yeah, I know your mom on a first-name basis, too."

"Yeah," I say, my focus dropping to the floor momentarily. "It's just ..."

"I know," he says, "I don't know how we missed each other."

"Yeah," I say. "I don't either."

His eyes stay in mine, until I purposefully drop my gaze, reminding myself that he's the reason I haven't seen him in seven years.

"I'll just go get my shoes." I point upstairs.

"Okay," he says, rocking back on his heels. "I'll just be down here. I'm not going anywhere."

The way he says his last words makes me pause. They're raw. They're uncensored. And if I'm not mistaken, they're not about him staying in the kitchen.

I start to turn, but then I stop. And I look back at him. He doesn't notice me. I watch him pull out a can of soda from the refrigerator. For a moment, my mind is transported back to Sweet Home. I remember him doing that same thing at my house—when my daddy wasn't home. And in that moment, from somewhere deep inside, I feel this pang of jealousy. Natalie has had this—*him*—for the last handful of years—and I haven't.

Suddenly, I notice his eyes smiling at me from over his soda can.

I think I jump, but I'm not sure if I actually do. I am immediately embarrassed, though. I didn't even realize I was staring ... or more so, that he had noticed.

I toss my attention to the carpet and smile, awkwardly. Meanwhile, he sets the can down and lets go of a wild grin. And with that, I turn and head up the stairs with the yellow roses still in hand.

I get my tennis shoes on and head back downstairs. But when I reach the bottom stair, I catch Berlin sitting at the kitchen table. His attention is somewhere beyond the glass sliding door. He doesn't notice me, but I'm happy he doesn't. It gives me some time to evaluate what I'm walking into.

He's got a scar on his right cheek. It's new. For a second, I wonder how it got there. He also has a scar on his arm—from his dirt bike accident. It happened when he was thirteen. He was going too fast, and he wanted to turn, but the bike didn't. He flew off and landed in the emergency room. I guess they are a little

The Life We Almost Had

dangerous, after all.

And I remember that hair. Although it's much shorter now, I remember how I used to run my fingers through those wavy locks. He would rest his head in my lap and stare up at the stars, and I'd stare at him and dream of the life we were going to have together. And as my fingers weaved a thoughtful web, I just remember feeling this need to love and care for this boy for as long as I knew how. I had never felt that way before. And I just remember thinking that I could never love someone more than I loved him. And so far, I haven't.

His eyes are still planted on something outside that door, while my gaze slowly grazes over his face. He has facial hair now. The boy I knew only pretended to shave. For a moment, I wonder how different his face would feel if I were to run my hand along his jaw—just like I used to.

The thought is almost too much. I clear my throat to get his attention ... or to regain my own—I'm not sure.

He turns, and instantly, I feel the weight of his stare.

"I'm ready," I say.

His eyes linger on me for longer than they should, but then before I can say anything else, he's up and on his feet. "All right, then."

He takes his soda with him, and when he gets to the front door, he opens it and gestures toward the porch.

"You look the same, too," I say, making my way through the door's frame.

"What?" He pulls the door closed behind us.

"You look the same," I say, turning back. "I mean, not exactly the same, but the minute I saw you, I knew it was you. You look how I pictured you would look."

His curious eyes cut to mine. "You've pictured me?"

I shake my head, as if to scold him.

"Do you picture me a lot?" he asks.

I've probably thought about him more than I'd like to admit in the last seven years. But I won't tell him that. Instead, I just give him a look that says he's pressing his luck.

He playfully grabs at his heart, and it makes me laugh.

"When I was younger," I say, "I would always imagine what both of us would look like when we were all grown up. ... You never did that?"

"Umm," he hums, as if he's thinking about it.

"You mean you never once wondered what I would look like all grown up?" I interject.

He stops on the sidewalk and looks up into the pale blue sky before leveling his eyes on me. "No."

"No?"

"Nope. I think I just thought you'd always look like you. ... And you do. You look like Iva Sophia Scott, age twenty-two and a half. Beautiful, as always."

I try not to blush. Meanwhile, he walks past me and opens the passenger-side door to his truck.

I don't even attempt any words after that, as I climb in and wait for him to get in, too. And when he does, he turns the ignition, and an old country song comes over the radio. As fate would have it, it's a song we used to always sing together. He looks up at me and smiles. It's enough to know he remembers, too.

But after that, he turns the music down and starts driving.

"What ever happened to the Chevelle?" I ask.

"I've still got her. But I only take her out on special occasions now. No sense in puttin' the miles on her."

I think about the cherry-red car for a second and how much fun we had in it. And for some reason, I get a tiny bit sad thinking about not ever having the chance to ride in it again.

"I did drive by your house, you know," he says. His voice is sober now, and suddenly, he has my full attention.

"What?"

He nods. "Your house in Sweet Home."

"You drove all the way back to Sweet Home just to drive by my house?"

He shakes his head. "No, I drove all the way back to Sweet Home ... just to see you."

I look down at the floor. "Everybody eventually leaves Sweet Home."

"Where did you go?"

"Chandler," I say.

He nods once more.

"When?" I ask.

"What?"

"When did you drive back there?"

"The day I got my license. That was the plan, right?"

I swallow down the lump growing in my throat, and I force my attention outside the window. "You stopped calling. I didn't realize there was still a plan."

The cab of the truck grows eerily quiet then, but I don't dare tear my stare away from that window.

"Iva?"

I don't want to look at him.

"Iva?" This time, my name comes even softer off his lips. And this time, I feel my eyes slowly gravitating toward him.

"You know why I stopped calling, right?"

I don't say a word, but I keep my eyes on him.

"Did you think I just stopped calling?" he asks.

I let several moments tick away in silence, while I gather up the courage to ask him the question I've been wanting to ask him for seven years now.

"Why?" I ask. "Why did I never hear from you again?"

His glance cuts to me, and then he breathes out a heavy sigh and returns his stare to the road ahead of us.

What had I missed? Why would he think I would know?

All of a sudden, there's a pained expression on his face. "Your dad answered the phone one night."

My heart drops in my chest.

"He told me to stop calling you."

"What?" My word comes out sounding a little broken and a little angry, and probably because it is.

He nods. "It was a Tuesday—a couple months after I had left."

I laugh once, not because it's funny, but because I can't believe that was the reason we lost touch. I stare at the road past the windshield. Little yellow line after little yellow line keeps disappearing under the truck.

"But I guess," he says, "looking back, I understand why he did it. I wasn't really the type any daddy would want his fifteen-year-old daughter hanging around."

I push back the tears threatening to fall. I had hated him—this man now sitting beside me—for so long. I had both loved him ... and hated him ... for so long.

His words tear at my heart. I had no idea Daddy had done that. I could have suspected something like that, but for some reason, I never did—not in the least bit. And I was so hurt that he stopped calling and answering my phone calls that one day, I just turned that part of me off. I stopped waiting for him. And every time I found myself thinking about him, I told myself he wasn't worth it. And as it turns out, I ended up telling myself that he wasn't worth it every day since the day he left.

"So, he told you to stop, and that was it?" I ask.

His eyes land on me, before he shifts his concentration back to the road.

"You never cared about what he did or didn't like before that," I say. "Why did *that* stop you?"

"Well, to be honest, it didn't," he says. "I called you three more times after that. And each time, he answered. And the last time, he threatened to get a restraining order if he ever caught me talking to you again. And that scared me a little because I thought if that happened then I would for sure never have a shot at seeing you again. So, I did what he told me to do. And that hurt like hell." He looks over at me and finds my eyes. "Iva, it hurt like hell."

I have to tell myself to breathe.

"But the day I got my license," he goes on, "I was there, at your house. The only problem, of course, was that you weren't."

All my focus dashes to the window and to the world rushing past us. He's driving too fast, but then again, what's new?

I'm at a loss for words. And all that hate ... All that hate I had stored up for him—it has nowhere to go now. For seven years, it ran through my veins. For seven, long years, it coursed through my blood, giving me a reason to move on from that little boy I used to love.

But now, I feel all that hate leaving my body, dripping from my fingertips. And with it, I feel this strong urge to press it back into my skin, just so I'll still have a reason not to love him.

"I just don't understand why he didn't like you so much," I say.

He takes his eyes off the road. "I think it was my cool, teenage swagger and my sexy, long hair."

I try to laugh, but it hurts too much.

It's quiet again after that, and all I can hear is the soft hum of another old country song pouring out of the speakers.

I don't hate Daddy.

And I no longer hate Berlin.

Now, I just blame myself.

Maybe there was something I could have done to change my daddy's opinion of him. I could have tried harder. I was just so busy being with Berlin that I didn't think to try.

I look over at him. His focus has returned to the road. I study the way his jaw moves with every thought—the way it always did. He's like riding a bike for the first time in years. It feels weird and a little awkward, but it all comes back. Gradually, I'm remembering him—piece by piece.

"I'm sorry I wasn't there," I say.

His eyes wander back to mine. "No, it wasn't your fault. Time just got in the way of us, I guess."

His last comment strikes a cord in me, somewhere deep inside. I inhale sharply and then force my attention out the window again.

"I cried for three days straight," I say.

I don't look his way, but I can tell he looks at me.

"When you didn't call, I cried for three days," I say.
"But then that fourth day ... you didn't," he says.
My eyes slowly drift back to him.
"And then you went to high school," he goes on. "And you probably had a good, respectable high school boyfriend with a good haircut and a nice Carhartt jacket. And your daddy liked him. And then you went to college, and you did well, I'm assuming because I know you and because, well, you're about to graduate." He pauses. "And I'm assuming that now you're probably involved with a guy who has promised you that he can give you a safe, suitable life."

He stops, and I feel my forehead fill with little wrinkles. He's wearing a challenging stare now that juggles both me and the road.

"Does a *suitable life* not sit well with you?" he asks.

I clear my throat and sit back in my seat, while I force my eyes straight ahead.

"I didn't think so," he says. I can hear the smile in his voice.

"It wouldn't with me, either," he adds.

I look over at him, and the first thing I notice is that daring smile hanging off his lips. I don't know what to think of it. I let it go, though, and I turn my focus to the window and to the grassy breaks in the row of little white farmhouses, instead.

"So, you do have a boyfriend then?" he asks. There's a hint of hesitation in his voice, but he hides it well.

"If I did, I don't think he'd take too kindly to you showing up with roses ... or whisking me away to some place out in the middle of nowhere." I never thought to ask where we're going or even what he has planned for us today.

He studies me before letting go of a mischievous grin.

"Channing, Kansas is not the middle of nowhere, Miss Scott."

"No?"

"No," he confirms. "The middle of Nowhere is actually in southwest Oklahoma."

"What?" I'm suddenly intrigued with his babbling.

"Nowhere, Oklahoma. You've never heard of it?"

I can't even hide my amusement. "How do you even know that?"

"Well, when you not only live in Channing, Kansas, but you're also from a string of little towns just like Channing, Kansas, you learn you've gotta have a comeback for the inevitable small-town joke."

A laugh unexpectedly falls from my lips.

"Hey, I've got an idea," he says, glancing over at me.

Before I can say anything, he's spinning the wheel and making a U-turn in the middle of the highway. I can smell the chemical scent of burnt rubber hanging in the air.

"Let's take the bike, instead. You can drive."

I grip the *oh-shit* handle and study his face. And after only a few seconds, I know that he's serious. "Berlin, no." I shake my head. "I can't drive it. It's been years. The last one I drove was your daddy's."

"Nooo," he says, forcing his hand to his heart. "Say it isn't so."

He takes another sharp turn, and I grip the handle harder. I had almost forgotten what it's like to ride with Berlin Elliot.

The Life We Almost Had

He opens my door, and I slide out of his truck. We're at the same barn we were at last night. But this time, I notice there's a small shed off to the side.

"I didn't know your grandparents had a farm," I say, eyeing the big, red barn.

"They didn't—not when I knew you, anyway," he says. "They bought it back a couple years ago. Like I said, my dad grew up here. It means a lot to him." He runs his fingers over his hair. "It was a little bit of an ordeal. The guy who owned it was dead set on keeping it." He pauses for a moment—long enough for me to take notice. "But everybody's got a price."

I look at him, but he keeps his stare straight ahead. And as we make a path to that little shed, a strange feeling pours over me, reminding me that we lost a lot of time. There's a part of me that feels as if I can still predict his thoughts, but then the other part of me is just staring at this man wondering what else I don't know.

We eventually stop in front of the shed, and he takes a small key from his keychain. And with that key, he opens the padlock and slides away the door.

"Uh-uh," I say, once I get a good look at the massive motorcycle in front of me. "There is no way I'm driving that."

"Whoa, whoa, whoa. First of all, this isn't a *that*. This is a Harley. Second of all, why on God's green earth wouldn't you want to drive a Harley?"

"I'll break it. Berlin, I haven't touched a motorcycle …"

He clears his throat. And all of a sudden, he's giving me this look as if I should choose my words a little more wisely. I start again.

"I haven't touched a Harley in my life."

"That's better." He smiles, approvingly.

"But come on," he says. "If you know how to drive a bike, you know how to drive a Harley. Let's go."

"Don't I need a special license?"

He pushes his lips to one side. "Nah."

I laugh. "That's comforting."

"Don't worry. I'm a little better at sweet-talking than I used to be."

I smile at him. Then, I look up to the low-hanging ceiling of the little shed and curse my stars.

"Come on." He hops on the bike and straddles the back portion of the seat, while patting the spot in front of him. "Take me for a ride, Miss Scott."

I stare into his eyes, and all I can think of is being fifteen and riding on the back of his bike, trying to chase the sun and get home before Momma and Daddy realized I was gone. Then I feel my chest expand with a breath, and shortly after, I force out a protesting sigh. But he just smiles back at me.

"Fine," I say, climbing on. "But don't say I didn't warn you."

He laughs and hands me a helmet. I put it on and start the bike just like he taught me to do on his daddy's motorcycle so many years ago. I'm absolutely shocked I still remember. And as I ease off the clutch, we jump forward, but it's not as bad as I pictured it could be. I don't run into the side of the shed. I don't run us into the barn or a tree. I stay on the little graveled path, and then I ease us onto the county road. I go slow at first, but then as it comes back to me, I go a little faster, and

The Life We Almost Had

a little faster. I had forgotten how fun this is.

"See, once you learn, you never forget," I hear him yell over the engine. "And once you get a taste of it, you always want more."

He leans in behind me and gently squeezes my thigh. His touch sends a shiver through my body.

That always worked on me.

"You hungry?" he asks.

I nod my head, and the big helmet nods with it.

"Let's go into town first," he yells, pointing to the right.

I nod again and lean to the right before feeling the smooth pavement under the wheels, as we leave the gravel road.

I follow Berlin's directions and pull into a parking spot right in front of a little diner with red awnings shading its big, front windows.

"How was that?" he asks, taking off his helmet.

"Not so bad," I say, after I've got mine off, too.

"Not so bad," he repeats. "I know you liked that. You always hide your cards."

"What?"

"You hide your cards. You've always done it."

"I ... don't hi ..."

Our eyes meet, and it makes me stop.

"Like that very first day," he says, "that day I sat next to you on the bus. You acted like you didn't like me sitting there."

I shake my head. "I *didn't* like you sitting there."

He keeps his eyes in mine. He's got a knowing,

little grin on his face. I would hate to say he was right, so I don't. Instead, I push past him and walk to the door of the restaurant. He follows close behind.

We sit down in a corner booth, and a girl, maybe a little younger than us, comes to our table wearing a black apron. The girl looks like someone, and Berlin seems to know her well. She smiles at Berlin and takes a long look at me.

"You look different, Berlin," she says, eyeing him again.

He runs his hand along his jaw line. "Must be the shadow," he says, winking at me.

The girl narrows her stare at him. Then without saying another word, she flips up a page from her little pad and takes our orders.

"Mary, you still got those banana milkshakes?" Berlin asks her.

The girl nods. "Yep."

"Good, we'll take two of those, too."

"All right," she says, spinning around. She heads back toward the kitchen, just as my eyes find Berlin's.

"Banana shakes?"

"Yeah, your favorite flavor, right?"

I just smile at him.

"You know her?" I ask, gesturing toward the girl, now taking an order at another table.

He bobs his head once. "Isaac's sister."

"Oh," I say. "That makes sense. They look a lot alike."

"Yeah," he says, chuckling, "they do."

"So, why did you leave Sweet Home?" he asks.

I sit back in the padded seat. "That last flood. Daddy called it quits after that—farming in the river bottoms, anyway."

He nods, as if he might have suspected that.

"We bought some land far away from the river and never looked back."

He takes a drink from his glass. Meanwhile, I plant one elbow on the table and rest my chin in my hand.

"I still can't believe you came back—just like we planned," I say.

He methodically sets down the glass. "Yeah, but the thing is, I hadn't planned you wouldn't be there."

Without even thinking, I let go of a sigh. "Yeah, me neither."

I watch him fidget with the straw in his water.

"And you came even though my daddy said not to call anymore."

"He said not to call. He never said anything about not stopping by."

A wide smile crawls across his face.

"What would have been different if I had been there?" I ask.

He lifts his shoulders and then lets them fall. "Maybe everything."

Those two words take the air right out of my lungs. And I let the next several moments just fall silently to the old table's hard surface between us.

"I hated you for a long time," I say.

He takes a breath and then nods. "I believe that. And I'm sorry. I should have done more. I wish I would have."

"No," I say. "You were just a kid. And if my daddy would have threatened me that way, I would have done the same. I just thought ..."

"That I stopped calling because I wanted to?" he finishes.

I timidly lift one shoulder.

"No." He shakes his head. "Iva, if you only knew."

My eyes find an anchor in his. There's a lot being left unsaid between our stares, but then again, there's also a lifetime of words being silently uttered, all at the same time. But they're all jumbled up, and I can't tell one from the other. And after a little while, I'm forced to give up.

I drop my gaze. "So, can you tell me what you do now?" I ask, sitting back again.

He pushes his glass more to the center of the table and sits back in the booth. "I drive."

"You drive?"

"Yeah," he says.

"Okay. Like ... a bus? Like a tractor trailer?"

"No, like, uh ..." He stops, as if he's thinking. "You know what? I'll just show you."

I give him a puzzled look.

"So mysterious," I sing.

He lowers his head and laughs to himself. "So, what about you? Tell me about school."

"Um, well, I graduate in May with a degree in fine arts."

"And you still paint ... and draw?"

I nod. "I do."

Isaac's sister stops at the table and places our burgers, fries and milkshakes in front of us. We thank her, and Berlin talks to her about Isaac for a minute. The way they talk, it's almost as if Berlin is her older brother. I've never seen him this way. It warms my heart a little.

"How's your sister?" I ask, when the girl leaves. I know I hadn't finished telling him about me, but I was anxious to change the subject.

"Elin's good. Married. ... Was married. She's now

divorced and has two kids."

I nod. It's hard to picture Elin married with kids. It's even harder to picture her divorced. I think I always had this story made up in my mind about her. In my head, she was always going to be a model and live in New York City and never marry but have hundreds of men who liked her. *Miss America.*

"Her kids are great," he goes on, tearing me out of my own thoughts. "One's four, and one's five. They can be little shit-stirrers sometimes, but I wouldn't trade 'em for a lighthouse in the woods."

I give him a knowing look. Back in Sweet Home, there was an eccentric old man who built a lighthouse in the only wooded area there was, south of town. Everyone called him Mr. Keeper. He mostly kept to himself, except for one day out of the year when he'd come into town and he'd pass out handwritten flyers about the history of lighthouses. People didn't understand him, but after a while, he just kind of morphed into the town's woodwork. And soon, he was as ordinary as the mailman. The only other person in town that could have matched Mr. Keeper was Claire Blanch. She used to walk a stuffed cat named Juniper on a leash down Market Street. I always thought she and Mr. Keeper would have made a good couple. I don't think that ever happened, though.

"But," I say, "the real question is: Would you trade 'em for a stuffed cat named Juniper?"

Berlin laughs out loud. "Iva Scott, I do believe your small town is coming out."

I smile to myself and take a sip of my milkshake. I'm happy he remembers. Then again, who could forget Miss Blanch and Juniper? Though, I do have to admit, it's a little weird hearing him talk about kids. That wild boy from Sweet Home actually did grow up. For a second, I mourn the loss of that crazy teenager, who was going to rule the world behind the wheel of his cherry-red Chevelle.

"Hey, do you still have McMarbles?" he asks.

I swallow down the ice cream and look up at him. "McMarbles?"

"Yeah."

"Berlin, McMarbles would be, like, twenty-five years old."

He shrugs his shoulders and gives me a sad look.

I shake my head. "McMarbles passed away during my senior year of high school."

"Oh," he sighs. He seems sincerely broken up about it.

"But in his last breath, he wanted me to tell you that he loved you and that he still loved your leather jacket."

He laughs. "That cat did love me. And he loved that jacket. What can I say? He had good taste."

I sit back and cross my arms over my chest.

"What?" he asks.

"He had a taste for something, but it wasn't your jacket."

"What? No. No," he repeats, moving his head back and forth. "I would never ... do that."

I keep my eyes on him.

"No, I only put catnip in the pocket one time."

I nod once, but I'm careful to keep a serious face.

"Okay, maybe twice."

I clear my throat.

"It was only because you loved that damn cat so much. And I thought if McMarbles liked me, then you would like me, too."

My hand goes to my mouth to try and cover my smile.

"I was right, though. You liked me because McMarbles liked me. Right?"

"Well," I say, "it didn't hurt."

"But McMarbles wasn't the only reason you liked me."

"No?"

"Nah, not even close."

"Was it the fast car and the dirt bike?" I ask.

"Yeah, that, and my awesome collection of ..."

"Oh, my gosh," I say, cutting him off. "Your Troll dolls." I shake my head. "Why did we like those ugly things so much?"

"I literally have no idea," he says, his voice breaking into laughter.

"But they weren't yours," I say.

"Yeah, but Elin didn't miss 'em."

My stare instantly shoots from my fries to him. "You're drunk. I remember that day like it was yesterday."

It looks as if he's thinking, and then he erupts into more laughter. And I know he remembers.

"She stomped all over the house looking for them," I say. "And there we were, hiding with all those stupid dolls in the back of your closet."

"She never did find those damn things," he says.

"What? Where are they?"

"Still in a shoe box in the back of my closet."

I give him a knowing look.

"Okay, fine, they're in four shoe boxes in the back of my closet."

"I can't, Berlin."

"She doesn't even miss 'em," he says. "*Now,*

anyway," he corrects.

I only stop laughing when Isaac's sister comes back to give us the check.

"I know what it is," the girl says, eyeing up Berlin. "I know what that new look on you is all about."

Berlin takes a long look at me, and then he rests his eyes back on the girl. "Okay, Mary. Go ahead. What is it?"

She takes the pen she's holding and starts chewing on the cap. "You've got that same look that I get when I finally find something that I've lost."

Berlin's eyes don't leave the girl for nearly three, breathless seconds. But then, he smiles, and his gaze gradually falls back on me.

"I think you just might be right about that, Mary," he says.

Mary smiles and sets the check on the table, before disappearing into the kitchen again. Meanwhile, Berlin keeps his lustful stare on me. It's heavy—his eyes in mine. But then again, it's also freeing ... and strange and wonderful. I missed him. I think I missed him more than I allowed myself to believe.

"You ready to blow this Popsicle stand, Miss Scott?"

He slides a bill into the check folder.

"Yeah," I say, collecting myself again. I grab my helmet and scoot out of the seat. Then, I make my way to the door.

"Thanks," I say, once we get outside, "for lunch."

Berlin looks down at the asphalt under our feet. "Iva, I owe you a little more than just lunch."

I get lost then in the honey-colored dream in his eyes before a car horn thrusts me back to reality.

"Here," I say, "it was fun going down memory

lane, but you should take these before my luck runs out." I throw him the keys.

"You sure?" he asks.

"I'm sure."

He gets on the bike and sticks the key into the ignition.

"Where are we going now?" I ask.

He looks up. "How do you feel about building a swing set?"

I nod and glance down at the ground before finding his eyes again. "I could do that."

I watch, then, as a happy smile slowly fights its way to his chiseled face. "Good."

I hop on the bike behind him after that and make myself comfortable.

"I should probably warn you to hang on tight," he says. "I drive a little faster than you do."

"Berlin, please don't kill us."

"Baby, have I ever killed us?"

I roll my eyes and pull on my helmet. "Don't call me *baby*."

"All right, beautiful."

I roll my eyes for a second time, even though I know he can't see them. And a second later, we rocket launch into the street.

I throw my arms around his waist, so I don't die. I can't say he didn't do that on purpose. In fact, I'm pretty certain he did. But I also can't say that I hate it ... or the way his muscles feel against my arms. Suddenly, I'm a teenager again, and it's just me and him, and nothing else in the world matters.

I rest my head briefly against his back. And at the same time, I push away all the thoughts that remind me that, now, everything's just a little more complicated than it was when we were fifteen.

We pull up to a house a couple miles outside of town. It's off a gravel road and at the end of a long, white-rock driveway.

The bike comes to a stop, and I pull off my helmet. He was right about the fast part, but I should have expected that. Berlin's only gear is fast.

"Berlin, whose house is this?"

"Elin's," he says, taking off his helmet.

I look at the house. It's breathtakingly beautiful—two stories, big wraparound porch, modern, but it still has a farmhouse feel.

"What does she do?" The question just falls out of my mouth. And I only half regret it.

"Preschool teacher," he says, knocking the kickstand into place.

I keep my eyes on the house, as my brow wrinkles. "What does her ex-husband do?"

I can tell he laughs a little.

"He manages the mechanic shop in town."

My head automatically tilts a little more to the side. Something's not adding up.

I slowly swing my leg over the bike, still keeping one eye trained on the big house in front of us.

"You okay?" he asks. There's a sincerity in his voice, but somehow, I can tell he's amused.

"Yeah," I say. "Yeah, I'm fine."

"Okay." He nods once. "Well, let's go inside."

We leave our helmets with the bike, and I follow him to the front porch.

"Elin's at work," he says, opening the door. "Kids are at their dad's."

I walk inside. The inside is just as beautiful as the outside. *Me* seven years ago wouldn't even hesitate asking Berlin the question I so desperately want to ask him: *How on earth do a teacher and a manager of a mechanic shop afford a house like this?* But the *me* today hasn't seen this Berlin in seven years, and the question just doesn't seem right.

I follow him through a great room with a vaulted ceiling. It leads into a dining area with a big, wooden table and an intricate light fixture that looks like art suspended in air. And on the back wall, there are two big, glass doors that lead outside.

And by now, it's no surprise that the backyard is just the same as the rest of the house—beautiful. There's a stone path, lined with purple flowers leading to a little fountain. And beyond that, there's a big, in-ground pool and endless stripes of green grass.

"That's where the swing set is going." Berlin points to a grassy spot opposite the pool. There's already lumber set out in piles.

I nod. "Okay."

He smiles at me and then walks toward the lumber. I just follow him, noticing for the first time, the covered patio and large, stone fireplace on the other side of the fountain. Padded outdoor furniture is arranged in a circle, and there's even a television mounted above the fireplace.

Not many places in the small towns I've been to look like this one. I'm kind of in awe, really. But mostly, I just want to know how—how they can afford all this.

Before I know it, I'm at the pile of wood, and I take a second to redo my hair into a messy bun.

"You really are beautiful," he says, gaining my attention.

My eyes flicker up to his.

"I kind of feel as if I'm dreaming," he adds.

All of a sudden, I have this crazy, strong desire to be in his arms. I loved this boy. And now, this boy whom I once loved with all my heart has turned into an attractive, beautiful-hearted man. And I'm at a loss for what to do about it.

I softly clear my throat and pick up a drill.

"So," I say, trying to shift the mood, "swing set."

He eyes me suspiciously for a second, but then he nods. "Swing set," he repeats.

"Have you ever built one of these?" I ask.

He shakes his head. "Nope."

I laugh.

"I was hoping *you* had," he says.

His eyes rest in mine for several more seconds.

"It can't be that hard," I say.

I step back and look at the pile of wood.

"I printed off some instructions." He pulls out a folded up piece of paper from his back pocket.

I try not to laugh. "Well, that's a start."

I walk over to him, as he unfolds the paper.

Our arms are nearly touching, while I look over his shoulder at the instructions. I can almost feel his breaths pressing into my skin. And suddenly, a chill runs up my spine.

With that, I leave him and pick up a board. And I can tell he studies me as I do it.

"Do you have screws?" I ask, trying not to look as flustered as I am. I can't feel this way about Berlin Elliot anymore. I can't. And I won't.

"Yeah." He gestures toward a little bucket near the

fence line.

I walk toward the bucket.

"So, what's next ... with you? What's the job?" he asks, laying a board on top of another board.

Out of habit, I run my tongue along my crooked tooth at the base of my mouth. I do it when I'm nervous. "I'll be working for this painter."

"Really?"

"Yeah," I say, grabbing some screws. "He's really good. He does amazing work, and in the art world, he's pretty well-known." I set the board down and pick up the instructions and study them some more. "I can't even believe I have the opportunity. I mean, I'll be working on the side, too, probably at a coffee shop or something like that, but it's really an opportunity of a lifetime—to work with him. I couldn't pass it up."

"That's really cool."

He sounds sincere.

"Iva Scott, the famous artist," he sings.

I breathe out an easy smile.

"So, what are you doing tomorrow night?" he asks.

I look up from the paper, but before I can answer, he starts screwing two boards together.

When he's done, he plants his eyes on me.

"Are you asking me out again?" I ask.

He shrugs, and I smile a little wider.

"Um, well," I say, my smile fading, "I should probably spend some time with Natalie. That's why I'm here, after all."

He looks a little hurt by my comment.

"You were just a bonus," I add.

His face glows with a soft grin. And then he lifts up a longer board.

I quickly realize he'll need me to hold it if he's

planning on screwing it to the other ones. So, I do.

"Did you know that it's Isaac's birthday tomorrow?" he asks.

"Uh, no," I say.

He drives a screw into the end of the board, and then he goes to the other side.

"And he usually spends his birthday with Natalie," he adds.

"Oh," I say. "I didn't know that."

"Well ..." He gives me a quick glance before securing the long board in place. "You could always surprise her and tell her you found something else to do, so she can go hang out with him."

I lower the board to the ground and just stare back at him with a word hanging on my lips. I don't know what the word is exactly, so it never actually does leave my lips.

"It's just a thought, anyway," he adds, with a little half-smile.

"And what if I were to say that I did, in fact, have something else to do, what exactly would that something else be?"

"Well," he says. "It could be anything you want. As long as it's with me."

"With you?"

"Yeah, of course," he says. "Who else do you trust in this town?"

I laugh and drive a screw into another set of boards. "Well, I'm not all too certain I trust you, either."

He stops what he's doing and cocks his head.

"Well, I know it was a while ago, but once upon a time, you did trust me with your heart."

My gaze goes directly to his. All of a sudden,

The Life We Almost Had

everything seems a little more serious.

"Tell her it's okay to go out with Isaac, that you've got other plans," he says, setting the drill down.

I feel my stare floating back toward the boards that are now starting to resemble a swing set.

"I'll show you something that will remind you of home—Sweet Home," he adds.

Then slowly, he walks over to me and takes the drill from my hand and sets it down. Then he takes my hands in his. I let him do it. I can't *not* ... let him do it. And immediately, my eyes go to our interwoven fingers.

I don't move. I just stand there, while a flood of memories fill up my head. I'm miles away from home, but suddenly, I feel as if I'm there. And after a few moments like that, he gently lets go of my hands and then wraps his arms around me.

I breathe him in. I've missed this—this feeling of being in his arms. He's more filled out and a little taller and stronger, but being in his arms feels the same—just the same as it did seven years ago. And for that moment, he's mine again.

We stay like that for a long time. I don't think either one of us wants to be the first to move. I think we've waited far too long for this reunion. And I'm almost afraid that if I let him go, he and this dream will dissolve into the afternoon sun.

"Berlin."

We both hear the voice coming from the back door at the same time, and instantly, I pull away from his arms.

A woman stops just outside the door. I recognize her immediately. She's the same girl I remember idolizing when I was younger. Her hair is a little blonder, and she's a little thinner. But other than that, she's the same girl. *Miss America.* But now, she looks surprised, and I don't blame her. I'm sure it's like seeing a ghost.

"Iva," she says, looking straight at me.

"Hi, Elin."

Her mouth is cocked open, and I can tell there's a question on her lips.

I peek up at Berlin, and he just smiles at me.

"Well, how does it look?" Berlin asks, gesturing toward the swing set and breaking the silence.

Elin rocks back on her heels. "It, um, looks great," she says, crossing her arms over her chest and letting go of a wide smile.

After that, we all just kind of stare at each other, until Elin uncrosses her arms and then points back toward the inside of the house.

"Um, I'll just be inside," she says. "It looks really good," she adds, one more time, before rushing off.

When she's gone, I catch Berlin's fiery gaze. I'm happy he still has the same, brown, wild-boy eyes I once fell in love with.

"I think she was a little surprised to see me," I say.

Berlin starts to nod. "But did she look more surprised than I looked yesterday?"

I laugh. "No," I confirm, "I think you've got her beat."

He bows his head briefly but then finds my eyes again. "I've missed you."

My focus rushes to the grass at our feet. I contemplate saying those three little words back to him. I want to. I want to so badly, but I also don't want to complicate this.

I take a step back toward the swing set.

He notices my hesitation. I can feel him carefully

studying me.

"You don't have to say it," he says.

And with those words, my heart breaks for him. He knows. He knows I missed him, too. He doesn't need to know the woman I am now to know the girl still inside of me missed him more than words can say. But even so, he deserves to hear me say it. I just don't have the courage.

"I'm just happy you're here," he says. "And that your daddy raised a woman who feels at home with a drill in her hand." He lets his eyes trail off to the swing set. "It does look pretty good," he adds.

I follow his lead to the boards and let a handful of silent moments pass between us before I hear the sound of my own voice.

"I've missed you, too, you know," I say, keeping my stare glued to the unfinished swing set.

He doesn't say anything, and after a while, I find my eyes settling in his.

"I know, Iva Scott," he says, nodding and smiling faintly. "I know."

Chapter Ten
It's the Long Hair
Thirteen Years Old
Iva

"**H**ere's the hammer. What do you need it for anyway? You got some Frankensteins you need to build?"

He looks at me as if I'm one letter away from loony. "My mom is hanging pictures, and she can't find ours."

I stick my banana Popsicle into my mouth, suck on it for a few seconds and then pop it back out, when my eye catches on something covered in the garage.

"What's under that big tarp anyway?"

His gaze follows mine to the garage, and then just like that, it's back on me. "You mean that big, gray one?"

"Yeahhh." I almost say it as if it's a question. He's

got this wild look in his eyes, all of a sudden, and I don't know what to think of it.

"That's where we keep the bodies."

I accidently swallow a piece of my Popsicle, and it makes me cough. "What?"

"Yeah, you wanna see?"

He takes my hand before I can protest and leads me toward the big tarp. I drag my feet, but he's stronger than I am, and in the end, it does no good.

"Look," *he says.*

He takes a corner of the gray tarp with both hands and pulls with what looks as if it's all his might. I know there aren't any bodies. But what if there are? I force my hands to my face and cover my eyes, as banana Popsicle juice runs down my arm.

Meanwhile, Berlin laughs hysterically. "You believed me."

"I did not." *I open my eyes to a cherry-red car—an old one—like the kind I've seen in the old car magazines my grandpa has in his attic.*

"It's mine," *he says, proudly.*

I look at him. I know this car isn't his. He can't even drive.

"Well, it will be mine, when I get my license—that's what Dad says," *he clarifies, before I even have a chance to question him.* "He says if I can fix it, I can have it."

I walk around the front of the car. The terrified part of me quickly melts into awe. I don't know a thirteen-year-old who already has a car. "This is pretty cool." *I open the door and sit in the driver's seat.* "What kind is it?" *I ask, licking the banana juice off my hand.*

"It's a 1972 Chevelle. It was my dad's first car."

I run my fingers over the steering wheel and then over the knobs to the radio. "Can I ride in it?"

He walks closer to me. "Sure. After I get it to run, you'll be my first passenger." *He stops at the open door*

and leans against its frame.
"You promise?" I ask.
"As sure as the sky is blue."

"Hey."
I hear his voice, then I jump up and throw the Seventeen *magazine down onto the bed.*

"Berlin! How did you get in here?"
"I walked through the door."
I shoot him a straight face.
"I knocked," he says, chuckling. "The door was open. I brought the hammer back. It's on that desk in the hall downstairs." He points toward the stairs.
"Oh," I say, running my fingers through my hair. I'm sure it's matted to my head from lying down.
"Where's your folks?"
"Oh, um, some city meeting or something."
I watch him. He hesitates, then takes a step into my room and starts scanning the walls. He's never been in my room. My parents have never let him. And I've always felt okay with that because it made me feel safe—safe to display my set of My Little Ponies proudly on the shelf in the corner, safe to throw my bra on the cedar chest at the end of my bed, safe to pin my drawings to the wall.
"Did you do all these?" he asks, his eyes now scanning the sketches.
I panic. I don't know what to say. Do I tell him I did them? Or do I lie and say I bought them? Seconds draw out, and eventually, his attention moves to me. Where would I buy these? That's ridiculous.
"Yeah." I can barely hear my own word. "I did."
"These are good."
Most of them are of the ocean, which I've never been

to. I've seen it in pictures and in photos, so mostly, it's what I imagine it looks like. Others are drawings of people—mostly my momma and daddy and Angel and Angel's momma and daddy.

"She looks better in your drawing," he says.
I look up at the one his eyes are planted on.
It's of his sister.

My heart sinks. He must think I'm a creep now. I panic even more when I think about the picture I drew of him, but then I breathe a sigh of relief, remembering it's still safely tucked away in my sketch pad.

"I didn't know you could do this," he whispers to himself. "I've never known anyone who could do this."

He genuinely looks as if he's in awe, and it makes me smile. No one's ever seen my drawings or paintings—no one except my parents.

"I want to be a famous artist," I say. His words have given me a new air of confidence.

He smiles back at me. "It would be cool to know someone famous."

The room is quiet, as he stops at each drawing and stares into it for a little while. I'm so nervous. I wish I could read his thoughts.

"What do you want to be?" I ask him.

"Hmm?" he hums, before taking a seat in my desk chair. I see him notice the bra on the chest. And I see that his eyes get stuck on it. It doesn't help that it's hot pink.

I quickly jump off the bed, grab the bra and throw it into the hamper.

Berlin just chuckles and drops his gaze. "Pink's my new favorite color."

I look at him with scolding eyes. "Tell me your dream, Berlin Elliot," I say, plopping back onto the bed.

He smiles and then gradually lets it fade. "I don't know," he says, shaking his head. "I just like cars and motorcycles and going fast—that's really all I like."

"Well, I'm sure there's something like that out there that you could do."

He nods. "Yeah, you're probably right."

Our conversation grows quiet. I watch him, trying to imagine what he's thinking, as his eyes travel up to the ceiling.

"Sometimes, our greatest dreams are born under the stars—when they are all we have to light our path," he says.

I just stare at him with a puzzled look on my face, and eventually, his gaze levels off and comes to rest in mine. His words sound pretty, but I have no idea what he's talking about.

"My grandpa always says that." He shrugs. "He has this thing about stars."

I look up at the sporadically placed neon stars on my ceiling. Some are plain. Some have stripes. I thought the stripes made them more unique. But before I can get another thought out, I hear the screen door downstairs open, and immediately, I go into panic mode again.

"You have to leave," I say, in a hurried whisper.

He sits up. "Where am I supposed to go?"

I look to the window.

"Iva Scott, don't go thinking I'm gonna jump out that window. Do you know how far down that is?"

I suck in a sharp breath, taking a second to think. "Okay, just stay in here, until I give you the clear, and then you can run out downstairs."

He nods. "Yeah, that sounds better."

I hurry toward my bedroom door.

"Wait!" he says, stopping me.

"What?"

"What's the sign?"

"What sign?"

"How will I know to go downstairs?" he asks.

"Oh, um ... I'll uh ... turn on the blender."

He pauses and makes a funny face. "O-kay."

I turn toward the door again, but before I leave, I swivel back around. "And no touching anything ... or snooping."

He puts two fingers in the air. "Scout's honor."

I shoot him a baffled look. "I think that only works if you're a Boy Scout," I whisper.

"Okay, fine, Elliot's honor, *then."*

I narrow my eyes at him. "Yeah, I'm pretty sure I can't trust that, either."

"Iva, I've already seen your bra and your underwear, I think it's ..."

"What?" I quickly scan the room and notice my Supergirl *underwear in the corner.*

"Oh, my gosh!" I run to them and scoop them up. Kill me now.

"Just touch nothing," I whisper-shout to him, before escaping out the door. This is the most embarrassing night EVER.

I get to the bottom of the stairs before I hear Daddy's voice.

"Oh, we get a welcome party tonight," he says to Momma, as he takes off his jacket and hangs it on the coatrack.

"No," I say. "No party. Just me." I try to say it casually. "How was the meeting?"

"It was long," Momma says, slipping off her shoes at the door.

I walk into the kitchen and open the freezer. I'm looking for things I can toss into the blender. I grab the ice cream and some frozen blueberries. I throw them on the counter and peek into the living room. Momma and Daddy are both sitting on the sofa now.

I quickly scoop out some ice cream and toss it into the glass pitcher. I pour the blueberries in next, and I look one more time into the living room. Then I close my eyes and press start.

The sound of the blender bounces off every wall of the house. I never noticed it before, but tonight, this old blender might as well be a freight train.

I nervously watch the ice cream and blueberries turn into a thick, blue heap.

"What are you making?"

I jump, and at once, lose my breath, almost knocking over the blender in the process.

I look at the ice cream and blueberry mixture and then back at my daddy, now standing in the kitchen doorway.

And then I see him—Berlin—coming down the stairs.

I quickly try to avert my eyes back to the blender, but it's too late. It all happens so fast. Berlin notices my daddy. My daddy turns and notices Berlin.

Oh God.

"What the hell are you doing here?" *Daddy says. His voice is stern and kind of scary.*

"Um, I was just returning the hammer, sir," *Berlin says, eyeing the hammer on the hall desk.*

Daddy glances at the desk in the hall. "Then how come the hammer is there, and you're upstairs?"

"Um, no one was here, so ...," *Berlin stumbles.*

I cringe, as his words hit my ears.

"I was just trying to find ...," *he continues, before being cut off by Daddy.*

"Son, you best be leaving."

Berlin nods and then takes the rest of the steps to the front door.

"And ...," *Daddy says.*

Berlin stops, but he doesn't turn around.

"If I catch you upstairs or even in my house again, period ..." *He stops there, and the world goes silent, except for the water drops falling into the porcelain sink. I hold my breath.* "I just better never catch you here again.

The Life We Almost Had

Are you hearing me, son?"

Berlin slowly nods. "Yes, sir."

He escapes through the door after that, leaving me and Daddy alone again.

And I thought the underwear was the worst thing that could have possibly happened to me tonight.

"Daddy, he really was just returning the hammer. It's just that the door was open and no one was downstairs."

Daddy doesn't look at me.

"What's going on?" Momma leans against the banister.

"She can't see that boy again," Daddy says, walking past Momma.

He disappears into the living room.

There are tears starting to well up in my eyes.

"What happened?" Momma asks.

"Berlin was just returning the hammer," I say. "He was upstairs because he was trying to find someone to tell ... that he had returned it. That's all."

I can tell she studies me. And I can tell she believes me.

"We'll talk about this later, okay?" she says in her empathetic voice.

I nod and slowly head back up the stairs, leaving the ice cream in the blender.

When I get to my room, I notice, out of the corner of my eye, something move. I look out my window and into Berlin's. He's holding up a piece of paper.

I wipe the tears out of my eyes and then read: I'm sorry.

I try to smile, hoping he doesn't notice my red eyes.

I go to my desk and write some words down onto a piece of sketch paper: It's not your fault.

He leaves the window and goes to his desk. He's gone for several seconds, and then he reappears with another sentence: Your dad hates me.

I turn the sketch paper around and write on the back in big, charcoal letters: It's the long hair. *Then, I hold it up in the window and shrug.*

He seems to consider it for a second, and I'm afraid he doesn't realize I'm kidding.

I scribble I'm joking *onto a new piece of paper and hold it up to the window.*

It looks as if he tries to smile, but the smile never quite reaches his eyes.

Chapter Eleven
That First Cut

Present

Iva

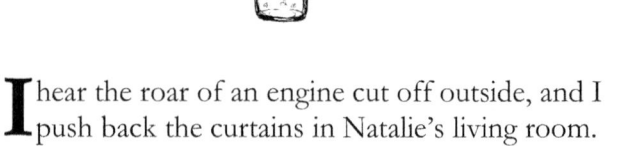

I hear the roar of an engine cut off outside, and I push back the curtains in Natalie's living room. The sun is setting, but it's still light out.

There's a car parked on the curb, and before I know it, I find myself standing outside on the narrow sidewalk, staring at it.

I can tell Berlin is watching me. He's leaned back against the passenger door of the car; his arms are folded; his legs are crossed out in front of him.

My eyes leisurely meander from the trunk to the hood, and then eventually, to the old, vinyl seats inside.

"Well," I say, "here she is."

I look over at him, and he just nods and smiles. "In the flesh."

My eyes fall back on the shiny, black exterior.

"But the Berlin Elliot I knew had a *cherry-red* Chevelle."

His eyes meet mine briefly before shifting to the car.

"Well, things change," he says, his words deadpanning into the concrete at our feet.

My gaze instantly goes to his, and for a moment, we don't say a word—even though I sense the silent whispers falling unspoken between us.

"You wanna go for a ride?" he asks.

I press my lips together and move them back and forth. I'm trying to hold back a smile. He already knows my answer.

"Get in," he says, opening the passenger door.

I gently breathe out and then walk toward him, before sliding onto the black vinyl. And before he gets in, I run my fingers over the dashboard, just like I did so many years ago. Unlike the outside, everything in here looks exactly the same. I like that it does.

He opens the driver's side door, and I quickly take my hand back and then watch him smoothly move behind the wheel.

"I thought you only brought her out for special occasions," I say.

He cuts a glance in my direction before pulling away from the curb. "That's right," he says, grinning.

We drive for a little while, with neither of us saying another word. If I'm honest, I'm almost afraid to say anything, in fear my words would betray me. I love this moment. I want to take it and shrink it down so that I can carry it around with me in my pocket forever. It feels so comfortable. It feels like home. I lost it once. And it hurts to think of losing it again.

For minutes, all that's audible is the soft purr of the engine and the whispered murmurs coming from the radio.

"You cut your hair," I say, breaking the silence.

He looks over at me. "You just now noticed that?"

I smile, and my eyes wander back to the window. "Do you remember that time my daddy caught you coming down the stairs, after returning that hammer?"

His laugh catches in his throat. "That is a memory I will never forget for as long as I live."

"Do you remember what you did that night?" I ask.

"Yeah," he says, nodding once. "I remember that, too."

There's a little girl on a bike with training wheels on the sidewalk outside my window. I follow her, until she disappears down another street. "I saw you walk out your front door the next morning, and all your beautiful hair was cut off." I return my gaze to him. "I was so sad."

"Well, I figured if it meant your dad liking me more, and if your dad liking me more meant I still got to hang out with you, then ... It was just hair." He plants his stare on the road ahead and shrugs a shoulder. "But we all know how that worked out. ... I guess it wasn't the hair."

I watch him. He doesn't take his eyes off the road. "I was kind of happy it wasn't," I say.

"Really?"

"Yeah, I liked that you grew it long again."

A slow smile burns across his face, and I remember

just then how much I love that smile. I quickly swallow the thought down.

"It's weird seeing someone sitting over there," he says. His eyes are on me now.

"What do you mean?"

"Well, after you, I never let anyone sit in the passenger's seat.

I can feel the questions flooding my face.

"Yeah, I know. Strange but true," he says. "I think it was just my way of holding onto you."

I inhale and then carefully force it out. I thought I would know exactly what to say to his every word if I ever got the chance to see him again. I thought I had this all planned out. God knows I had years to do it. But here I am, in this moment, and I don't know what to say—much less how to feel. It's been years. We were young. So much has changed. I just wish I would have found him sooner.

"What about your friends?" I ask, trying to change the subject, fast. "Didn't any of your friends ever ride with you?"

"I always made 'em sit in the back. And I kept a box on the front seat, so nobody really ever questioned it. And then, I got my truck, so ..." He looks my way. "That's weird, isn't it?"

"It's not *that* weird," I say, glancing at the speedometer. He's speeding, as usual.

He chuckles to himself.

"What was in the box—that sat on the seat?" I ask.

"Oh, just my CD collection."

I look at the dash just to see if anything had changed since the last time I was in here.

"But you don't have a CD player in here," I say.

He shoots me a swift glance and then grins. "And

The Life We Almost Had

you would be the only one who's ever noticed that."

I meet his charming stare and force my teeth into my bottom lip. "I don't even want to know the type of people you were hanging out with."

"Well, Isaac was one," he says.

I nod. "Enough said."

He laughs, and I do, too.

"So, tell me all the trouble you've been up to lately," I say, when our laughter fades into that black dash.

"Honey, we ain't got enough time for all that."

I roll my eyes at the *honey* part.

"No," he says then, shaking his head. "I left that stuff behind—trouble, that is. Well, most of it, anyway—with my teens."

"No. Berlin Elliot, the craziest boy I knew?"

"Yeah, well, I never said I wasn't still crazy. I just cut back, you know, just to save a few years on the end of this old yard stick."

I keep a watchful eye on him.

"Okay, what about girls then?" I ask. "I know this is a small town, but you must have every girl in it just waiting for you to give her a chance."

He looks at me, and I swear I see him blushing. But there's something about his eyes and the way they speak so powerfully without saying any word at all. Then again, there's always been something about his eyes.

"Nah," he says, shaking his head. "I probably damn near ran off every girl in this town."

I look up, and briefly, our eyes meet before he focuses back on the road.

"Come on, Berlin, I've never known you not to be a gentleman. I expect you to have broken some hearts, but please don't tell me you meant to."

His eyes seem heavier, darker. "Maybe you should

hear the whole story first."

"Berlin," I scold.

"It's not that bad," he assures me.

I give him a hesitant look. "Fine, tell me your story."

"All right." He brings his other hand up to the steering wheel, so that both hands are now resting on the top of the wheel. But it's not until we get about a hundred more yards down the road that he starts talking.

"I left Sweet Home, with the full intention that I'd see you again," he says. "And then, you know, the time came, and I went back, and you weren't there." He pauses and shifts gears. "After that, I didn't really expect I'd see you again. I mean, I hoped it." He shrugs. "But I didn't think it would ever happen. And God knows, if there was anyone left in the town to ask, I would have asked every last one to find out where you had gone." He sits back in the seat and rests one arm on the ledge of the open window. "But anyway, after you, everything just became a little less serious. With you, I had it all figured out. With you, I had a reason to have it all figured out. You were it. It was gonna be you—you and me. It might have been a little wild, maybe even a little crazy here and there, but it was all going to be okay because it would be me and you. And that's how life was gonna go."

I force out an unsteady breath. "Berlin, you never told me this."

Instantly, a serious expression takes over his face. "Iva Sophia Scott, you knew how I felt about you."

"Yeah, but we were kids. I had no idea that you put that much thought into it."

"Yeah," he simply says. "We were kids. But we still

The Life We Almost Had

had hearts." Our eyes meet briefly. And I smile because I feel vindicated. I loved him. I knew I loved him, but I spent so many years telling myself that it was only puppy love that I started to believe it.

"Well, anyway," he goes on, "without you, at the time, I just lost the taste for all that—all that love stuff. I didn't care—I mean, I tried—but in the end, I just didn't care whose heart I broke or if I drove too fast to live long enough to have a white picket fence and two rug rats." He pauses and takes a deep breath in before continuing. "You were my drug, Iva. I wanted you. As soon as I saw you, I wanted you. And I wanted you every moment I could get you. But you were also my heart—that soft piece that made me want to be a better man. And I really liked that soft piece, damn it." He stops there, but I can tell he has more to say, so I don't dare interrupt. And I wouldn't know what to say anyway. I hadn't anticipated his words. I couldn't have.

"And anyway, that's why I think I wasn't the greatest boyfriend after you," he says. "I was selfish. And I did pretty much what I wanted, when I wanted to do it. And that was it. And each heart was just like the last. It would break; she would cry; and I felt bad, but I didn't feel too much else."

He finishes, and there are tears floating in the backs of my eyelids. I try desperately to push them away before they fall. There are no words for how I feel. I'm sad I missed so much time with him. I'm scared I've missed too much. I'm terrified of missing all the rest. My heart is both breaking and melting for the boy I used to know. My teenaged self prayed every night that this boy would be a restless wanderer without me. But now, I just feel sad for ever wishing that upon him. And yet, I'm so happy that our love meant that much to him.

And I wish I could tell him that. I wish I could tell him that he just recited my life in these past seven years, as well. But I'm too afraid. I'm too afraid it's just a little too little, a little too late.

"It's that first cut, I guess." His words force my attention back to him.

I don't say anything; I just try to smile. I know that's enough for him. And in the next moment, we're pulling off onto the side of the road.

"Anyway, this is it." He stops the Chevelle and eyes a spot through my passenger-side window. "It's just across the field."

I have no idea what *it* is exactly, but I don't think to question him.

He gets out, and I follow his lead, and we walk across the field in silence, until we get to a line of trees.

"It's just through here," he says.

It's starting to get dark, so I follow him closely into the trees. We go about another couple hundred feet to a wooden dock. It's suspended in the air, above a bluff painted with green leaves. And out from the bluff, far below us, is a river that in the twilight looks like shiny, black oil. It carves its winding path in the dirt and weeds and flowers below us. I can just make out the dark and light greens spattered with orange and white from where we are, perched like birds above the valley.

"It's beautiful," I say.

He turns my way, and his lips curve up just right. "Yeah," he says. "That she is."

I quickly peer back down at the dark river and try not to blush. I know what he's thinking. And I should kill his thoughts. But something in me won't let me do it.

"Do you see that light over there?" He points

across the valley.

I follow his finger to a spot on the far bluff.

"Yeah, I do."

"It's a lighthouse," he says.

I look closer, and immediately, a smile takes over my face. "It is," I say, once I've got a good look at it. "But why?" I ask.

He shrugs. "I don't know. Maybe it's Mr. Keeper."

I watch the white light on top of the slender, little building spin around in circles.

"Well, you must know who it is, right? This is a small town."

He shakes his head. "I've never asked," he says, shoving his hands into his pockets. "I think I just always wanted to believe it was Mr. Keeper."

I smile and plant my eyes back on the light swirling around in the distance.

"I think it is," I say. "When everybody left Sweet Home, he came here."

He meets my gaze, as a grin smolders on his face. And we stay in each other's eyes for a few, long heartbeats, until I force my attention to the lighthouse again.

"How did you find this place?" I ask.

After a short pause, he chuckles to himself. "Sometimes, I look for places that don't have people. ... And I wander a lot."

That's all he says. I look over at him. His stare is somewhere far off.

A restless wanderer. I remind myself again to be careful what I wish for.

"What do you think Natalie and Isaac are doing tonight?" I ask, in an effort to change the subject.

He transfers his weight to his other leg. "Same as

they always do on his birthday."

"And what is that?" The mood has shifted, and I'm grateful.

"They'll go to some car show if they can find one. Then they'll go to Amelia's Tacos and Burgers for dinner, and then they might go see whatever movie is playing at the Walt. And then, you can use your imagination after that, I suppose."

"Oh, okay," I say, squeezing my eyes shut, begging my imagination not to go there.

"It's true," he says. "Same thing. Every year."

"They sound like two old people who've been married for sixty years."

"And they're *not together*," he says, using air quotes.

"Right," I say, sarcastically.

Our conversation grows quiet. And in that time, an owl coos off in the distance.

"Tacos and burgers?" I ask.

"Yeah, I was wondering when you were going to say something about that. It's actually a pretty good place."

"Okay," I say. "I'll take your word for it."

"Hey, speaking of those two, you wanna maybe go out with them tomorrow night? It could be like a double date, but no one is really seeing anybody."

I lower my head and smile to myself.

"It'll be fun," he adds.

I look up and meet his soft, brown eyes. I don't even have to answer. He already knows I'll be there.

His lips turn up, and then his gaze travels back to that lighthouse in the woods. I hate that I'm enjoying this time with him—knowing what I know. I hate it. But I also kind of love it, too. So much feels the same. But then again, so much has changed.

The Life We Almost Had

When I loved him, his Chevelle was cherry red.
It's black now.
When I loved him, we dreamed under the stars.
We have no dreams together now.
When I loved him, Sweet Home was still sweet.
It's home to ghosts now.

Chapter Twelve

Angel's Tree House

Fourteen Years Old
Iva

"You know who built this tree house?" *I ask. I lie down on the boards that make up the little floor, and I kick my feet up onto the wood railing. Berlin lies right next to me and does the same.*

"Who?"

"Angel's daddy."

"Who was Angel, anyway?"

"The girl who lived here before you." I turn my face so that I can see his. "She had your room."

"Oh," he says. "Were you friends?"

"Yeah." I look up into the hole in the roof and at the dozens of branches that crisscross above us in the dark.

"We were."

"Do you miss her?"

"Yeah," I breathe out, "some days."

I pick up the jar of lightning bugs we caught just a few minutes ago, and I examine the little parts of them that keep lighting up and fading out and then lighting up again. Then I tilt my face toward his; he's already looking at me. "But if she would have never left, I might not have ever met you," I say.

He smiles. "That might be true."

"Angel was like that," I say.

"Like what?"

"Always watching over me."

I don't say anything else, and eventually my thoughtful stare wanders back to his.

"You're pretty," he breathes out.

My eyes narrow in on him. I'm trying to figure out if he's just messing with me.

"You are." He says it as if he's never thought of it any other way.

"Okay," I say, looking away, feeling awkward. I'm pretty sure my momma is the only person who's ever called me pretty.

"What?" he asks.

"I don't know. Friends don't usually tell friends that they're pretty."

"Are you blushin'?" he asks.

"What? No." I press the jar of lightning bugs to my stomach.

"You are."

I cover my cheek with the palm of my hand. I know I'm blushing. My cheek feels as if it's on fire.

"Do you like me, Iva Scott?"

"What?" My eyes dart to his. One hand is still glued to my cheek; the other is glued to the lightning bug jar.

"I like you," he says.

My stomach starts to feel flip-floppy, so I sit up and lean my back against the railing. He follows suit and does the same, leaning his back against the railing opposite of me.

"And I've wanted to kiss you ever since I saw you in that window that first night. ... But then, I thought that all was a given."

"A given?" I ask.

"Yeah," he says, "I hang out with you every day. We stand together, waiting for that bus every morning and then we sit together on the way to school—every day. And then after school, we hang out in this old tree house. So, yeah, I thought it was a given."

I lower my head and smile to myself. I can't even control it. All those Seventeen *magazines couldn't prepare me for this moment—my moment—when all my dreams come true—when Berlin Elliot says he likes me.*

My gaze slowly rises to meet his.

"Can I kiss you?" he asks.

I sink my teeth into my lip. I'm trying my best to fight off a crazy grin, while my mind goes back to that first time he sat next to me on the bus. I have been secretly wanting to kiss him ever since then.

"Have you ever kissed anyone before?" I ask.

I'm curious. I'm hoping I'm his first kiss. But I also want to know what I'm going up against. I don't know the first thing about kissing.

He shakes his head.

I let go of a thankful breath.

"Have you?" he asks.

I shake my head.

A few moments pass, and then he carefully crawls across the wood floor and then sits down right next to me. My heart is pounding, and I can't take more than a shallow breath, but I also can't take my eyes off him. He's the cutest boy I've ever known. And he wants to kiss me.

The Life We Almost Had

He lifts his hand to my face, and his fingers graze my skin, starting at my temple and coming to rest at my chin. There's this new look—like hunger or want—in his brown eyes, as his stare follows the path of his fingers.

My heart is about ready to explode in my chest. I almost can't take it.

And then without warning, he looks into my eyes, and a wave of anticipation suddenly washes over me. And in that second, I wonder if he can see the hunger and want in my eyes, too. I want this boy. I love this boy.

After several breathless heartbeats, I watch his eyelids slowly cover his eyes. And then he leans closer. I close my eyes, and before long, I feel the touch of his warm lips.

He moves his mouth over mine, and I do the same. And then, he pulls away, leaving my lips feeling tingly. It was only a moment, but it was the best moment of my life. And with my eyes still closed, I quickly memorize everything. It's a Tuesday night in Angel's tree house with Berlin Elliot—My. First. Kiss. And it was perfect.

"I guess we're more than friends now," he whispers.

I open my eyes and press my fingers to my lips, as he finds a place next to me. And we stay like that—in the perfect silence—until he reaches for my hand and weaves his fingers through mine.

So," he says, "I guess I can tell you now that I like your butt, too."

"Berlin Elliot," I scold, gently elbowing his arm.

I can't stop smiling. My mind is still on the kiss. But then, my eye catches on the lightning bugs, and I start to unscrew the jar.

"What are you doing?"

"I'm freeing them," I say. "They only get to shine for a little while."

He looks down at me and smiles.

"That's why I like you, Iva Scott."

Laura Miller

I rest my head on his shoulder, and I set the jar's lid onto the boards beside me, as one by one, those fireflies fly away. But what I don't tell him is that I'm hoping one of these lightning bugs makes it up to heaven and tells God that the boy I want to marry is Berlin Elliot.

Chapter Thirteen
Like the Boy

Present
Iva

"So, you two knew each other before this weekend?" Isaac asks, eyeing Berlin and I from across the table.

We're at some small bar downtown on our *double date*.

I glance at Berlin, and for a moment, our eyes meet.

"Yep," Berlin says, returning his attention to Isaac.

Isaac keeps his cryptic look, but now he also narrows it in on Berlin.

"Were you a thing when you used to know each other or something because …"

"We were next-door neighbors," Berlin says, interrupting him.

"Ohhh," Isaac says, drawing out the word. "The next-door-neighbors' thing."

"No," Berlin says, grinning, "it was a little more than that." He looks over at me, and I just shake my head and smile.

"Berlin was the love of Iva's life," Natalie all but shouts across the table.

All eyes go to her.

Instantly, I feel as if I want to crawl under the table and hide until everyone in the bar leaves. Berlin, on the other hand, doesn't really seem as if he's at all affected by her statement.

"I'm sorry, Iva. I didn't mean ...," Natalie stutters.

I open my mouth, but nothing comes out.

"It's okay," Berlin says, taking my hand under the table.

Immediately, all my attention goes to his hand and his fingers now interlocked in mine.

"I already knew that," he says.

The feel of his hand is like an old memory you get to touch again. Suddenly, I can smell his boy cologne hanging in the warm, summer breeze, as we lie in the grass and weave our bodies together. I swallow hard and try not to let everyone at the table see my memory, too.

"It's true," I say, clearing my throat. "He already knew that. Then again, we were, like, fourteen."

"Fifteen," Berlin corrects. "Well, I last saw her when I was fifteen. She was the first person I met when we moved to Sweet Home. In fact, the evening before we officially met, I watched her change her own bike tire. And I knew, right there, we were going to be friends."

"What?" I turn to him. "I didn't know that. You watched me?"

"Yeah, a little creeper-ish, I know. But I just had never seen a girl change a bike tire."

"Berlin!" A girl yells from another table. And just like that, she's hovering over us. "I didn't know you were back in town."

I look at Berlin. *Back in town?*

"Yeah, just for a little while," he says to the girl.

"Well, isn't that nice," she says, pulling out a napkin from her purse. "Look, I don't want to interrupt you all, but can I get you to sign this for my aunt. She just adores you."

Berlin looks a little embarrassed, but he also looks a little too comfortable with that question for it to be odd.

"Sure," he says.

He squeezes my hand before letting it go and taking the pen and the napkin from the girl.

"Jill, you know that ain't for your aunt," Isaac says, prodding the brunette.

The girl rolls her eyes, but otherwise, ignores Isaac, though I know we all notice her blush.

I watch Berlin sign the napkin, while Isaac and Natalie talk to each other. And just as he's finishing, I look up and catch the girl's stare on me. I think it's a curious look, but I can't be sure. Either way, she quickly averts her eyes and takes the napkin from Berlin.

"Thank you," she says, pressing the signature to her chest. "She's just gonna love this."

"Okay," Berlin says with a nod.

And with that, she vanishes just as quickly as she had appeared.

"Okay, anyway, so, let me get this straight, then." Isaac seems determined to go on with his questioning, but *I'm* wondering what in the hell just happened. And why isn't anyone else wondering the same thing?

I look at Natalie. She's lost in her phone now, and she doesn't seem the slightest thrown off. *What on earth is going on?*

"You guys had this thing," Isaac continues, "whatever it was, when you were in high school, and then, you moved away," he says, eyeing Berlin, "and then ... you just never saw each other again? And then, like, what, a half a decade later, she just shows up here?" he asks, now staring straight at me.

"Yeah, that's about right," Berlin says, taking my hand again.

I really should protest his hand-holding. I'm not sure why he thinks, after seven years, he can just take my hand like that. Then again, I'd be lying if I said I didn't like it.

"So, you really liked this girl?" Isaac asks. He's addressing Berlin now, as if they're the only two people at the table.

It's a moment before Berlin says anything.

"Yeah," he says, eventually, squeezing my hand. His action sends an electric shock sprinting through my body, starting at my fingertips. God knows he's gorgeous. And I loved him. It's hard not to feel this way—no matter how much time we lost.

I watch Isaac. He keeps his focus solely on Berlin. I can tell he wants to say something else on the topic, but he never does.

"Natalie, I think this is your favorite song," Isaac says in her direction.

Natalie sets her drink down and listens over the

loud hum of the bar sounds.

"I can't even hear it," she says, almost yelling.

"It is," he assures her, "trust me."

He scoots out of the booth and takes Natalie's hand. "Come on, let's dance."

Natalie smiles at me. "I guess we're dancing then," she says. And right before Isaac pulls her away, she whispers *sorry* to me.

I smile, letting her know it's fine.

After they're both gone, I sit there, staring at a hole in the wood on the table's surface. Everything feels so raw, as if someone's just scraped back the first layer of my skin. And I don't know what to do about it. I came here just a couple days ago thinking that Natalie and I would spend all day at the pool, working on our tans. And then at night, we would paint the town red and dance until our feet hurt, and then we'd hobble home, with our heels in our hands and stay up all night talking about all the stupid adventures we had ever had ... and will have.

But that was all before I looked up from that street the same day I arrived here. At first, he was just an attractive guy that caught my eye. But then, I saw his face. And that's when my heart nearly stopped. I almost couldn't believe my own eyes.

"You wanna get some air?" I hear Berlin's smooth, deep voice, and it easily drags me out of my thoughts.

"Yes," I say, faster than he can even get the words out.

He chuckles, and together, we slide out of the booth and head for the bar's back door. And I might be crazy, but I feel as if every eye in this place follows us out.

There's a wood picnic table a little ways from the

door. We go to it and take a seat on the table part, planting our feet on the long bench.

"You can't *not* love 'em," he says, elbowing my side.

I nod, knowing he's referring to Natalie and Isaac.

It's dark, despite the glow of the lights from the bar. And in the far distance, you can see a tiny spattering of stars in the sky.

"What was that about ... in there?" I ask.

"What?"

"That girl ... wanting your signature?"

"Oh," he says, not bothering to elaborate.

"Berlin, what do you do?"

He smiles up at the sky.

"I drive a car."

I feel my head cock to the side.

"What kind of car?"

"A stock car. It's not a big deal. I'm still working my way up."

"But people know you."

"Yeah, well, we are in Channing, Kansas. Everyone knows the mailman, too."

I shoot him a curious look, but soon it melts into a warm smile. "You found something to do with fast cars, after all."

He nods. "Yeah. Yeah, I guess I did. But then again, you said I would."

He lies back against the boards that make up the table's surface.

"What do you think McMarbles is doing right now?"

I hear his voice, and then I lie back next to him. We're nearly shoulder to shoulder.

"I think he's looking down at us, thinking that we have no idea what we're missing."

I can tell he looks at me now, but I keep my eyes trained on that black sky.

"You think he's got all the plastic milk cap rings he could ever want?" he asks.

This time, I turn my head and meet his soft stare. He smiles at me, but right before it gets too serious, I look away.

"I think he does," I say.

It's quiet then, but it's a comfortable quiet, so I welcome it.

"Do you remember that day of the tornado?" he asks.

Instantly, I choke on a laugh.

"Geez, Iva, tornados aren't funny."

I try unsuccessfully to compose myself.

"Okay, fine, it was funny," he says. "I mean, it wasn't, but it was," he adds.

"I don't think I could ever forget that, even if I wanted to," I say.

"You were so scared."

"Well, you know, it was a tornado, and all," I remind him.

He drops his gaze. "I was more afraid of you dying on your own accord than by the actual tornado." He moves his head back and forth against the wood still warm from a sunny day. "I remember it, like it was yesterday. You were running around trying to snatch up everything soft you could find. And then ..." He stops and grabs his midsection and chuckles to himself. "And then you threw it all at me. And do you remember what you said to me?"

I wait for his eyes to find mine. "I do." I nod. "Unfortunately, I do."

"You said: *If we don't make it, I just want you to know*

that I was gonna marry you, and we were gonna have two kids, and we would be the happiest two people in all the world."

I listen to him recite my own words back to me.

"And then you said ...," he goes on.

I feel the weight of his stare, and I can tell he's waiting for me to finish his sentence.

I sigh because I remember, because I don't want to say it, because I *do* want to say it.

"I love you," I say. "I said: *I love you.*"

He presses his tongue to the inside of his mouth and forces his cheek out, as if he's in deep thought. "You did." He nods. "And you know what I learned that day?"

"Isn't it pretty obvious?"

He laughs. "No, not that. I already knew that."

"What?"

"Never underestimate this boy, Iva. I know more than I let on."

I shake my head in a scolding way. It, of course, doesn't faze him.

"No," he goes on, "I learned that we say what we already should have said when it's almost too late to say it."

His words are sharp and painful, and they force me to look his way.

"So, um, in perfect human fashion ..." He stops and drops his gaze. "I'm gonna just throw this out there."

My heart jumps into my throat. I try with all my strength to swallow it down. I have no idea what he's about to say, and I have no idea if I'm prepared to hear it, either.

"Iva, it's been fun trying to win you back." He moves his fingers so that they touch mine, and then slowly, he covers my hand in his. I close my eyes and let the feel of his touch flow over every inch of my skin.

"But if I'm honest with you," he says, "I was doing it because I told myself that if I ever ran into you again, I would do just that—I'd win you back." He turns his head and rests his eyes in mine for a moment, but then all too soon, he shifts his focus to the black sky again. "Shit," he quietly curses, "I've thought way too much about you in the last seven years that I, at least, had to do me right by trying."

He stops and clears his throat. And in those couple seconds of silence, I feel my heart slowly slipping deeper into my chest. I was expecting this, but I don't think I was as prepared as I thought I would be. We were kids. *Just kids.* And now, he sees it, too.

"But, Iva," he says, "being with you this week, I realize that I don't love you like that boy back in Sweet Home loved you."

I take a deep breath in. *I can do this. I can hear this.* I already knew it. And I need to hear it—straight from his mouth. We've grown up. We've grown apart. We've chosen our own paths—paths that don't lead back to one another anymore. And maybe ... Maybe he *is* in love with someone else.

"Iva ..."

My breathing has become this shallow sequence of tiny breaths, like the pattering of rain on a window. And suddenly, I realize that all that's running through my mind is closing the door I secretly fought for so long to keep open. And somehow, amongst the storm, I manage to find the soft, warm glow in his eyes.

This hurts like hell—just like it did the first time.
But I know it's necessary.
"I don't love you like that boy anymore," he

whispers.

"Iva! Berlin!"

Instantly, both of our attentions move to the little bar's back door.

It's Natalie.

"Iva. Berlin," she calls again.

I let go of a long-held breath. Berlin sighs.

"We're over here," he says.

Our hands fall apart, and we sit up and watch Natalie walk—not so gracefully—over to us.

"You guys wanna head out?" She plops down onto the table's surface.

Berlin and I look at each other. I wonder if he can tell that I'm asking him to make the call.

I'm almost thankful for Natalie's interruption. I had already heard enough.

"Yeah," Berlin says, "okay."

"Okay then," Natalie proclaims, pulling on my arm. "Help me back to the door, Ives. My heels can't take the mud in this sea of ... mud." She stretches out her arm over the grassy space between the table and the bar.

And with that, I give Berlin a small smile before taking Natalie's arm.

After Isaac drops Natalie and me off at Natalie's house, I help Natalie to her room.

"You know, I don't have a thing for Isaac, despite what everyone says," she says, kicking off her heels. "I mean, not a serious thing, anyway."

"I know," I lie.

"I mean, he's cool," she says. "It's just ... He's Isaac, and I still remember him as that scraggly, little boy that cried his eyes out the whole first week of kindergarten."

I watch her collapse, with all her clothes on, into her bed.

"Well, I'd say he's probably grown up a lot since then," I offer.

"Yeah," she says, pulling the covers up over her shoulder. "Maybe."

She slides her hands under her pillow and closes her eyes, and I quietly make my way back to the door.

"Iva."

"Yeah?"

"Can you keep a secret?"

Her eyes remain closed, but her expression is happy.

"Yeah," I say.

"I love Isaac," she whispers.

I smile. I'd tell her I already knew that, but part of me doesn't want to burst her bubble.

"Iva?"

"Yeah?" I say.

"Have you told him?"

"What?"

"Have you told Berlin, yet?"

I breathe out a sigh she probably doesn't hear.

"No," I say.

"He's in love with you."

I don't think I hear her right.

"What?"

"Berlin. Is. In. Love. With. You." This time, she pauses after every word, as if that will help me understand.

Her eyes are closed. I'm half-wondering if she's dreaming.

"Isaac told me," she says. "He said Berlin is in love with a girl he used to know from the town he used to live in. And he said that town is Sweet Home." She breaks and yawns. "And that girl is you."

I shake my head in disbelief, as my heart crashes against my chest. I want to tell her it doesn't really matter, based on the conversation we had tonight, but I can tell she has already drifted off to sleep.

I carefully turn, and as I leave the room, I switch off the light.

When I get back to the guest bedroom, I notice I have a text message.

It's from Berlin.

Instantly, I feel a wave of excitement rush through me, but then just as quickly, that wave turns to dread. And I find my finger anxiously hovering over the phone.

I take a deep breath and then click on the message: *I'm still here tomorrow. You wanna hang out?*

I'm a little taken aback. I thought he just said he didn't want to hang out ... or ... Or maybe he thinks he still has to finish the conversation. Or maybe this is his way of saying he still wants to be friends.

Either way, I'm relieved. I thought once he figured out that seven years was too long a time to make up that I would lose him for good. I can barely get my fingers to type fast enough.

Natalie goes to work at noon.

I send it and stare at the phone.

A moment later, it lights up.

I'll be there at noon, the message reads.

I smile and then set the phone down. But I can't

stop thinking about what Natalie said. Had he really held on that long? And had it really taken him just a couple days to change his mind?

I feel tears welling up in my eyes. I don't want our story to be over. But I know it almost is. And I know it has to be. But at least we have just a little more time.

Chapter Fourteen

He's Wrong

*Fifteen Years Old
Iva*

"What's your favorite color?"
I look up into that hole in the roof above us, and I think about his question. Nights like this—summer nights in this tree house with Berlin Elliot—are my favorite.

"Rain," I finally say.
He looks at me and smiles.
"Rain isn't a color."
"Sure it is."
"Well, then what is the color of rain?"
I turn my face toward his. "Rain, silly."
He narrows his eyes at me in a playful kind of way.

"That's why I like it," I say. "Can you think of anything that's the same color?"

"Hmm," he hums. He interlocks his fingers in mine and looks up toward the sky. "Water."

"I knew you were going to say that."

He shrugs.

"Water is water," I say. "But rain ... Rain is everything that it can take with it—like the muddy silt from the river and the green maple leaves from that puddle in my backyard. Everything it can take, it takes a piece of. So, it's not just one color. It's the color of everything water once touched. And nothin's like it."

"But you're wrong."

I turn my face toward him and catch the way he's looking at me. That look—it's the moment he first said his name; it's the night I saw him through his window for the first time; it's the way he looked at my drawings; it's our first kiss; it's that moment he said I love you, without even saying a word.

"What do you mean?" I ask.

"Your eyes are the color of rain," he says.

He looks into my eyes, as if he's trying to look past them.

"They're the color of everything they've ever touched—rain," he says.

His words make me smile. I swear I don't know how I got so lucky the day this boy showed up across the street. I squeeze his hand tighter and lay my head on his chest.

Moments pass, and we just lie there, in the warm breeze, listening to the leaves in the trees rustle all around us, until I kick my feet up against the wood railing.

"I have a taste for something," I say.

"Like what?"

"I don't know, like ... Maybe chocolate milk."

"Chocolate milk?"

"Yeah."

"Well, what about that mason jar of orange juice you've been sippin' on?"

I shrug and set my sights on the jar sitting in the corner. "I've been drinking that all day."

"Okay, well, let's go see if we have some," he says, starting to get up.

I follow him down the ladder nailed into the tree, and then we make our way to his kitchen.

His parents are out at a restaurant in the next town over, and Elin is out with her boyfriend. My parents are at my grandma's across town. So, it's just me and Berlin tonight. Of course, my parents think I'm at home studying for my driver's permit. But they already taught me everything there is to know about driving before I turned twelve, so really, it's their fault I got so bored I came over here.

Berlin goes to the fridge, while I take a seat on one of the barstools.

"Why does it always smell like toast in here?"

Berlin glances up at the toaster and then lifts his shoulders. "I don't know. We like toast."

I give him a crooked but satisfied smile, and he pulls open the refrigerator door.

"Nope," he says. I hear him slide some things over on a shelf. "No chocolate milk."

I push my lips into a pout and feel my body slump.

"You got any at your house?"

"No," I say, "I don't think so. I drank it all."

"Well, let's go to the store and get some then."

I look at him as if he's crazy.

"You want to walk to the store? It's like ten miles."

"It's not ten miles. It's more like five. But we don't have to walk."

"What do you mean?"

"We can take my dad's bike."

I just stare at him from under my eyelashes. "Your

daddy said you can't drive it in town. You don't have a license."

"Oh, it's late. No one will notice. We'll just go real quick and come right back."

I think about it for a second—exactly a second. I know it's probably a bad idea, but I really do want that chocolate milk, and anyway, almost everybody is probably already asleep or holed up in their houses for the night anyway.

"Okay, but real quick," I say.

"Iva, really, who are you talking to? Of course it'll be quick."

I roll my eyes and slide off the bar stool. "Don't kill us."

"Never, baby."

We get to the garage, and we each grab a helmet. I always wear the green one. It's really Elin's, but she never uses it. I pull it over my head and watch Berlin straddle the bike. And after he starts it up, I hop on behind him.

We zoom over the gravel on his driveway and then onto the street, and eventually, onto the highway. It's just like being on those dirt roads in the bottoms—really isn't any different, except a little smoother ride, I guess.

We're headed to the grocery store that's in Holstein. Sweet Home doesn't have a grocery store of its own. There's a convenience store at the corner of our street and Market—near the railroad tracks—but it only sells alcohol, candy bars and Clearly Canadian. And anyway, it's already closed by now.

It doesn't take us long at all to get inside the city limits, and on the whole ride, we never once come across another car.

I notice the speed limit sign reads thirty, as we zip past it. But Berlin doesn't know limits. Fast is his only speed. So, we keep going forty-five.

I love the way the air is warm even when it's dark

outside. That's my favorite part about summer.

I breathe in deeply and wrap my arms tighter around Berlin's waist. He's wearing his leather jacket. He always wears it when he's driving—even when it's ninety degrees. And I've never said it to him, but I love him. I love him so much it hurts.

Then I hear it—the loud, harsh shrill of sirens. I hear them even before I see the red and blue lights bouncing off the pavement in front of us. Immediately, the blood runs cold in my veins. We're dead.

Berlin looks back, noticing the officer's car, and then before I can think anything else, we're pulling into the gas station.

Berlin cuts off the engine and straddles the bike. He pulls off his helmet next, so I do, too. And then we just sit there, awaiting our fate, as my heart pounds in my chest.

It feels as if a thousand years go by before the officer even gets out of his car.

"What is he doing?" I whisper to Berlin.

He shrugs and shakes his head. I can tell he's nervous. I'm nervous, too.

I hear the door close behind us. Then, I hear the officer's footsteps getting closer to the bike. And all of a sudden, he's standing right next to us.

He's tall and big and intimidating. Then, I notice his face. It's Officer Brad. He plays basketball at open gym with my daddy every Wednesday night. Inside, I secretly breathe a sigh of relief because I know now at least we have a better shot of getting out of this than I thought we had.

"Berlin Elliot." Officer Brad's deep, booming voice fills the space around us, sending chills down my spine.

Berlin nods, acknowledging him.

"Iva Scott," Officer Brad says next, turning and casting his scolding eyes in my direction.

I push my lips to one side and force my eyes to

Berlin's leather jacket.

"I'm not even gonna ask you for your license, boy, because I know you ain't got one."

He stops there and just stares at Berlin. Berlin is brave, and he doesn't cave. He just sits there and looks as if he's preparing to face whatever's coming next. I admire him for that. I know he's scared; he has no idea that my daddy plays basketball with him.

"Why don't you two get in the car," Officer Brad says. And with that, he walks away.

Berlin turns and looks at me.

"He's friends with my daddy," I quickly whisper to him.

"Iva, that doesn't help," he mumbles. "In fact, that might make this worse."

I push out a defeated sigh. Then, I swing my leg over the bike, and Berlin does the same, and slowly, we walk to the squad car and slide onto the slick back seat.

I sit next to Berlin in the middle, holding his hand, while Officer Brad stands outside of the car, playing with his walkie-talkie.

"My dad is going to be so pissed," Berlin says, letting his head fall against the back of the seat.

I look at him, trying not to smile. I know it's not funny, but my heart is racing, and we're in the back of a cop car, and it's all because of chocolate milk.

"Oh, shit," he says, regaining my attention, "your dad is gonna kill me."

I try desperately to swallow down my smile.

"Iva," he scolds, "this isn't funny."

"No," I agree, shaking my head, "it's really not."

Berlin forces his head against the back of the seat again, closes his eyes and lets out a long sigh. Meanwhile, Officer Brad continues to hang out outside the car.

"This is not funny," I say. "Now, how in the hell am I supposed to get my chocolate milk?"

I want to smile, as Berlin's serious stare falls back on me, but I manage a pout instead.

Suddenly, Officer Brad is behind the wheel, and I hear Berlin clear his throat. Right away, my eyes get big. I know Berlin is about to say something, and by the look on his face, I know it's probably not going to be the wisest thing he's ever said.

"*Officer.*"

Oh, gosh. Here we go. *If we weren't already in trouble, we're definitely about to be in trouble now.*

"*I know I shouldn't have done what I did,*" Berlin says, "*but have you ever had a girl next to you that you just couldn't say* no *to?*"

Officer Brad peers up into his rearview mirror. His eyes are fierce, and he's got this stone-cold look on his face. I quickly avert my attention from the mirror.

"*Well, it's just, sir,*" Berlin goes on, "*she wanted a chocolate milk, and I didn't have any way of getting her one without the bike, so ...*"

I covertly peek back up at the mirror. I can just barely see Officer Brad's face, but it looks as if he's trying not to smile. Instantly, I let go of a thankful breath.

"*Is there any way we can stop at the IGA before it closes and just get a chocolate milk?*" *Berlin asks.*

Oh, gosh. *I swallow down a laugh before it has a chance to escape out of my mouth.*

"*Please,*" Berlin goes on. "*I mean, my dad's already gonna have my hide.*" *Berlin glances over at me.* "*And her dad ...*" *He stops.* "*Who the hell knows what he's gonna do to me? Hell, you'll probably have to show up at my house tomorrow to clean up a murder scene.*" *He pauses to shake his head and look down at the old, blue carpet covering the floor. And for the first time, I see a different kind of worry in his eyes.*

"*So,*" *he goes on,* "*can you just grant a poor kid's last, dying wish? I just want to make her happy tonight.*

The Life We Almost Had

And if that chocolate milk is going to make her happy, well, then ..."

"In and out," Officer Brad says, sternly, surprising both of us.

I look over at Berlin. There's a smile on his face now. In fact, you'd never know he was in the back of a police car, just a few seconds removed from detailing his own murder.

We pull out of the gas station, leaving the bike behind. And sure as his word, a minute later, Officer Brad is pulling right up to the IGA's doors.

"I'm timing you, son," Officer Brad says, looking down at the watch on his wrist.

Berlin jumps out of the police car, even before Officer Brad can get his last word out. And I watch as he dashes through the grocery store doors.

It's a few long, silent, awkward moments before Officer Brad starts talking again.

"Your daddy's right about that boy."

I meet his stare in the rearview mirror, and my heart breaks a little. I know my daddy doesn't like Berlin, but I'm not exactly sure why that is. If he really knew him, like I knew him, I know he would like him, too. And anyway, it's my fault we got in trouble tonight.

I sigh, and my defeated gaze falls to my folded hands in my lap. I start to fidget with the end of my tee shirt when I hear his voice again.

"He's wrong about him, too."

I look back up and into the rearview mirror, and Officer Brad is wearing the most subtle smile. And gradually but surely, a smile finds my face, too. And not even a second later, Berlin opens the back door and rushes into the car, sliding across the back seat, stopping only when his hips touch mine.

"Did I make it?" Berlin asks.

"No," Officer Brad growls, pulling away from the

grocery store, not even bothering to look at his watch. His stern voice is back again. But then I look into that rearview mirror, and I swear I see him smile.

Officer Brad keeps his eyes on the road, but I turn my attention to Berlin. He looks a little disappointed, but then he hands me the milk, and all the disappointment melts away.

"I told you we'd get it," he whispers in my ear.

I take the milk and shake my head.

I think I just fell a little more in love with this boy. And for the first time, someone has actually told me that it's okay to do that.

I think I just fell a little more in love with this night, too.

Chapter Fifteen
Your Place

Present
Berlin

"**H**ey," she says, jumping into my truck.
"Hi."

She seems happy. To be honest, I really didn't know what to expect after our conversation last night. I do hope to finish that sometime soon.

"Where are we going?" She looks over at me, as I pull off the curb.

"I was thinking my place."

Her eyes are on me fast.

"Your place?"

There's a curious surprise in her voice. It's cute. I

bow my head and smile to myself. "Yeah, I want to show you something."

"Like what you do for a living?"

I look her way and nod.

"Well, it's about time, Mr. Elliot."

We drive for a few miles, and it's not too long, and we're already outside of town. Houses are scarce out this way. Actually, everything is scarce out this way. So, we talk about our days and Sweet Home and high school, until I pull off the highway and onto the county road. Channing is known for its covered bridges. We go over a little one with a red roof. She makes a comment about how much she likes them and how they're kind of like art. But then I turn into the driveway, and all of a sudden, she stops mid-sentence and sits up in her seat.

"Where are we going?" she asks.

She glances over at me, and I give her a funny look.

"I thought we were going to your place," she says.

The long driveway is lined with apple trees. I didn't put them there, but it was one of the reasons I bought the house.

"Well," I say, "we were, but then I got to thinking: Maybe I should try my luck, see if these people are looking to unload a house on somebody today. You never know."

She looks over at me and gives me a quirky smile. I expected that.

The apple trees stop at a clearing, and then you can

see the house. Her eyes stay planted straight ahead.

The house is newer. Apparently, there was an old farmhouse here before it burned down in the early 90s. The people who bought the property after the fire built this house. It's more modern-looking than I'm used to. But I like it just fine. It's a stone and stucco two-story, and they did a nice job on the landscaping. A set of brothers who grew up here and own the local landscaping business put in the trees and the flowers and the lighted stone walk. It's nothing like Tom Stewart's place; he's got family money and owns the only bank in town. But it's not really what you'd expect a twenty-two-year-old to have, either. Hell, sometimes I wake up and wonder whose house I wandered into the night before.

I watch Iva. She's taking in the world outside her window, not saying a word. I'd pay to know what she's thinking right now.

I park in front of the three-car garage, and then I get out, walk to her side and open her door.

She silently steps out of the truck. I can tell she's suspicious, even as she tries to hide it. But I don't blame her. The wild, long-haired boy, who was always dressed in black because it hid the grease stains best, doesn't really belong in a house like this. Hell, the man who bought it doesn't either.

We take the stone path to the front door, and I gesture for her to go inside. She does, but it's not before she hesitates, giving me a long, questioning look.

I just smile and follow after her. And once I'm inside, I set the keys on the entry table and take off my jacket and throw that on a chair.

Then I notice her eyes travel around the room. They start at the vaulted ceiling in the entryway, and then they move to the staircase that spirals up to the second floor. And finally, they land on that ridiculously big, glass chandelier hanging from the ceiling. Elin picked it out. Actually, she picked out about everything in this whole place, except for that old grandfather clock in the hall. That was the same grandfather clock that sat in Grandma's living room for nearly fifty years. It was her most favorite possession. People say that if there were ever a house fire, they'd take their birth certificates or photos or something like that with them. Well, I'd probably leave all that stuff behind, just so I could get that clock out of here.

"Do you want something to drink?" I ask, walking into the kitchen.

She doesn't answer. I wait for a good, few seconds, and then I make my way back into the dining room.

"Iva?"

"I'm in here."

I follow her voice to the den.

"Berlin, what are these?" She must sense I'm in the room because she never takes her eyes off the wall.

"This is you," she says, pointing at a framed photograph.

I stare at the photo on the wall.

"Yeah," I say, nodding.

"This says NASCAR." She turns back and looks at me.

"Yeah," I say.

"Berlin, this is a little more than *working your way up*."

I shrug. I don't know what else to do.

"This is more like *you've made it*," she says. She looks at the frame and then back at me. "Berlin, this is NASCAR."

I nod, and she laughs to herself. "You're famous. Like, legitimately, you-have-your-own-Wikipedia-page famous."

Her eyes study me with this certain kind of sparkle. I recognize it. I've seen it before, like on the day I taught her how to ride my old dirt bike or when she took that first ride in the Chevelle or like the first time I kissed her in that old tree house.

"Well, this explains the house."

Her eyes find mine.

"It's beautiful, by the way," she adds.

I nod once. "Thanks."

She looks at me then, as if she wants to say something else.

"What?" I ask.

"Elin's house?" she says.

I nod, and I can see the understanding slowly washing over her.

"It was a birthday present," I add.

"Oh." An easy smile races across her pretty face. But I can tell she's still got another question in her.

"What is it?" I ask.

She pushes her lips to one side before giving me a shy look. It's cute.

"Your grandparents' farm?" she asks.

I nod again. "Christmas present to my dad."

Her entrancing stare stays locked in mine for several, long heartbeats.

"Not bad gifts," she says.

I shake my head. "They didn't complain."

She laughs softly to herself. "But how did this all happen?" Her eyes are back on the pictures on the wall.

I take a second and lean against the doorframe. "Well, with the dirt track, I guess. And then it just kind of evolved from there." I stop and shrug. "My uncle was always interested in it. He never did it, but he knew some people, and he got me started in it."

She moves down the wall, pausing for a few moments at a time to examine each photo. Elin framed them all for me and hung them on the wall, just last summer.

"You were so young," she says.

I nod. "Yeah, it all went fast—no pun intended."

She peeks back at me and gives me a silly smile. "Why haven't you mentioned this?"

I shrug again, but really, I didn't tell her because I wanted to surprise her. I wanted to see that sparkle in her eyes.

I watch her, not even trying to hide my grin. I can't honestly tell you if I got more pleasure in winning those races or watching her look at these photos.

After carefully inspecting each one, she goes to the trophies next, pausing to look at every one of those, too. Then, when she's done with that, she finds a cushioned chair across the room and makes herself comfortable.

I follow suit and sit down in the desk chair and lean back.

"How? And when? And ... How? Start from the beginning."

"Well," I say, taking off my cap and tossing it onto the desk, "I picked it up in high school, and it just sort of stuck." I run my fingers through my hair to break up my hat head. "I got a late start. Most kids start racing when they're seven or eight, but cars and speed always came kind of natural to me."

I meet her eyes, and she smiles and nods her head.

"But it wasn't until I placed pretty decent in the

Busch Series that I got noticed," I say. "And the next thing I knew, I was a full-time driver and rubbing elbows with Carl Edwards. If you would have told me four years ago, I'd be there, doing that, I would have told you that you were batshit crazy."

She opens her mouth, but nothing comes out, at first. "I just ... I just can't wrap my head around all this."

Her eyes don't leave mine for a long while, but then, eventually, I watch her gaze travel back to the photos on the wall.

"My dad ...," she says, her words trailing off. "He's never gonna believe this."

"What?" I say, feigning shock. "I could have sworn he thought I was gonna make something of myself."

Her attention immediately falls back on me, and she laughs. "Yeah, especially after that night Officer Brad brought us both home."

I lower my head and laugh, too.

"I can just see them," she says, closing her eyes, "those blue lights reflecting off your leather jacket."

I watch her smile break across her sweet face.

"Isn't it funny," she says, "that when you close your eyes, sometimes you can see something from so long ago, just as if you're there, looking at it?"

Her lips lift a little more, but her eyes remain closed.

I fold my hands behind my head. "What else do you see?"

She breathes in, keeping her eyes closed. "I see your room: your bed on one side; your desk in the corner; that shelf full of model cars; the window. And when I look out of it, I see those yellow curtains draping over my window, blowing in the breeze."

"Iva, why are you in my room?"

She opens her eyes, and they seem to stumble upon me—slowly, gradually, like raindrops sliding down the glass. "I'm in your room a lot," she says. "It's just always there, on the back of my eyelids. I don't even know why."

"Iva," I say and then pause for whatever reason, "I didn't finish what I was saying last night."

Her smile fades a little. "Berlin, you don't have to."

I cock my head a little to the side. "No, I do."

She sits back in the chair and rests her hands in her lap. She looks nervous. It makes me nervous. And for a split second, I wonder what she's thinking.

"I was saying ..." I lean forward and rest my elbows on my knees. "I was saying: I don't love you like that boy from Sweet Home loved you anymore."

"I heard that," she sings, softly, her eyes now glued to that hardwood floor.

"Iva."

I wait for her gaze to slowly make its way back up to mine. And when it does, I go on.

"I love you, as the man from Channing, Kansas." I sit up and rub the back of my neck, as an anxious breath flows past my lips. "And I know this is all too late and maybe the wrong timing. I mean, I don't even know what your plans are after school. I don't even know how you feel about all this ... But ... At least you know where I stand. At least now, you know. Nothin's changed. I still love you, Iva."

I watch her chest rise. And then I watch it fall, while time ticks out its slow and steady waltz on that old grandfather clock in the hall.

"Berlin ..." She cautiously shakes her head. "It's only been a week."

I study her face; I try to read her expression. I just want to know if she feels the same way I do.

"Yeah," I admit. "I had one week with you just now. But the truth is, I've had roughly ..." I pause to add up the time. "I've had roughly 150 weeks with you." I bring my fist to my mouth. "And that's 149 weeks and 6 more days than I needed to know that you were something I was never gonna forget."

She breathes in. I breathe out. And then her stare turns down to the hardwood again, as she fidgets with the hole in her jeans.

"Berlin, I'm moving to New Zealand next month."

My eyes find hers.

"You're what?"

I sit up even more in my chair.

"That's where the painter lives. He's a friend of a professor. And he's really good. I'm going to work for him."

Now, *my* eyes are on the floor. And suddenly, I'm at a loss for words.

"I'm sorry I didn't mention it sooner," she says.

I nod, but I think it's purely out of habit. The truth is, I have no idea what I'm nodding to. I press my hand to my chest. I don't feel well, all of a sudden.

"There aren't any good painters ... in the United States?" I ask.

There's a break before she speaks. "There are. It's just ... he's one of the best. And he's offered me a job."

I slowly bob my head. And then I clear my throat. "You thirsty? You want a beer, some wine or something?"

I think I just need to get out of the room for a second. These walls are closing in on me.

She swipes her eye with the back of her hand.

"Okay," she whispers.

I get up and leave the room. She doesn't follow me. I'm glad.

When I get into the kitchen, I rest both hands on the edge of the countertop, and I hover over it, breathing in, breathing out, trying to hold it together. *I can't lose her again.*

After a moment, I hear her footsteps, and I stand up and turn around.

"Maybe you could come." Her words are barely over a whisper. She's stopped in the doorway, leaning up against the frame.

I meet her beautiful, blue-gray eyes. They're full of so much. I never understood them. I knew I never would. They would always be a mystery, and I welcomed that.

"I have a contract." I can hardly get the words out.

Instantly, her gaze turns down, and I can almost see the hurt weave down her face.

"Oh," she says.

"It's two years," I add.

She looks back up at me, but she doesn't say a word. She just nods and lets her eyes wander to a place outside the window above the sink.

I force out a breath. I never expected to find her again. But I did. And she's even more than I remember. So, how am I supposed to just let her walk away? The thought sounds impossible.

"This life has never been on our side, has it?" she asks, rescuing me from my thoughts.

I shake my head, and despite myself, I smile. "No. No, it hasn't."

"This week was fun," she says, but I can hear the sadness in her voice.

I nod, but I can't get the words out to agree with her.

"How long are you there—in New Zealand?"

Her attention strays to the window again. "I don't know," she says, lifting her shoulders. "I haven't really thought that far ahead."

I chew on the inside of my cheek, before I catch sight of the refrigerator. It's a welcomed distraction.

"Beer? Wine?" I ask, pulling on the door.

"Oh ... Um, wine, I guess."

I grab the bottle of wine and find a glass in the cabinet.

"I'm sorry, Berlin."

"No, it's ... uh ..." I pour the wine and hand her the glass. "It's not your fault. It's just ... We finally stumble onto each other again, and now ..." I stop when I remember something. "Wait, you asked me to come with you."

Her eyes quickly find mine, and all of a sudden, her look turns shy. "Yeah."

"Does that mean what I think it means?"

She smiles a sweet smile and lifts one shoulder. "Maybe the girl from Sweet Home kind of likes hanging out with the man from Channing, Kansas."

I can't control my wild grin, and for several, perfect seconds, neither of us says another word.

Iva Scott still likes me.

I just watch her, staring back at me, and I try to soak up every, last piece of this exhilarating charge hanging in the air before reality smacks me in the chest again.

"Come to Sweet Home with me tomorrow," I say, breaking the silence.

I can tell she's trying to read my thoughts.

"For old times' sake," I add.

She pushes her hair back from her face. "It's like, five hours from here, right?"

"Yeah, we could go in a day and come back," I say.

My mood has shifted. I can think about tomorrow—if she's in it. And for now, I just won't think about the days after that.

She's thinking, probably calculating the risk—the fallout, everything that could go wrong, how many different pieces our hearts could end up in—if we drag this out. And as her teeth press into her bottom lip, my only thought is: *I hope she calculates into the equation the regret we'd carry with us if we didn't.*

"Have you been there recently?" I ask.

She shakes her head. "Um, no. I drove through it once years ago, but I didn't stop."

"Aren't you curious to see what your house looks like, if that tree house is still there, if the ghost of McMarbles is still sitting in your bedroom window?"

She laughs, and it fills the room with life again.

"We could leave in the morning," I say. "We could get there by noon, stay for a couple hours and be back by sunset. Give the place a proper goodbye. What do you say?"

I watch her chest rise and then fall like a wave in the ocean. Then, finally, she nods her head. "Okay."

"Yeah?" I say.

"Yeah," she agrees.

My heart nearly jumps out of my chest.

"Okay," I breathe out, grinning. "We can leave at six."

"Six?"

"Yeah, what's wrong with that? I was thinking five, at first."

"No, six is good. I just don't think I know what six in the morning looks like."

"Well, dear, you're about to find out."

Chapter Sixteen

One Hundred

Fifteen Years Old
Iva

"Hey," *I say, taking a seat on a stool in the corner of his garage.* "You wanna go walk up the street and get some Clearly Canadian?"

It's the only nonalcoholic drink the store at the corner sells.

"Okay," *he says, from under the Chevelle's hood.* "But why don't we drive there?"

He closes the big, metal hood, and it hits its base with a loud thud.

"What?"

"Yeah, let's go for a drive. It's only up the road."

"Wait. It's fixed?"

"Yep." He proudly shows off his white teeth.

I'm in the passenger's seat before he can even get another word out. I've been waiting for this day for probably as long as he has. This car means freedom. In a little less than a year, Berlin and I will have the freedom to go anywhere in the world we want to go together.

I watch him get in and turn the key. The engine rattles to a start, and this time, it doesn't cut off. I look over at Berlin with wide eyes.

"It's going!" I shout.

"Yep, it's going."

We slowly back out of the garage and then onto the street.

"Want to see how fast she'll go first?" He looks over at me with a devilish grin on his cute face.

I just smile, and he already knows that's a yes.

We cross the railroad tracks to the bottoms. Berlin is still only fifteen and neither of us needs another ride in a cop car, but over here—on the other side of the tracks— it's a different world. The rules of the rest of the world don't really apply on this side. This is where Berlin taught me how to drive his dirt bike and then his dad's motorcycle. Over here is where I drive my daddy's tractors and trucks from one field to the next. Over here, age doesn't matter. In fact, the only thing that anyone ever asks over here is: Can you reach the pedals?

I grab my seatbelt and grip the seats, as we quickly climb up the speedometer.

This side of the tracks is purely river bottom. It's flat, flat and more flat. And the roads are straight, straight and more straight.

I watch the dial on the speedometer climb to fifty and then seventy and then to eighty and then eventually to ninety. I have nothing to reference our speed. There are no trees or houses down here, and all the fields look the same.

But then, ninety comes. Ninety is when it starts feeling fast. I close my eyes before we get to a hundred. And I only open them when Berlin yells out the number.

"One hundred!"

He lets off the gas after that. And just as he does, a flash of something that looks an awful lot like my daddy's white truck catches my eye.

"Berlin!" *I reach for his hand.* "Did you see who that was?"

"Who?"

Before I can answer him, I look in the side mirror and see the truck making a U-turn in the road behind us.

"Shit!" *Berlin says, eyeing the rearview mirror.* "Shit!" *He pounds his palm on the steering wheel.*

We slow down, until we come to a stop on the highway. Nobody is worried about blocking the road. There are never any cars down here anyway.

Daddy pulls up right behind us and gets out of his truck. He looks pissed. But I'm so frozen in my own skin that I don't even think to move. I wish we could just drive—drive until it's just me and Berlin, drive our way out of this. But I know, no matter how far or fast we go, we'll never be able to outrun my daddy.

I watch Daddy swiftly walk through the tall weeds on the side of the road. The weeds almost look offended as they bend and then quickly snap back in the wake of his big work boots. But in the end, those weeds do nothing to slow him down. And before I know it, he's opening my door.

"Get out," *he says to me, in a stern voice.*

I briefly glance up at Berlin. He looks pale—as if he's just seen a ghost.

I wish I could stay right here with him.

"Out," *Daddy says again.*

With that, I slide off the vinyl seat and out of the car.

"Get in the truck," *he barks. His words are short and*

to the point.

I slowly make my way back to his truck, dragging my feet in the weeds. And when I finally get there, I climb onto the seat. And then I watch the scene unfold in front of me. I'm scared for Berlin, but I feel powerless to help him.

Daddy slams the door of the Chevelle and then says something to Berlin through the open window, but I can't hear what it is he says.

It's less than a minute, and Daddy's back in the truck. And the whole way home, he doesn't say a word. The silence is terrifying. And I'm scared when he does eventually start talking that he's going to say I can't see Berlin anymore.

Maybe we should have just kept driving.

I let go of an inward sigh. I'd find a way to see Berlin, though. Even if Daddy did say I couldn't, I still would. I can't even count anymore how many times I've been forbidden from seeing him. We find a way, though. Love always does. I love that boy with all my heart. And someday, I'm going to marry him. And Daddy's just going to have to learn to love him, too, because in the end, there's nothing he can do to make me stop loving him.

We get home, and Daddy still hasn't said a word to me. I almost wish he would just say something and get it over with. Each silent second that passes makes everything I touch feel more and more like shattered glass.

I carefully slide out of the truck, and I head into the house and straight up to my room. Still, Daddy hasn't said a word, so I don't, either.

Berlin's light is already on. I turn on my light and wait for him to notice.

Within a few seconds, he's at the window, holding a Clearly Canadian and staring back at me with a question written on his face.

I lift my shoulders and then let them fall, and I don't know why, but a smile takes over me. And as if it's contagious, he smiles, too.

Then he holds up a piece of paper that reads: I'm sorry.

I go to my desk and scribble down the words: She got to 100!

He holds up another page: She did!

He flips it around: I thought he was going to kill me.

I write quickly: What did he say?

He gets another piece of paper and writes something new: Stay away from my daughter.

I breathe out a sigh of relief. It's not like he hasn't said that before.

I look across the way and notice another message: You guys really have 8 guns?

Oh, God. *I mouth the words.*

He cocks his head, as if he's still waiting for my response.

I bite my bottom lip. And then hesitantly, I hold up nine fingers.

What? *He mouths.*

I grit my teeth together and slowly nod.

Shit, *I see him mouth.*

I go to my desk and then jot down a sentence onto my sketch paper: You wanna come over?

He bends down and uses his knee to write something else: Are you trying to kill me?

I smile. And eventually, he does, too.

Six months ago, I convinced my parents I needed a fire escape, in case there was a fire in the kitchen and I couldn't get out. I had never thought about a fire or having to jump out my window because of one, but when I came up with the idea for Berlin to use the ladder, it got me thinking. So, by the time I actually had to present it to my parents, I honestly was terrified that I was going to die a violent, fiery death alongside my shelf of My Little Ponies and Cherished Teddies. So in the end, it was an Oscar-worthy performance—only it really wasn't a performance at all. Either way, I got the ladder. And I got more time with Berlin, too.

He holds up a piece of paper with only one word written on it, this time: Midnight.

Chapter Seventeen
Stay Broken

Present
Iva

"Iva, you've been spending a lot of time with Berlin the last couple days."

I look over at Natalie. She's painting her nails for the second time tonight.

"What?" I ask.

She glances up at me.

"You and Berlin."

I sit back against the headboard of the spare bed—the bed I've been sleeping in all week. "I know, I'm sorry. I'm leaving the country soon, and we really haven't spent that much time together, have we?"

"What?" she says, giving me a strange look. "No, come on, please. The minute you told me that you found the boy from Sweet Home, I knew I wasn't going to see hide nor hair of you for the rest of the week. I could care less about that. Because you know why?"

I smile at her. "Why?"

"Because now, I've got an excuse to go to New Zealand. And I'm gonna be there—a lot." She wags the brush from the polish at me. "You just better get a big bed, so I have somewhere to sleep when I get there."

"Okay," I promise. "I will."

Her eyes quickly find mine. "But seriously, you and Berlin?"

"We're just catching up." I try to sound happy, but I know it comes out sounding anything but happy.

She gives me an unsatisfied flick of her eyes before going back to her nails.

"What was wrong with the purple anyway?" I ask, trying to change the subject.

She gazes down at her fingers. "It was too girl-next-door-trying-to-have-a-punk-rock-attitude."

"O-kay ...," I say, with a raised eyebrow.

She goes back to her paint job.

"Natalie, why didn't you tell me Berlin was a NASCAR driver?"

I watch the features on her face scrunch up, as if she just tasted a lemon. "You said you knew."

"No." I shake my head. "I never said that."

"Yeah, when I said he was risky, you said that you didn't qualify driving fast as risky, or something like that."

"No, I ... I just knew he liked driving fast. I didn't know he did it for a living."

"Yeah." She shrugs her shoulders. "He's kind of a

local celebrity around here, I guess."

I wait to see if she's joking. I don't think she is.

"Natalie, he's kind of a national celebrity."

"Meh," she says, waving her hand in the air, "if you're into that sort of thing."

She's onto her toes now.

I laugh and slide my feet closer to me, so that my knees are bent. "So, he's been doing this since high school. How have you never mentioned that you know somebody who races cars ... not even once?"

Her lips turn down at their ends. It looks as if she's really thinking hard about it. "I don't know. I kind of just found out about it myself. I mean, he wasn't really a big deal until just recently. Until then, I thought it was more of a hobby, to be honest. And anyway, I don't even really know what NASCAR is. I mean, yeah, I know it's got cars and that they drive in circles, maybe; I don't know. But I'm sure as hell not going to randomly go up to you and say: *Hey, this guy you don't know*—or I thought you didn't know—*drives a car, and he drives it fast.*"

I stare at her, even though she never glances up at me once. I'm half amused and half dumbfounded.

"But just out of curiosity, why did you never think to introduce me to him?" I ask. "I was always trying to set you up with people—before, of course, I knew the extent of the *Isaac situation*."

"The *Isaac situation*," she repeats, with a certain kind of pleasure in her voice.

"I don't know," she says next, looking up at the ceiling for a brief second. "I thought you'd want some artsy type of guy, who went to Juilliard and spoke at least two languages or something. And I love Berlin like a brother; don't get me wrong. But he just didn't seem like your type."

I chew on her words for a minute. "Is that why you never tried to set me up with anyone?" I ask.

She smiles through her puckered face. "It's really hard to find a guy who speaks proper English around here, much less a whole other language altogether." She pauses and sits up tall in her chair. "But I guess I was wrong. Apparently, you like the rough and fast ones."

I playfully roll my eyes at her and go back to my sketch pad. I'm drawing the lighthouse that Berlin and I saw a couple days ago. I do that, until something else tugs at my curiosity.

I let the pencil go idle, and I look over at Natalie. "So, why doesn't he have a girlfriend? I mean, he's attractive and successful. How is he not taken?"

She clears her throat, and at the same time, tightens the nail polish bottle with just the pads of her fingers.

"Let's just say," she says, locking her eyes on me, "I'm lookin' at the reason now."

"Uh-uh." I shake my head. "I'm not buying it. It's been seven years, Nat."

"Look, Iva, what's there to buy? It is what it is. I mean, guys are different than girls. They're not survivors, like we are." She sets the polish onto the desk beside her. "Our hearts break, and we pick them up, glue 'em back together and march onward. Guys' hearts break, and they just stay broken—until *we* put 'em back together."

She looks at me; she has this new, serious air about her now.

"But can't someone else put him back together?" I ask.

"Not like you can," she says.

I sit there, soaking up her words. I don't want to

believe she's right. Everything would be a whole lot easier if she were wrong.

"When did you get so romantic anyway?" I ask her.

"Oh, come on. I'd throw this pillow at you right now if it wouldn't mess up my beautiful, sassy-but-not-too-sassy-red nails."

I laugh and reposition the sketch pad on my knees.

"He'll be all right," I say to Natalie ... to myself.

"Yeah," she says. She seems to study me. I go back to drawing, trying not to let her stare affect me.

"You told him, didn't you?"

With that, I set the pencil down.

"Yeah."

I don't look her way, but I hear her breathe in and then loudly exhale.

"What did he say?"

"I don't know," I say. "What could he say? I'm leaving. He's staying. My life is there. His is here." I shrug, trying not to look as sad as I feel.

After a few moments of silence, she walks across the room and sits down on the bed beside me.

"Do you really like him?"

I gnaw on my bottom lip, out of habit, I think. "Seven years ago, I couldn't even bring myself to picture my life without him. And nearly every day since the day he left Sweet Home, I prayed for this—just to have one, last chance to see him again. I thought that if I saw him just one more time, I'd be okay." I pause to gather my thoughts. "And now, I've gotten my second chance, and it's about to end, and I don't think I'm going to be okay. I don't think I want it to end."

"Even after he broke your heart?"

I stretch out my legs and cross them in front of me. "It was my daddy."

"What?"

"Daddy threatened him with a restraining order."

"Get out!"

She roughly shoves my arm.

"Yeah," I say, rubbing my bicep. "It wasn't his fault."

"And you never knew?"

I shake my head.

"Wow." She sits back against the headboard, too.

"But I don't know," I say, "this last week, it was even better than I had imagined it could be. It was like old times but better. It's as if ..." I pause, thinking about how I want to say my next sentence. "I know this sounds crazy, but it's as if now we know it was real."

Natalie gathers her legs to her chest and rests her cheek on her knee. "Iva, you know I'm not going to tell you to stay here. You can't stay here. You had this dream since you were a little girl, even before you met Berlin, and now you have the opportunity of a lifetime."

"I know," I sigh. "I know."

"Maybe he'll go with you."

I shake my head. "No, he can't. He has a contract. Plus, he loves it. And it fits him."

"But what if *you* fit him, too?"

I suck in a big breath and then slowly force it out. "Maybe it's just not meant to be."

Her eyes turn down to the sky-colored comforter we're both sitting on.

"Well, how long's his contract?"

"Two years," I say.

"Oh," she sighs. "Well, did you figure out how long you want to be in New Zealand?"

I manage a silent *no* with the shake of my head.

"Well, you could come back here after you've become famous." She smiles a big smile. "Or ... maybe he could go there in two years."

"Maybe," I say, not feeling too optimistic about that last option.

She doesn't say anything after that, and I follow her roaming eyes until they stop at a spot near the corner of the bed.

Maybe he could come to me in two years. But he'd still be leaving behind his career, his dream, his niece and nephew. And who knows how long—if ever—it will take me to make a name for myself.

"Natalie, this is crazy. It hasn't even been a week, and I'm thinking about how to fit Berlin into my life."

"It's not crazy. You grew up with him. You probably know him better than anybody. And he's a good catch." She lazily shrugs her shoulders. "I would be trying to fit him into my life, too."

I smile, but I don't feel it.

"Nat."

"Yeah?"

"I told him I'd go back to Sweet Home with him tomorrow."

"Sweet Home?"

"Yeah, I know it's our last, full day together, and I can always tell him I can't ..."

"Uh-uh," she interrupts, stopping me. "Go. You need to go." She smiles softly, kind of like the way my momma always does. "I'll just see you in the Land Down Under."

I take a breath. "Well ... technically, it's the Land of the Long White Cloud."

"What?" She wrinkles her nose.

I just lift my shoulders.

"Anyway," she goes on, "isn't Sweet Home, like, quite a drive from here?"

I push my lips to one side and nod. "Yeah, it is."

"All right. Well, have fun," she says, patting me on the thigh.

"Thanks, Nat."

She stretches out her legs again.

"He's the boy from Sweet Home!" she shouts unexpectedly into the room, making me jump. She's got a crazy look in her eyes now.

"I know," I say, starting to laugh. "I feel like the luckiest ... and the unluckiest girl in the whole world—all at the same time."

Natalie puts her arm around me and squeezes me tight. "Sometimes it's just life's way of keeping us balanced, Ives." She pushes a strand of my hair away from my face. "But we make it. We always do."

I force out a heavy sigh. I barely even realize I'm doing it.

"But what is it about Berlin that you like, out of curiosity?" she asks.

I meet her inquisitive stare. "What do you mean?"

"I mean, when I come to visit you, we go to coffee shops with these artsy bands playing in the corner or some wine bar in this cool, little renovated building downtown. But here, the best place, honestly, is a barn in the middle of nowhere."

I laugh once. I didn't realize I came off as having a type of place or a type of guy, for that matter.

"I don't know," I say. "When I think about Berlin, I just have so much love for him; I don't even know what to do with it. And I've missed him so much. And now that I've found him, it's as if all the world is right again. So, I don't think it makes any difference really where we are or how different we might seem. In the end, we're just two people from the same place who fell in love."

I finish, and Natalie looks almost teary-eyed.

"Do you think you would pick him out of a crowd, if you didn't grow up with him?" she asks.

My gaze briefly falls to the bed. "Yeah," I say, "I think I would." I feel my eyes lift and venture to the street outside the open window. "There's just something about him that draws me to him. And I don't know if it's the way he looks at me or that he always knows the right thing to say to make me smile ... or that he remembers that banana is my favorite flavor." I stop and laugh to myself. "Or maybe it's just that when I look at him, I see the other piece of me— that piece that's not afraid to drive the Harley or to dream about being a famous artist or even to fall in love. And in the end, no matter what I do or how far I go, my mind and my heart and my soul just always wander back to him. Even my daydreams can't escape him. It's as if everything just always leads back to him.

So, yeah, he could be in a crowd of a million people, and I think I'd still find him, and I'd pick him."

Chapter Eighteen

I Can Do This

*Fifteen Years Old
Iva*

I come into the house crying. I normally don't openly cry in front of anyone, but I'm too sad to care right now.

"Honey, what's wrong?" my momma asks. The little wrinkles in her forehead let me know she's worried.

"Nothing," I say, roughly. I know I'm being short with her.

"It's that boy, isn't it?" my daddy chimes in. "I told your mother you shouldn't be hanging out with that kid, with his dirt bike and his wild self."

"He's not wild! And they're good people," I shout, before looking down at the hall floor. "But it doesn't even *matter anymore; they're moving."*

My daddy sits back in the living room chair and doesn't say another word. But I can tell by his expression, he's a little too pleased.

With that, I storm up the stairs and fly into my room, slamming the door behind me.

I don't want Berlin to leave. He's the best thing that's ever happened to me in this tiny town. If he goes, what will I do? There will never be anyone like him.

I bury my face into my pillow to muffle the sound of my sobs.

I love Berlin. He can't leave.

"Honey."

I hear my momma's soft rap on the door. I want to ignore it. I just want to be left alone, and I really want to tell her that, but the words never come.

After only a few moments, I hear the door creak open, and then I feel her sit down next to me on the bed.

I shift onto my side, but I keep my eyes trained on my frilly, yellow pillowcase. "Berlin's leaving."

She rests her hand on my arm. "I know, honey."

My eyes flicker up. "You knew? Did you know before I knew?"

"I only found out today, too," she says. "I talked to Carol."

A breath lifts my chest, and then a sigh quickly follows.

"It's going to be okay, honey. There will be other people who will move in next door. Maybe it will even be a girl your age this time. And you guys will be best friends ... maybe even for the rest of your life."

I press my face back into my pillow. She doesn't understand. I don't want anyone else. I want Berlin. He is my best friend. He will be my best friend for the rest of my life.

"Can Daddy give his daddy a job?" I ask. The

thought just comes to me.

"Oh, sweetie," she says, in her mom voice—the kind that lets you know she's about to gently tell you bad news. "Daddy doesn't have a job to give, and even if he did, it's not the kind of job that Berlin's dad would want."

My heart sinks a little further in my chest. I didn't even think it had any further to sink.

She soothingly rubs little circles into my tee shirt. "It really will be okay. I promise."

I roll my face back into my pillow. She doesn't understand. She'll never understand.

"Momma, why does Daddy not like them?" My eyes are full of tears, and my voice sounds like sandpaper.

"Who?"

"Berlin's family."

"Oh, Iva, your daddy likes them just fine."

I position myself so that I can see my momma's face. And with a stern look, I let her know that I know she's not telling the whole truth.

She gets it.

"Your father is just protective of you," she says. "A boy moving across the street is a daddy's worst nightmare. That's all. He likes them just fine." She stops and laughs softly to herself. "If your daddy had his way, he wouldn't have you get married until you were old enough to get the senior discount at Victor's."

"But, Momma, nobody's talking about getting married."

"I know. I know. It's just ... It's how daddies think."

I stare up at the ceiling and at my neon stars. "Well, maybe I could visit him, after he moves."

My momma lets out a sigh, and in that long, unspoken breath, I can hear the words: That will never happen. *But it doesn't matter because as soon as I said it, I knew it, too. There's no way that Daddy would let me go visit Berlin in some strange place if he doesn't even like me playing basketball with him in the driveway right outside the door.*

I'll just have to wait until Berlin turns sixteen and he can drive here himself. Maybe, then, it will be as if he never left.

But that's more than six months from now. That might as well be a lifetime away.

I turn over on my side, away from my momma.

"It really is gonna be okay, honey," she says, standing back up. "You'll see."

She leaves the room and closes the door behind her, while I try to wipe the tears out of my eyes.

I have to wait a whole half of a year to see him. That thought in itself is enough to crush me, especially since I haven't gone a day in the last three years without seeing his face.

It feels as if someone is sticking little needles into my heart. I've never felt this way before. I press my hand hard to my chest to try and stop the pain, but it doesn't do much good.

I never knew you could love someone so much.

I squeeze my eyelids shut, and tears seep out of the corners of my eyes. How am I going to do this? *I lie there and think about all the things we're going to miss, like homecomings and prom and graduation. When I pictured those things, I pictured him beside me. And how am I going to be able to look out my window and not see him? Like, what if I look across the street one day, and no one is there? Or worse, what if I look across the street and someone else is there—in* his *room?*

I stop my thoughts right there. I can't even think about that. I just have to get through six months. That's what I need to focus on. And until then, we can talk on the phone every day. And we can plan all the cool things we're going to do when he can drive and we can go anywhere we want to go. And maybe by that time, I'll have grown into my body and my hair won't be so frizzy and my face will be just like those girls on the cover of Seventeen *magazine. We'll see each other for the first time in months, and it will be like a movie. It'll be perfect.*

I can do this.

Six months.

Just six, long months.

I miss him already.

I'm drawing at my desk. The title at the bottom of the sketch paper is Berlin's House. *I have a drawing that I did years ago. I titled it* Angel's House. *You put them side-by-side, and they don't look that much different from one another. There are just a few minor changes that most people probably wouldn't even notice. For instance, Angel's family had an American flag waving off the front porch. When Angel left, they took that flag with them, and Berlin's family never replaced it. So, there's not a flag in the second drawing. And Angel's curtains were a pale blue. Berlin's curtains are navy. In Angel's driveway, there's a maroon Mercury Cougar sedan. It was usually in the driveway. And it just so happened to be there the day I did the drawing. I was glad, but I would have drawn it there anyway because I always liked that car. It had a little cougar decal in its grille, and I always thought it made it look so expensive. But in Berlin's driveway, I drew the old muscle car his daddy drives—and his motorcycle, too. And I drew one side of the unattached garage open, so that you could see Berlin's cherry-red Chevelle. And I drew Berlin working under its hood.*

If you were to ask me which drawing I like better, I'd give you a quick answer. But I'd feel bad about it because Angel was like a sister to me when she was here—and she did save my life that one time. But Berlin has my heart.

I look up from the drawing and see Berlin in the window across the street.

He smiles and gives me that same suggestive look he always gives me around this time at night.

I smile, too, and nod my head. And with that, he shuts off the lights to his room and disappears.

I look at the drawings one more time, and then I slide both into a folder and set the folder carefully into my desk drawer. Then, I go to my mirror and comb out my hair and then put it into a loose bun. And after I'm done with that, I go to my second window—the one that faces the side of our house—and I quietly let down the rope fire escape ladder.

"Hey," he whispers up to me.

"Hey," I whisper back.

He starts his climb, and I wait for him. And after a few seconds, his hands are gripping the wood of the windowsill.

"Hey," he says again, his face now peeking through the frame.

I feel a wide smile edge across my face, as he climbs in, gathers the rope back up and drops it right inside the window. And before I know it, he's pulling me close to him and passionately pressing his lips to mine.

I savor his kiss. I know I don't have many more with him. I know our time is running out.

"What's wrong?" he asks, pulling away. He uses the tips of his fingers to lift my chin. "Have you been crying? Your eyes are red."

I lower my face, so that he can't see my eyes.

"I don't want you to leave."

Immediately, I feel his arms engulf me, as he squeezes

me into his chest. I breathe in the smell of toast. I'm going to miss his toast smell.

"I don't want to leave, either," *he says softly into my ear.*

"We'll still talk, right?" *I ask.*

"Every day," *he says.* "And as soon as I get my license, I'll be here, all right?"

I nod into his chest.

"It's only 186 more days," *he adds.*

I lift my head so that I can see the feathery gold flakes in his eyes. "You counted?"

He nods. "I might have."

I wrap my arms around his midsection, and after a few, long, silent moments, he walks me to the bed.

"Come on," *he says,* "I've only got one more night with you under these neon stars."

He sits down, and I smile and sit down next to him. And then we both fall back against the sheets, and he wraps me in his arms.

"You know I was thinking the other day," *he whispers in my ear,* "how lucky we were to have found each other."

He pulls me closer, and our bodies meld together.

"I've never met anyone like you, Iva."

I watch the moonlight filter into the room, wishing I could hold onto his words forever.

"You read girly magazines," *he says. His voice is raspy and barely over a whisper now.* "But there's oil on your fingertips."

I look at my hand, and sure enough, there's a stain from when I helped my daddy change a tractor tire earlier.

"You draw pictures of the ocean like someone who's lived her whole life on the shore, but you've never once tasted its salty water," *he says.*

I bring his hand up to my lips and kiss his tanned skin.

"And you're beautiful," *he goes on.* "And fearless.

And you see something in me.

What do you see in me, Iva?"

I close my eyes and wrap his arm around my waist again. "I see ..." I stop to take a breath. "I see a piece of art—made of metal and rubber and wood. But the thing is, it's one of those pieces that's never really finished. It just keeps moving and changing. And every day, it looks like something new and beautiful. So, I just keep hanging around and staring at it, waiting to see what it's going to be next."

I pause, and for a few heartbeats, I can only hear that tree branch scraping across the roof.

"Metal, rubber and wood, huh?" he asks.

"Mm-hmm," I hum.

"All right." I can hear his smile, as his warm breaths graze my neck.

"And most of all," I say, "I see love. I see love in your eyes—for this life, for your family, for Mr. Keeper and Claire Blanch—for people you don't even know ..."

"And for you," he whispers in my ear. "Most of all, for you." He presses his lips to my neck. "Iva, I love you so much. I've never loved anyone like I've loved you. And I just know I'll never love anyone like this again." He grows quiet and swiftly intakes a breath. "I just know it."

I turn around and still my lips against his, and then I gently rest a hand on either side of his face. "I won't either," I say. "I'll never love anyone like I love you." And as I say the words, I feel a weight, as if it's an anchor, tugging at my heart, and I know that what I've just said is true.

My heart will always long for him.

Tears slide down my cheeks.

I look into his brown eyes, and I run my fingers through his long hair. He doesn't fit in here; he never has. He doesn't know anything about farming or small-town norms. He doesn't know you don't wear black everywhere you go. He doesn't know you don't encourage Miss Blanch's weird tendencies. Just last week, he bought a new leash for her stuffed cat she parades around town. He said he had noticed that the old one was only hanging together by a thread. He doesn't care if you're the fire chief's son or a waitress at Victor's. He treats everyone the same. And we could be flying a hundred miles an hour down a long stretch of highway or lying perfectly still, looking up at the stars, and he's content, either way. I think I love that about him best. It doesn't matter where we are or who we're with or what we're doing, he lives his life all the same—his own way—all in.

"We have to stay together," *he whispers against my mouth, his breaths leaving a welcomed heat on my lips.* "Iva, I'll never move on from this—this thing we have. I'll never get over you. Even if I wanted to, I wouldn't know how to do it." *There's a broken piece to his voice, and it makes my heart ache even more for all the time we're going to miss.*

"Is that a promise, Mr. Elliot?"

I try to wear a brave face, even though my heart is breaking.

He looks into my eyes, and then I feel his lips press a desperate kiss onto my forehead. "That's a promise. I'll never get over you, Miss Iva Scott," *he says, his voice gravelly.* "As sure as the sky is blue, I'll never get over you."

Chapter Nineteen

You're Home

Present
Iva

I tiptoe down the last few steps to the front door of Natalie's parents' house. They know I'm leaving with Berlin today; I just don't want to wake anybody up at this ridiculous hour.

I carefully open the door, and then as quietly as I can, I slip through it. Berlin texted me a minute ago, letting me know that he was outside. It's dark out, and the air is a little cool. I pull my jacket closed and sleepily make my way down the sidewalk and to his truck.

The seat feels warm as I crawl onto it.

"Good morning, sunshine."

I look at him through tiny slits in my tired eyes. "No talking until after the sun comes up."

He laughs. "Whatever you say, beautiful."

I smile at that. I know I don't look beautiful. My hair is twisted up into a knot on the top of my head. I think I put mascara on, but I'm not sure, and that's all the further I got in the make-up department. And there's probably still sleep in my eyes.

Berlin keeps his word and doesn't speak the whole time the sun is slowly creeping up the horizon. Instead, we listen to the soft melodies pouring from the radio, while pinks and oranges light up the sky. It's been a long time since I've seen the sun rise. I've forgotten how pretty and peaceful it is. It's calm and quiet and untouched by the day.

"When you drove through it last, what was it like?" He breaks the long silence and my thoughts with his husky, morning voice.

I lift my head from my bent knee and look over at him. He's focused on the road on the other side of the windshield. I wait to answer him until after I study his face. He's dark, despite the fact that we're a long way from last summer. And he has a five-o'clock shadow now. It makes him look older, more experienced in this thing we call life. And I realize, for the first time, that he's got it—life—more figured out than I do. I'm still finding myself. And he's already found.

"Empty," I eventually say.

He chuckles. "It was empty when we were there."

I nod. "True."

"Did you go by the house?"

I shake my head before I answer. "No."

He nods, and I rest both my bare feet on the seat and hug my knees. "Are you excited to see it?"

He cocks his head to the side before he speaks—almost as if he's unsure of what he's about to say.

"Yeah, I am. But I'm afraid it's going to look so different that I won't recognize it anymore."

I lay my cheek on my knee again. "You'll recognize it. No matter how much it changes, it stays the same. I mean, some things aren't there anymore, but it's as if your memory just fills in the holes."

"What things are gone?"

I take a breath and think about it. "Um ... Victor's Café; the store at the corner; the bleachers at the baseball diamond in the park; most of the baseball diamond; and that little shed we used to hide in when we got caught in the rain on the other side of the tracks. Remember?"

He nods. "I remember."

"Well, it's gone." I shrug. "But I still see it."

He bobs his head again—as if in thought.

"We have a lot of good memories all over that little town," he says.

I turn my face, so that my other cheek is now resting on my bent knee and I'm looking out the window. "Yeah, we do."

Little does he know, I've had all those memories playing on repeat since the day he left.

The drive all but flies by, and four and a half hours in, we stop at a little grocery store in a town along the way to get sandwiches, popcorn and Gatorade.

"Do you ever get scared inside the car?" I ask,

offering him some popcorn, once we're back on the road.

"Inside my race car?" he asks, taking a handful of the popped corn.

"Yeah," I say.

He shakes his head. "Nah, you get used to it. Bad crashes really aren't that common, and the cars are a lot safer than they used to be."

"Have you? Ever crashed?" I almost can't get the words out.

"Yeah," he says, grinning at me. "But they've never been that bad."

I try to scold him with my eyes. "You can't smile about that. And you can't get into anymore crashes."

He laughs. "For you, I'll try not to."

I lower my head and smile to myself, before another question pops into my mind. I swear I've learned more about NASCAR in the last four hours than I ever thought I'd know.

"Does it get hot inside the car?"

"Yes. But you get used to that, too."

"What if you have to go to the bathroom?" I ask.

"You go."

"What?"

"Thankfully," he says, "I've never had to." He dips his head. "But some have, and they just go. And then they pour water on themselves before they get out of the car to hide it."

"No!"

He nods. "It's true."

"That is ... truly ... enlightening," I say. "Thank you for that."

He smiles wide. "You're welcome."

I look over at him. His eyes are on the road. He is

pretty cute. Actually, he's really cute. Most of the time, I think I just see him as the boy I grew up with, and every once in a while I get these flashes of the man he is now, and it literally almost takes my breath away.

"What about your number?" I ask. "Do you get to pick it?"

"Nope. Owner does."

"Hmm," I hum.

"And the whole paint job is just a few big stickers—even the headlights and taillights," he adds.

"The lights on the car? They're stickers?"

"Yeah, completely fake. All an illusion."

"What?"

He just nods.

"I feel as if my whole life's a lie," I say.

Berlin chuckles and switches his driving hand, before turning off the highway.

"We're not just drivers; we're magicians, too." He winks at me, and it makes me laugh.

And it's not long after that, and we're passing the sign that reads: *Welcome to Sweet Home, You can hang your hat, you're home.*

My eyes go from those words to the little city limit sign that reads: *Population: 137.* Only, the *137* is partially scratched out, and it's been replaced with a new number: *102.*

We hit a pothole, and the little bit of purple Gatorade that's left in the bottles in the center console sloshes around. I look at the clock in the dash. It's almost noon, on a Wednesday. But I'm not sure you could guess it by just looking. There's no one around. There are no cars. The buildings are empty and boarded up. I strain my eyes to get a good look inside the post office as we drive by. I think it might still be in operation. And if that's the case, it might be the only place still open on this whole street.

Another turn, and just like that, we're home again. Berlin stops along the curb in front of my old house. I peer out the window. It looks like home. It looks unloved, but it looks like home. Big pieces of plywood cover some of the windows, and weeds are just starting to grow up again in the cracks in the sidewalk after a cold winter. There's a little *no trespassing* sign on the old iron fence that has always wrapped around the front yard. And gone are my momma's yellow roses.

I look over at Berlin, and he's looking at his house across the street.

"Well, there she is," he says.

His house has boards in the windows, too. But he doesn't seem too upset about it. I can tell he's just happy to be here.

He opens his door and steps out of the truck. I follow his lead.

"Looks the same," he says, leaning against the truck.

I glance over at him and then up at his house. "Well, besides the boards and the weeds and the broken windows," I say.

"Yeah, besides all that," he says.

We stand there, just looking at his house. And I replay in my mind the time it was Angel's. And I remember that bird cage in the hallway and that big wooden table in the dining room. And then I think about when it was Berlin's house, and all of a sudden, I breathe in the smell of toast.

"Let's go inside." He pulls on my hand.

"Wait. What?" I ask, tugging back.

"Yeah, yours first."

He leads me to the front gate of my house.

"Berlin, we can't go in there. It's somebody else's, and it's probably not safe, anyway."

"We'll be careful. And no one will care."

I look up at the house, and instantly, an overwhelming sense of nostalgia and curiosity takes over my body. I want to see those rooms again.

"Okay, fine, but let's do it fast," I say.

Berlin looks back at me with a smirk. "That's the only way I know how to do most things, my love."

I roll my eyes at him and let him lead me through the wrought iron gate and then up to the wooden porch and weathered front door.

The door's lock has already been broken once. And now, the door is simply sealed by a piece of two-by-four nailed to both the frame and the door. Berlin easily pries the board from the door and pushes it open.

As the old hinges scream back to life, the first thing I notice is the faded wood floors. They have taken on a kind of ghostly look now—mostly from the dust. There's dust everywhere—on the wood baseboards, on the banister leading upstairs, on light fixtures still hanging from the ceiling. And with the dust, there are cobwebs dancing along the walls and crisscrossing in the corners.

For a good minute, we both just stand there, taking it all in. It looks familiar, but just like its outside, it also feels eerily untouchable. I'm afraid to disturb the little holes in the walls or to step on the creaky floorboards, and not only because I think it might be unsafe, but mostly because I'm afraid to feel this house's pain. I'm afraid to feel its lifeless soul touching me back.

But in the end, it is home. It's unloved and uncared for, but it's home.

The Life We Almost Had

I step toward what was the dining room. The table is gone. I close my eyes, and I imagine my momma and daddy and me sitting around our pork chops, talking about our days. I hear the laughter, and I hear Daddy going on about the weather. And I even see the scolding look from Momma to clear my plate.

I walk to the banister that leads upstairs. It's still the same banister, even though the paint is all but chipped away. I rest my hand on it. It moves ever so slightly under the weight. Years ago, it was fully capable of holding my backpack and all its books. But I wouldn't expect it to do that today.

Berlin follows close behind me. I can tell he's watching me. I like that he's giving me these few moments to get lost in this place one more time.

A warm breeze filters through the broken window, and I breathe in the smell of roses. I know it's not real because there are no roses. But for a good, few seconds, there were.

Berlin takes my hand, and suddenly, something about being here and feeling his touch makes me sad. I loved that boy that lived across the street so much. And I wished for him back for so long.

And now he is.

And I'm leaving.

He smiles at me—one of those not-so-rare smiles that makes my heart beat just a little faster.

The breeze dies down, and for the first time, I notice the musty smell of dust, mixed with stale air. And everywhere I look, there are only browns and tans and grays. But yet, I imagine blue curtains and red chairs and light yellow walls.

We walk into the living room. It's quiet and empty now. But somewhere in the background, I hear the weatherman on the TV talking to my daddy about rain. And then I hear Daddy talking back to him, telling him to bring the storm a day later. And everywhere I look I swear I see one of my momma's treasures—like that plant that hung from the ceiling in the den or that big, ugly flower vase that sat in the hall. And what once seemed odd and useless are now, suddenly, my most favorite things in all the world.

Berlin steps lightly on the floor. I know he's making sure it's not going to cave in on us.

I let go of his hand and start up the stairs.

"Iva, I'm not sure we should go upstairs."

I step on the first step. It seems all right. So, I step on the second, and then the third.

"I think it's fine," I say.

Berlin doesn't stop me, as I slowly make my way up the stairs. Instead, he walks right beside me.

We get to the top of the steps, and I turn to the first room.

I test the floor. It seems okay, too, so I go in. And the first thing I do is stand in front of that window. And I stare out of it and at the window across the street. And after a moment, Berlin comes and stands next to me.

"So, this is where it all began," he says.

"Once upon a time," I say, spinning around to look back at the empty spot in the corner, where I—and sometimes we—used to sleep.

"It looks so much bigger in here without the furniture," I say.

I run my fingers along the wallpaper border, until it curls up at its end and stops. It's my same wallpaper—blue and white waves—just like the ocean. Then I look up and notice the neon stars still stuck on the ceiling.

The Life We Almost Had

Some even still have their blue stripes. And finally, under the second window, I notice the rope fire escape ladder. We both see it at the same time. And I watch as Berlin reaches into his dark jeans and pulls out his pocket knife.

I don't say anything. I know what he's about to do. And I know he probably shouldn't, but I also know that it probably doesn't matter one bit to anybody whether that old rope is here or not. ... But it matters to us.

He takes the rope in one hand, and with the other hand, he starts cutting through the dusty, braided nylon with the knife.

I watch him, until the rope is free from the windowpane. Neither of us says a word about it.

After my room, I explore the rest of the house—the kitchen, the bathroom, the den—where my daddy would analyze endless farm magazines and almanacs. And finally, I find myself back at the front door, and I just stand there and stare at everything inside the house that I can fit into my line of sight. I want to remember it all—every doorway, every window, every scuff in the floor. I don't want to forget a thing.

"I think I like it more now than I did the last time I was here," I say.

Berlin chuckles. "Isn't that how it always goes?"

I smile at him. Then I stand there, just silently memorizing. And Berlin lets me do it, without saying a word.

"Okay," I finally say.

"You ready?"

"Yeah, I think so."

We walk back outside. And with the rope ladder still in his hand, Berlin picks up the two-by-four, lines up the nail holes and shoves it back against the door. It stays, as if we had never touched it at all. And then we make our way down the old porch steps.

I watch Berlin toss the ladder onto the truck bed, and then together, we walk across the street.

His front door is locked, and immediately, my shoulders slump a little. I want him to be able to relive his life here, just like I was able to.

We stand there for a moment.

"Maybe the back is open," I offer.

"Wait," he says, reaching into his pocket.

He pulls out his ring of keys.

"You don't."

"I do," he says.

He locates a gold key from his keychain and sticks it into the lock. The key turns, and the door clicks open.

"I can't believe you still carry that key around."

"It came in handy, didn't it?" he says, grinning back at me.

"Well, we're just lucky nobody changes locks around here," I say.

We both step inside, and the wood boards of the floor creak below our feet.

"Hey, you know what?" he says, stopping me.

"What?"

"I think that's the first time I've ever used that key."

I catch his giddy expression, and I just laugh. "I believe that." Locked doors in Sweet Home were like spots on a tiger.

I watch him walk to the center of the dining room, the first room in the house, and stop. He looks around. His eyes travel from the floor to the walls to the ceiling and then back to the floor again.

"It looks different without carpet," he says, turning

back toward me.

I smile and survey the empty walls with the wallpaper hanging on for dear life and the cobwebs in the corners and the dust as thick as a slice of bread sitting on the windowsills. "It's the carpet that makes it different?"

"Well, mostly," he says, taking time to wink at me.

I shake my head and walk into the kitchen. The appliances are all still here. In fact, only the refrigerator is different from when Angel lived here. Hers was a tan, almost yellow, color. Berlin's was always white.

I stop at the sink and stare outside the window when something grabs my attention.

"Berlin."

"Hmm?"

"Come here," I say.

Within a moment, he's standing beside me, looking out that same window.

"It's still here," I say.

"Well, hot damn." He runs his fingers over his lips.

"Let's go see it," I say.

I unlock the back door that's right off the kitchen. It sticks, but after a good, hard pull, it pops open. And then, we walk across the backyard to the little wooden ladder nailed into the old oak tree.

"It's smaller than I remember it," I say.

He shrugs. "It looks the same to me."

I climb up the ladder and crawl along the wood boards that make up the floor until I'm resting on its far side. Unlike the two houses, this old tree house surprisingly seems as though it's lasted the test of time, without much change or wear.

Berlin climbs up next and takes a seat on the opposite side. And he just stares at me with a big, wild smile stretched across his face.

"My first kiss was right here," he says.

I lower my eyes before meeting his gaze again. "Mine, too."

"Really?" He acts as if he's shocked to hear that. "With who, pray tell?"

I shake my head. "Just some boy I used to know."

"Well, it couldn't have been just any boy. I mean, it was your first kiss. He had to be something special, right?"

I stare back at him, trying not to smile.

"Was yours ... special?" I ask him.

"The kiss or the girl?"

I keep my eyes locked in his, but I don't say another word, while hushed seconds fall to the boards beneath us.

"The answer is *yes*, to both," he says.

There's a minute where neither of us speaks or even moves, for that matter. But then it's me who eventually bows my head and softly clears my throat.

"You think Officer Brad is still running up and down these streets?" I ask, looking through the space in between two railings.

Berlin peers through the railings as well. "I don't know if anyone's out there anymore."

Instantly, I choke down a laugh.

"What?" he asks.

"I'm sorry, I could just swear that I've heard that line in a movie about the apocalypse once."

"Well," he says, chuckling, "it could very well be ... the apocalypse. In the time it took you and I to drive here, the world could have ended. In fact, we could literally be the last two people left on this earth." His stare remains somewhere far off. "We wouldn't know the difference here."

My eyes catch on an old, glass bottle rolling down the middle of the street.

He's right.

"It'd be nice if somebody could bring some life back into this town." His eyes wander back to mine.

I nod. "You never know. Maybe that old lighthouse in the woods will guide everybody back here again someday."

He laughs to himself. "Yeah, maybe."

I stumble upon his gaze briefly before my attention strays to a piece of wood in the far corner of the little house. Berlin follows my stare there.

"Well, there it is," he says, "the first cut."

I softly smile, and then I move over to it and trace our initials in the wood with my fingertips, remembering the day he put them there.

Berlin moves next to me and watches me do it. And when I get to the last letter, I look at him. And I get caught in the words in his eyes. And I don't know if it's just being here or remembering how I loved him ... Or maybe it's just the man he is now, and all the time we've been spending together is just now catching up—but I can't look away. I'm mesmerized by the gold spinning in his gaze.

With a gentle hand, he moves my hair from my shoulder. And then his fingers carefully trace a path down my bare arm, leaving a trail of fire in their wake. My heart pounds in my chest. I forget to breathe. And before I can even get another thought in, I feel my eyes falling shut. And then it all happens so fast—the rush, the heat, the familiar sensation of his lips brushing against mine. Our actions are remembered, yet somehow new and raw. At first, the kiss is soft and gentle, and his touch is tender. But then it deepens, as he intertwines his hand in my hair and draws me closer to him. And all I want is more of him. Lust and passion sprint through my body. But mostly, I feel love—a love I thought I had lost forever.

I loved the boy from Sweet Home. And now, I'm back at the place where it all began with the man from Channing, Kansas. And I can't even tell them apart.

Suddenly, our kiss breaks, and he presses his forehead to mine. I'm out of breath. He is, too.

"I've been wanting to do that all week," he breathes out in a whisper. And after a pause, he adds: "I'm sorry if it was the wrong thing to do."

I lift my gaze to his. "I'm not sure it was—the wrong thing."

There's a subtle smile on his lips. I have no idea what he's thinking. I can't even tell my own thoughts apart. Everything about this moment is so overwhelming. And meanwhile, my heart is about ready to burst.

I love him.

The thought just dashes across my mind, as if finally, it were free.

I love him.

I haven't admitted that to myself for nearly seven years.

"It's been a good week," he says.

My eyes immediately turn down to the boards that make up the floor.

There it was—that moment that reminds us that this all is about to end.

It stings my heart.

"When you become a famous artist, you'll let me know ... where I can get your work." There's pain in his voice. My first instinct is to kiss it away, but that's overridden by seven years of absence.

I try to smile, instead. "When I become a famous artist, I'll send you my favorite piece ... on the house."

He lowers his head. "I can't wait."

I watch his eyes travel to a place in the distance, beyond the walls of this tree house. And it looks as if his mind goes there, too.

"We are more than a week, Iva Scott. Please don't forget that."

I meet his sultry stare.

"I won't," I promise.

It grows quiet again, and there's a part of me that wishes for this big, blue sky above us to swallow us both, so that we can live in this world, in this time, forever. It's an old wish. I've wished it before—in this same place, a long time ago.

"Iva."

He presses his lips together and furrows his brow—as if he's about to say something important.

"I love you," he breathes out.

And just like that, I lose my breath.

"And I'm always going to feel this way about you," he whispers. "This love," he clarifies, "it's always going to be here for you. But of course, you knew that," he adds, in a low voice.

I feel tears pricking the backs of my eyelids. I don't want this to end. I don't want this to end again.

He reaches for my hand. Then he intertwines his fingers in mine—just like he used to. The feel of his skin on my skin immediately makes me wish he hadn't done it. It feels good to be here. It feels good to be here, like this, with him. It makes me wish I had never accepted a job half a world away. It makes me wish I had dreamed all my dreams differently. It makes me wish we had never left this sweet, little town—that those seven years apart had never happened.

I stare at our hands and feel a tear slide down my cheek.

"I love you, too, Berlin Elliot."

I just say it. I forget the consequences, and I just say how I feel.

He looks into my tear-filled eyes.

"Then stay with me," he says.

There's a moment when I can hear myself breathing. I'm not thinking anything. I'm just replaying those four words over and over again in my head.

He squeezes my hand and rests his other hand on the side of my face. "Make a life with me, Iva."

A series of incoherent thoughts run through my mind then: *Sinclair Williams; Berlin; the bird on the broken fence; painting; plane ticket; Berlin; a dream; the ocean; New Zealand; Berlin.*

And then, my lips part, and a word comes out.

"Okay," I whisper.

He finds my eyes. There's caution written on his face—as if he doesn't know if he can trust his own ears.

"Okay," I say again. *Who knew that little word could be so freeing?* "I love you, Berlin. I want to make a life with you."

I can tell he doesn't quite know what to say. "You don't need time to think about it?"

I shake my head. "I have thought about it. I've thought about it every minute since I found you again."

"What about the internship? What about New Zealand?"

I shrug. "I want to be with you." An unexpected smile crosses my lips. "I don't have to go. Berlin, you're my dream. You've always been my dream. I can paint here just as easily as I can paint anywhere in the world." I laugh, despite the tears still in my eyes and those rolling down my cheeks. "Plus, here, I'll have my muse."

He looks at me—like really looks at me—like he did when we were just kids. It's that same look of a million wild and crazy thoughts all wrapped around one, central thing. And a long time ago, I deciphered that one thing is *love*.

He gathers me into his strong chest and firmly wraps his arms around me. "Iva, you are more than I could ever comprehend." Then he pulls away and finds my eyes. "It's always been you. Just so you know, it's always been you, Iva. There comes a day in every man's life when he looks up, and he knows he's met his match. And for me, I was just a boy when that day came." His voice breaks into a smile. "But I knew it, all the same. That day I looked up and saw you just across this street ... That was the day I laid down my armor ... and gave you my heart."

I wipe my eyes with the back of my hand.

"Iva, from here on out, we're gonna be okay. We're gonna make it this time." I feel his tender kiss on my forehead. "I'm not letting you get away again." He pushes a strand of my hair back from my face. "Plus, this time, there are no daddies threatening any restraining orders, and I've got a car. And I'll drive as long and as fast as I have to ... to get to you."

I look into his eyes. "Promise?"

He nods. "As sure as the sky is blue, Iva Scott."

He pulls me closer again and whispers in my ear: "I love you, baby. I love you with everything I am.

I always have.

I always will."

Chapter Twenty

I Saw Your Name

Two Months Later
Iva

I declined the offer to work under Sinclair Williams. And I canceled the flight to New Zealand. And on the fifth of May, I graduated from the university with a degree in fine arts—something I'm not quite sure how I'm going to use in Channing, Kansas, but right now, it doesn't matter. Right now, what matters is that I get to begin again the life with the boy I've always loved—with the boy who taught me how to love.

Natalie wasn't surprised when she heard the news that I wasn't going to New Zealand. She was sad that she no longer had a reason to go there, but she got over it pretty quickly. And Isaac acted as if he knew I would stay all along. Berlin's parents, too, didn't seem overly surprised. And neither did Elin. My parents, on the other hand, were a different story. Berlin came with me to tell them. My momma was happy—happier than I imagined she would be. And I don't know if it was because I'd be closer to home—at least now, she wouldn't have to take a plane to see me—or if it was just because she really did like Berlin. She never said it growing up, but she was, ultimately, the reason that Berlin and I got to spend the time together that we did back in Sweet Home. She was always in my corner when it seemed as if Daddy wasn't.

And I might be crazy, but as I was telling them my plan to move to Channing, I almost thought I saw something in my momma's eyes. It was almost as if, for a moment, she was someone else entirely. For the first time, I saw this glint in her far-off look that made her appear vindicated—as if she had believed this was always going to be the outcome.

My daddy, however, kept a straight face the whole time that Berlin and I talked. I was almost afraid for Berlin, even though he now towered over Daddy's shrinking frame. I just couldn't stop thinking about all the times I had to fight with him to see Berlin. I know he thought Berlin was never good enough for his little girl. And I don't so much hate that he thought that way anymore, but I was hoping that he would see him in a different light now that he's a man.

When we finished talking, Daddy looked at Berlin. I could tell he wasn't really thrilled about anything we had said.

"Well, just how do you plan on supporting

yourself?" he asked. "My daughter will do just fine. She's got a good education. But she doesn't need to be supporting you, too."

Berlin briefly glanced at me. He still had that same terrified look on his face he always had when facing my daddy, but at the same time, I could also see something new in his eyes.

"I think I'll be able to pull my weight, sir," he said, meeting my daddy's cold stare.

"Daddy, Berlin is a NASCAR driver," I interrupted then.

Daddy's eyes got as big as two, round saucers. Then he stared at me, and then he stared at Berlin. And then he pulled out his glasses from his shirt pocket and put them on. And Momma, Berlin and I watched as he found his phone and pecked out some letters.

A few, long minutes crept by before we finally heard Daddy mumble, under his breath, the words: "Well, shit."

Then he slowly set his phone onto the arm of the sofa, slipped his glasses back into his shirt pocket and didn't say another word, until we were leaving. It was then that Daddy stood up, and he shook Berlin's hand—for the first time ever. And then, he smiled a rare smile. And you could think that Berlin being a famous NASCAR star sealed the deal when it came to Daddy's opinion of him, but I know the truth. It wasn't the titles or the fame or the money. When the rubber met the road, it was the haircut and the slacks and the button-down shirt—that wasn't black.

I set down a box full of my clothes and swipe my forehead with the back of my hand.

It's move-in day, and it's nearly ninety degrees. But I can honestly say that today is my most favorite day of my entire life, next to the day I saw Berlin for the first time in seven years.

"Iva, Isaac wants me to open the shed tonight."

I look up from the box. "Oh, really?" I scrunch up my nose and plop down into a desk chair. It's parked in the hall, for now. It almost made it into the den.

"Yeah, I know," Berlin says, echoing my exhaustion. He glances down at his phone's screen.

"I was hoping for a relaxing night ... with you," I say.

He looks back up and pushes his lips to one side, as if he's thinking.

"It's fine," I say, before he has a chance to say another word. "Just tell him you'll do it."

His gaze stays in mine for a long moment. I know he's trying to read my thoughts. "You sure?"

"Yeah, it'll be fun. And *fun* sounds good, too," I say, smiling back at him.

"Okay, then. I'll let him know."

We get close to the path that leads to the barn, and I notice that there are cars lining the road.

"Berlin, why are people already here if it's not even open, yet?"

He pulls up to the barn and turns off the truck. "I don't know." He looks up at the big, wooden door. "I think Isaac said that he might get here early and open it up. He knows where the extra key is."

"Oh," I say, with a question still hanging on my lips.

I reach for the door handle, while Berlin gets out of the truck.

"Well, then why couldn't he just open it up himself … since, well, he did?" I ask, through the open window.

He smiles. "I guess it's just a nice gesture, you know, to ask."

I half-heartedly try to hold back a laugh. "A nice gesture? *Isaac Thrasher* and *nice gesture* don't really go together."

"I do believe you are absolutely, one-hundred percent correct about that, Miss Scott." He opens the door and offers me his hand. "Maybe it was Natalie's idea to ask, then."

I shrug and let him help me out of the truck. Then we walk to the barn hand in hand. And as soon as we get to the big door, I can see all the people inside. It seems as if everyone from the whole town is already here.

"Well, I guess there wasn't much going on anywhere else," I say.

"Oh, baby, come on, this is where you want to be—no matter what else is going on."

I laugh, and he leads me through the crowd of somewhat familiar faces. I'm still getting to know everybody.

The lights are all on, and there's a soft glow over every person and piece of wood surface. I can tell that Isaac is in charge of the music, as usual. There's some kind of folkish country pouring through the big speakers. And tonight, there's a karaoke machine in the corner.

All of a sudden, the music stops, and I hear Isaac's voice echoing off the walls. "Attention. Attention."

The crowd hushes to a soft murmur.

"I just want to let everybody know that the infamous Berlin Elliot has just entered the building with his beautiful childhood love, Miss Iva Scott." He points in our direction, and everybody turns to look at us.

I squeeze Berlin's hand, as I increasingly feel the weight of their stares.

"The thing is," Isaac goes on, refitting his blue Royals cap over his head. "The thing is, I always knew Berlin was looking for someone. And not just anyone, but someone in particular. He never told me outright, of course, but I knew it. Everywhere we went, his eyes would always be scanning the faces in the room. And he probably doesn't remember it, but once, years ago, he mentioned this little town he spent some time in, and that little town was Sweet Home, Missouri. And then along with it, he mentioned a name—Iva. And that's when I put two and two together." He takes a long swig of a bottle and then sets it down. "Berlin," he says, looking directly at Berlin now, "you'd make a piss-poor detective because all that time you spent looking for her, in the end, it was her who found you." He picks up his beer again and raises it in the air. "So, thank you, Iva, for saving my friend, here, from a life of always looking at the faces in the crowd, trying to find his other half."

Berlin squeezes my hand. There's a tender look in his eyes. Meanwhile, there's a tear in mine. Somehow, Isaac Thrasher, in his artful rambling, managed to pull on my heartstrings.

"He'll be taking autographs in the back all night, so

feel free to hit him up," Isaac adds, lightening the mood again. "You got aunts, uncles, Grandma, Grandpa, the family dog—make sure you get everybody a signature."

The crowd buzzes with a soft laughter, and immediately, Berlin turns to me.

"Tree house?"

I nod.

Isaac keeps hamming it up, while we slide out the back door. I'm pretty sure we go unnoticed.

We get to the little house, and Berlin takes my hand and kisses the back of it.

"I love you."

I smile.

"I love you, too," I say.

It's crazy how easy it is to say those words after all the time that has past. Then again, I've said them to Berlin, the boy from Sweet Home, a million times before. And also, I guess, it's easy to say words that are true.

I kick off my boots and climb up the ladder and find a spot on the boards. Berlin climbs up next and sits across from me.

"What?" I ask.

"Nothing." His grin is wide. "It's just that we've been doing this for quite some time now, Miss Scott."

"Doing what exactly, Mr. Elliot?"

"This," he says, glancing down at the floor of the old tree house. "Sittin' in tree houses, looking at each other from across the way."

I press my teeth into my bottom lip. "I like tree houses. And side-by-side is overrated. This way, I get to look at you."

He lowers his head and laughs to himself.

I listen to the way his voice breaks. In seven years,

he still has the same, sultry laugh.

"I thought you were the cutest thing when I first saw you," I say. "Of course, I'd never admit that then."

"No, you wouldn't," he says.

A spry grin edges, little by little, up his shadowed face.

"It was the long hair," he adds.

I nod. "It was ... among a few other things."

He breathes in an unhurried breath, and then he pushes it out through the space between his lips. "You want to know what I thought the first time I saw you?"

I nod.

"I thought ..." He pauses. "Now, remember I saw you before you saw me. You were changing that bike tire, and I thought ..." He brings his fist to his mouth. "I thought, I've got to find a way to talk to that girl. If it's the last thing I do, I have to talk to her because I can already tell that when she moves, the world stands still."

I fix my eyes on his.

"You still think that?" I ask.

He dips his head. "Every day."

"And you know, I was scared to death," he goes on, "to sit with you on the bus that first day."

"No, you weren't. I don't believe it."

"I was. I was so afraid that I would say the wrong thing, and you would think I was weird and you would never want to talk to me again."

"Well," I say, laughing, "I did think you were weird." I meet his stare. "But I happened to like weird."

He keeps his eyes locked in mine, but he doesn't say a word for several, faultless moments. And in those moments, I feel something that feels a lot like desire and love and want coursing through my blood, and I just know I've made the right choice to stay here—right here with this man.

He sits up. And I watch him, as he carefully moves closer to me and then takes my hand.

"Iva."

"Yes?" I say.

"I found you, and at the same time, I found *us* in Angel's tree house in a little town that's just as much a part of me as my own heart. And I was lucky enough to find you again ... here, in this old tree house where I spent so many of my days hiding away from the world, dreaming of you."

He pauses and slides his hand into his pocket and leaves it there. "Iva, I drive 200 miles an hour around a racetrack with dozens of other cars ... going 200 miles an hour, and that has yet to give me the thrill of just one of your glances."

He removes his hand from his pocket, and I can see now that he's holding something.

"Iva Sophia Scott. See, I know what it's like to have you. And I know what it's like to lose you. And that kind of thing," he says, pausing briefly, "that kind of thing makes a man who he is. Because I will never live another day of my life like I lived it before I knew you. You forever changed me. You are forever written into my very flesh. And plain and simple, you are my story, Iva Scott. I can't tell *me*, without telling *you*."

There are tears threatening to flood my eyes, as his sweet words puncture my soul, eternally leaving their footprints on my existence.

"And I don't know why this little girl from Sweet Home—this little girl, with her pink tennis shoes and her bright smile and her big dreams—was drawn to a boy like me, but I thank my stars she was. And the thing is, Iva, when I dream about my future, your name is written on every wall. Even when I questioned whether I'd ever see you again, I still saw your name." A slow-burning smile gradually pushes up his face. "And no matter what you say tonight, I'll still never be without you. I gave you my heart when I was only twelve years old. You didn't know it, yet, but I did. And somehow, I knew that I'd carry you in my heart for as long as I walked this earth. So," he says, positioning himself so that he's on one knee, "Iva Sophia Scott ..." He opens a red, velvet box, and I immediately gasp, as my fingers go to my lips. "What are your thoughts on forever?"

I can feel tears trickling down my face. And I try to speak, but nothing comes out. So, I try again.

"I think forever sounds pretty nice."

The lines start to blur after that, but it's not long, and Berlin has the ring out of the box, and he's taking my left hand.

I watch him slide the silver band onto my ring finger, and I just can't stop thinking how happy I am to have found him again.

A flash of shiny light distracts me, and for the first time, I notice the yellow diamond on my hand. It's in the middle, and it's surrounded by a string of white diamonds.

"Berlin, it's beautiful."

"The center stone is your mom's."

My eyes flicker up to his.

"What?"

"It's your mom's," he says again.

I look down at the ring. "I don't understand."

"When I went to ask your parents for their permission, your mom told me a story about her first love."

"The yellow roses," I whisper.

He nods. "He's the one who gave them to her."

I rest my hand on his knee. "What happened?" My eyes settle on the ring. "She never told me."

"I know," he says, taking in a breath. "Apparently, he was a lot like me. He drove too fast, and he was all sorts of different—too different for her daddy's liking. But she loved him. And she loved him up until the day of his seventeenth birthday, when he lost control of his car and the good Lord took him home. And then she just kept on loving him even after that day, too."

His gaze falters, and he pushes out a lungful of air.

"But she said they found a ring inside the glove compartment. And wrapped around the ring box was a letter, asking your mom to marry him. ... So, it meant a lot to her that you have it."

I look down at the canary-colored diamond. Tears are filling my eyes, making my vision blurry. "Thank you," I whisper, wrapping my arms around him.

"I love you so much," he says, kissing me softly in my hair. "But then, you already knew that."

I laugh, through the tears, and then he pulls away but keeps me in his arms.

"I can't wait to tell the world," he says, his grin wide.

"Well, let's go do it," I say, swiping the dampness off my cheeks. "Let's go tell the world."

His beautiful brown eyes come to rest in mine. "You're going to be my wife, Iva Scott."

I can't stop smiling.

"I've waited so long to say that," he adds.

I glance down at the ring on my finger, and then I wipe the remaining tears from my eyes. They're happy tears—every last one.

Berlin takes my hand, and we climb down the little ladder nailed to the tree and make our way back to the barn. And it's just a matter of moments before Berlin is opening the door.

The first thing I notice is the perfect silence. The talking and loud laughter that were present just a short time ago are gone now. And now, all eyes under the barn's yellow lights are on us.

Berlin looks at me and then turns his face back to the crowd.

"She said *yes!*"

The barn erupts with applause and cheers, and the next thing I know, Natalie is throwing her arms around me. She squeals in my ear and then lets go of me to hug Berlin. And for the first time, I see Berlin's parents and Elin and her kids. And then I see my daddy.

Everyone is here; I had no idea.

But then I see my momma, and the tears return. And immediately, I go to her, and I wrap my arms around her slender frame.

Chapter Twenty-One

So Lucky

Two Months Later
Iva

He can barely get into the door, and I'm running to him and jumping into his arms.

"Hey, baby," he says, kissing me on the neck. "I missed you."

"I missed you, too." My legs still wrapped around him, I kiss his lips. "You were amazing, by the way."

"No," he says. "I wasn't. It was a bad race. But it doesn't matter. I'm here with you now."

The phone rings, and I bury my face into his shoulder. It rings again, and I try to ignore it. But then I remember, I can't. I'm planning a wedding.

I fall out of his arms, run to the phone and pick it up.

"Just one second, babe. It's the caterer."

"All right," he says, setting his bag onto the floor.

I take the call, and by the time I get the chicken and the beef and the vegetarian dinners all sorted out, I go back into the living room. And he's asleep on the couch.

I sigh and cover him with a blanket. Then I sit on the corner of the coffee table, and I catch myself watching him breathe in and breathe out.

I love him. I love him no less than that little girl back in Sweet Home loved him. And that little girl loved him a lot.

I gently trace a winding path with my fingertips down his arm.

When I saw him across the street after those seven years, I first just saw a strikingly attractive guy. It wasn't until my eyes lingered just a little too long, that I realized I was staring at that fearless, wild boy from my past—who still had my heart.

And some days, I wish it all were still as easy as those days back in Sweet Home—when he was never more than just a window away and my daddy was the biggest inconvenience we had. I'd welcome my daddy's disapproving look today if that were the only hurdle Berlin and I had to face.

These days, Berlin is home three days a week. He gets back on Sunday night and leaves Thursday—every week. He's always traveling or training or racing. I do get to see him race, though. I'm thankful for that. I fly to wherever he is—whether it's Kansas City or Atlanta or Las Vegas—on Saturday night, and then I watch him race on Sunday. And then usually, I come back home by myself, while he does his post-race interviews and talks about the race with his crew. And I stay up and wait for him to come home.

I miss him a lot on the days he's not here, but I try to keep busy. I spend most of my time working and planning the wedding. With his schedule, I can't even imagine when he'd have time to plan anything, much less a wedding. And I know he feels bad about me having to do everything, but in the end, I really don't mind. I just wish I had more time with him. And sometimes, if I'm honest, I wish I had more time to draw and to paint, too.

I took a job at the library not too long after I moved to Channing. There aren't many options here, but at least at the library, they let me teach basic classes on art history and how to paint trees and bowls of apples and bouquets of flowers—the types of things you paint when you're learning to paint.

Berlin and I talked about moving. With his job, we could go anywhere really—as long as it's in the United States. But his family is here. And he loves his niece and nephew with every fiber in his being, and he sees them less than he sees me. I don't have the heart to suggest we go anywhere else.

I do wish there was an easy answer, though—an option that would allow us to stay here and him to race and me to make a living doing what I love. And even if I couldn't paint full-time, I would love to be surrounded by art at an art gallery or something like it.

He shifts on the couch, and the blanket falls to the floor, halting my thoughts. I pick up the cover and gently lay it across his midsection again. Then, I kiss him lightly on his cheek and delicately run my fingers through his hair.

I love art. It's my passion. But the thing is, Berlin Elliot is my heart. And I can't live without my heart.

"Geez, how long was I asleep?"

I look back at the couch and then up at the clock on the wall.

"Hmm, a couple hours."

I set the brush down and spin around, so that I'm facing him. His hair is flattened on one side, and his eyes are barely open. Still, he looks irresistibly handsome.

"Really?"

I nod.

"I'm sorry, baby." He sleepily walks over to me and kisses me on the lips. "What are you working on?"

I shrug. "It's just a picture that popped into my head the other day."

It's a painting of a shore and an ocean somewhere far away. It came to me, while I was working my normal shift at the library—where exactly five of the same people frequent on a daily basis. I wondered for the first time since I found Berlin again what New Zealand would be like. There, I was going to probably be selling coffee to locals and tourists. But there, I would also be learning to paint like Sinclair Williams, one of the best in the world.

"It's beautiful," he says, coaxing me back to the present.

I notice his look hangs on me a little longer than usual. "Is there something wrong, Iva?"

"What?" I ask. But then I shake my head before he

has a chance to answer my question. "No, nothing's wrong," I say. I think it's the truth, but I can't be sure.

He lightly kisses me again—this time, on my cheek. And I close my eyes and savor the feel of his lips on my skin.

"Okay," he says, nodding. I'm not sure he's convinced.

I know there are blue and white paint splotches all over my face and probably in my hair, too, but I give him my best put-together smile.

"I love you, baby," he says, in his raspy, sleepy voice. I don't think he intends it to sound ridiculously sexy, but it does, all the same.

He kisses me again. And this time, I throw my arms around his neck and kiss him back.

"I think I was just missing you, Mr. Elliot," I whisper against his face, breathing in his sweet cologne. "Next time, I'm coming with you—inside the car."

"Inside the car, huh?"

I give him an exaggerated nod.

"Hell, why don't you just drive?"

I pull away from him a little and meet his stare. "Deal."

The sound of his sultry laugh fills the room.

"Iva, every day that I get to come home to you is the best day of my life," he says, squeezing me into his chest. "Some days, I just can't believe the life I lucked into."

I rest my head on his strong arm. His muscles were something I had to get used to; although, I admit, it wasn't that difficult. When I knew the boy I knew in Sweet Home, he barely had a muscle to call his own.

I gently run my hand down his chest and stop near his heart.

"How did I get so lucky to find you again?" he asks, in a low growl.

I smile and nudge my cheek against his shoulder. "You must have done something right."

"Nah," he says, moving his head back and forth. "I'm pretty sure that if there was something wrong to do, I did it."

I laugh. "Then maybe you did all the wrong things right."

"Yeah," he says, in that same low voice. "Yeah, that sounds more like it."

He tucks a few strands of my hair behind my ear. "How are the wedding plans coming?"

I suck in a long breath. "Good," I say. "I think everything's going to plan. Natalie and Elin have been a big help with everything here."

"That's good," he says, briefly casting his eyes to the floor. "I'm sorry I can't help more."

"It's fine. I understand. And I enjoy it—most of the time."

His stare lingers.

"And how's the library?"

I shrug. "It's going."

He uses his finger to lift my chin, so that he can see my face. "Iva, don't forget, I've known you since you were twelve years old. I know when something's bothering you. You can tell me if you don't like it here."

My gaze quickly falls to the floor. "I do," I say, looking back up. "I do like it here. I'm just getting used to it, that's all."

He keeps his light brown eyes on me. "Baby, you'll tell me, right? You'll tell me if you're bored here or if you want to do something different. I mean, I don't have any art connections, but I can try ..."

I stop him. "I'm fine. I love you. I choose you, Berlin."

For a few seconds, his narrowed eyes study me, but then soon, a little smile starts to edge its way up his face. And before I can think another thought, he picks me up, so that one of my legs is on either side of his waist. Then, he grabs my backside, and I let out a high-pitched cry.

"Well," he says, "in that case, I've got three days with my sexy fiancé. And then come Sunday, she's gonna drive my car. And then I'm either gonna be out of a job or we're not gonna make it to see Monday. So, I say, let's make the most of these three days. What do you say, pretty girl?"

I scrunch up my nose and bury my face into his shoulder, while he presses his lips into my hair.

"I say that sounds like a dream," I sing, with a wide, happy grin.

Chapter Twenty-Two

You Need to Go

Two Months Later
Iva

"Hey," I say, walking into the room. "How was your flight?"

"Good. ... Long."

He toes off his shoes at the door.

"How's it been back here?"

"Lonely," I say, throwing my arms around his neck and reaching up on my tiptoes to kiss him.

He sets his things down, wraps his arms around me and lifts me up into an embrace.

"Oh, I missed you so much," he says, kissing me on my lips.

The Life We Almost Had

After a long while, he gently sets me down and then gives me a half-worried look. "What's wrong?"

I force out a puff of air. "Oh, it's just wedding stuff, that's all," I say, trying to play it off.

"What kind of wedding stuff? You sound like you have bad news."

"Well, good and bad."

Little wrinkles form on his forehead. "What is it?"

"Good or bad, first?"

"Give me the bad, so it makes the good better."

I squish my lips to one side, not wanting to tell him. I don't really feel like talking about it all now. He just got home, and all I want to do is forget everything but him. "The caterer bailed. She said it's too many people. They can't do it."

"Rose's?"

I nod.

"Why?"

"Well, Berlin, it's, like, five hundred people. It kind of makes sense. You had to go and make yourself famous." I fold my arms across my chest, and at the same time, feel my lips pushing up my face. "And famous people don't get married in small towns."

He walks by me and plants a kiss on my cheek. "The only famous person I see here is Moose."

I look over at his lazy tabby cat. "Moose knows how to do famous."

"He sure does," he says.

Berlin plops down into a kitchen chair and just stares back at me.

"What?" I ask. I keep my smile, even though the caterer thing really did wreck my world today.

"Can we just elope?"

I muster up a fake pout and then walk over to him

and straddle him on the chair. He wraps his arms around me, and I fall into him.

"That would have been a better question four months ago—before I did all this work," I whisper near his ear.

"So, it's too late then?"

I use his shoulders to push myself up, and I meet his silly, defeated grin.

"Damn it," he says, shaking his head.

I fall back against him with a playful groan.

"So, what's the good news?"

I press my teeth into my bottom lip and smile. "I think I found a dress."

"Really?"

"Mm-hmm."

"Can I see it?"

"Uh-uh," I say, moving my head back and forth against his shoulder. "It's a surprise."

He laughs. "I'm already trying to figure out how to keep my manhood intact while I watch you walk down that aisle. And you're not helping any."

I laugh, too. "I'm sorry, baby."

"Well, my manhood aside, that is good news. I'm happy for you, babe. ... Oh, hey," he says, patting my backside. "You packed for Nashville?"

"Nashville?" I push myself back up.

"That get-together thing before my race. You're coming, right? All the girlfriends are coming."

I look at him sideways. I'm not sure if he's messing with me just yet or not. "Berlin, I have my art show this Saturday."

"That's *this* Saturday?"

I nod.

"Well, can't you just move it? Aren't you the only

one in it?"

I feel my body involuntarily slump. "Yeah, but invitations have already been sent out, and ..."

"Oh!" he says, sounding excited for me. "Well, how many people are going?"

My shoulders sag even more. "I only have three RSVPs, and one is your sister."

He's quiet for a few moments after that. And I'm not expecting them, but tears start to sneak into the backs of my eyelids. I'm not sure what triggered them, necessarily, but if I were being completely honest with myself, I'd say that they had been waiting to fall for some time now.

He immediately wraps his arms around me and pulls me into his chest.

"Iva."

I brush away the tears with the back of my hand and try to gather myself.

"You ..." He stops, and it makes me take notice. *Something is wrong.*

I look into his eyes. They're sad, and instantly, a shot of fear races through my body.

"You're not happy here," he says.

It's not a question. It's a statement. And it's true. But I don't want it to be true.

His lips part, but no words come. There's something else he wants to say. And my heart sinks. I don't want to believe I'm not happy here. I love him. He's my happy.

I'm terrified of what he's going to say next.

"You need to go to New Zealand." His voice is scarcely over a whisper.

I watch the honey swirling around his toffee-colored eyes. "What?"

"I, uh ...," he says, but then stops. "I was talking to some people this past weekend. They're really into art, and I mentioned this Sinclair guy, and they knew who he was. And they were impressed that you did, too." He pauses again. "Baby, apparently this guy has more connections than I could ever dream of having when it comes to art. You need to go and paint and be where people appreciate you." His voice is gentle, yet sure.

"But ..."

"You're not supposed to be here," he says.

"But your contract."

He doesn't say anything. He just nods once. And right then, my heart breaks. He wouldn't come. If there's anything that means as much to him as I do, it's racing, and I know it. And even if he said he would, I would never let him give it up. He was meant to race. He was meant to do this with his life.

But it still hurts. I try to hold back the pain, but the more I try to hold it in, the more my throat aches. And soon, a sob escapes me. And then another. And another. I'm terrified. I'm terrified to leave him. But I think I'm more terrified to stay. And I think he sees that, too.

"Iva." His eyes are red, like the color of the sun at sunset. "I see you crying at night. When you're looking out the window, I see you crying. And I saw the letter."

"What?"

"I saw the letter you got a couple weeks ago—the one from Sinclair that said the opportunity was still there. And I saw the way you looked at it—with regret. Iva, I don't want to be the reason you regret anything. Life's not meant to have any regrets. You were meant to dream big dreams. And you were meant to paint those dreams. And the bottom line is that you can't paint those dreams here."

I try to control the flood of tears now racing down my cheeks. "I can't leave you," I whisper. It takes every ounce of energy I have to utter those words.

"You can," he says. And for the first time ever, I see tears in his eyes.

I shake my head. "No, I can't."

"But you will," he says.

And with those three, little words, everything changes.

It's as if I can literally feel my heart being ripped out of my chest. This can't be happening. This is just like the first time. All those feelings of losing him are rushing back.

I shake my head, even though I know he's right.

"I want you to go," he whispers. "It's an opportunity ... to be noticed, to do what you love for a living."

I briefly force my eyes shut. "I don't want you to want me to go."

"Iva, if you only knew how hard this is for me." A tear falls down his cheek. I kiss it away. And then we just sit there, listening to each other breathe, consumed by the fragile uncertainty that hangs in the air.

"What if ...?" I say, brokenly, through my tears. "What if I go for a little while, and then I come back? What if I do that?"

There's a moment where I forget to breathe. And then, he tries to smile. And I can't tell you why, but him smiling makes his eyes look even sadder.

"I would like that," he says.

"Then, I'll come back," I say.

I try to push away the tears with a smile of my own.

"Berlin." I place a hand on either side of his face, and his eyes quickly find mine. "But what if I have to be there awhile?"

My gaze casts down to the little space between us. I want him to say he would come to me.

He lifts my chin, and it forces my attention back to him. "Then you buy the best piece of New Zealand real estate you can find, and you paint a beautiful life there."

It's not what I wanted to hear.

"And I'll come to you," he says. I meet his dark stare. "Once this contract's up, I'll come to you."

Instantly, a raw smile rushes to my face. His words are a warm comfort. But I also see the fear in his eyes. It's the same fear I know is in mine, too. We jumped into this too quickly. Without a thought, we thought we could just forget the seven years that passed between us and pick right up where we left off. But that's hard to do. I love this boy no less than the first day I fell in love with him. But we've each planned our life without the other.

"Nothing changes," he whispers into my ear. "You hear me?"

I nod.

"I want you, Iva. I always have. I always will. The heart wants what the heart wants, and it wants you. Plain and simple. It's already made that pretty clear." He presses a kiss into my hair, as a rogue tear slides down my cheek. "You've never asked me to be anything I wasn't. You just took me as I was. And some days, I still can't figure out why your heart picked me. But I'm so happy it did." He pulls me closer to him. "Thank you for loving me—for who I am, and for who I'm not." There's a pause, and then I hear his deep, rasping whisper in my ear: "But now, it's my turn to love you for who you are. And you're an artist, Iva. And budding artists don't live in Channing, Kansas."

I breathe in the smell of his cologne, and I close my eyes. It's the smell of home, of love, of Berlin Elliot.

My heart is breaking.

"This isn't the end, Mr. Elliot," I breathe out, tears consuming my cheeks.

I feel his head nod against my face.

"This isn't the end," I say, one more time, pulling back and meeting his red gaze.

He shakes his head. "I don't believe in endings—especially when it comes to you, Miss Scott."

It's a Friday afternoon. I pick up my carry-on luggage, and I feel my chest lift with a breath.

In words, this isn't the end. Nobody said it was. Not me. Not Berlin. But it doesn't take away that fear in my heart—that fear in my heart that comes with leaving him on the other side of the ocean.

Berlin knows I'm leaving today. He's in Nashville, getting ready for a race, as I stand here. We spent every moment we had earlier this week wrapped up in each other's arms. And each moment made me question this decision that much more. But I'm also excited. I'm excited the opportunity is still open to me. I'm excited to learn more about my passion. I'm terrified to leave, but I'm excited for this new adventure, too. I've been dreaming this dream for a long time. And today, I get to live it.

I glance down at my hand. Next to the canary-and-white-diamond ring on my finger, there's my passport and a one-way ticket to Christchurch, New Zealand.

I take one more, long look at the home Berlin and I shared for exactly four months and eight days. It was such a short time, but it might as well have been a lifetime because in those four, short months, we got to live out a dream we thought we had forever lost.

But then again, maybe it was never really found. Maybe we were still just dreaming.

My eyes get stuck on the couch in the living room. I love that dumb, big couch. I don't even know how many times Berlin and I drifted off to sleep, while some old movie from the forties played on the television in the background.

I swallow down the ache in my throat, as my stare gradually wanders up to the big glass doors that lead to the backyard. There's a porch swing there, where we spent every warm night we had remembering Sweet Home and the life we shared there. And intertwined in those memories were always the dreams of the life we were going to have here, too.

Sweet Home was our beginning. But every piece of this house tells a story about our second chance. And there's a part of me that wishes I could take the whole thing with me.

I close my eyes, as if to keep it all in. And then, slowly, I force out a breath, and I shut the door.

The unknown is a scary place. But Berlin and I made it through seven years. We can make it across an ocean.

Chapter Twenty-Three

The Time in Between

Two Years Later
Iva

I look down at the diamond ring I've been wearing for a month now. But I can't stop thinking about him. And you would think *him* would be the man who gave me the ring. But tonight, *him* is Berlin Elliot.

Some people dream about a second chance with the one that got away. I used to be one of those people.

But I don't dream that dream anymore.

I got my second chance.

But as it turns out, second chances aren't really all they're cracked up to be. It's true. It's one more opportunity to dance around the room before the song ends. And it's fun and exciting and beautiful. It's everything you wished it could be ... and maybe even more.

But then, it ends.

The song must end.

It always does.

And then you're left just humming the words to an empty room and an empty heart.

Two years ago, it was a clean break, like that of an ax splitting open a log. I didn't know it at the time, but the moment that ax hit the wood, that was the end of us. Looking back, it was more swift than it seemed. But it was no less painful.

Berlin and I talked on the phone a lot at first. I'd stay up until all hours of the morning just so I could hear his voice. And I'd go to work, and then I'd go paint. And I could barely keep my eyes open, but I was happy.

And I can't even tell you exactly when it all started unraveling. All I remember is that there came a day in the middle of the afternoon when I stopped, and I glanced up at the clock on the wall. And I just stared at that clock and thought about him resting his head on his pillow half a world away. And that's when I realized that it had been a month since I had last spoken to him.

The realization almost shattered me. I had no idea where the time had gone.

We had planned so many things—life, trips, adventures. But then, he got into the heart of his race season. And I started helping more with art shows in the evenings. So, by the time I got home at night, he was just starting his day; he was literally a day behind. And soon, we were talking on the phone less and less, mostly because of the time difference. And we never could get our schedules to match up, so we could see each other. I flew home a couple times in the last two years, but he was always in another big city and in another big race, and each time, we missed each other, and I returned to New Zealand, with only having seen his car on the television. And we talked about him coming to visit after the season was over. But we never made it that far. And truthfully, I don't know who raised the white flag first. I don't know if it was me or him. But I really don't think it was ever a conscious decision on either of our parts. In the end, I think we both just fought so hard that eventually, we ran out of fight.

As it turns out, an ocean is mightier than we had once believed.

It was a Tuesday, nearly a year after I had first left the States when he left a voicemail—the voicemail that sealed our fate. It was in the middle of the night. The message said exactly two words: *I'm sorry.* And with those two words, I knew what he had done.

It was the day he re-signed his contract.

I cried myself to sleep that night. And the next day, I took off his ring. I put it in my momma's red, velvet box, and I tucked it away in the drawer in my nightstand. And no matter what I tried to tell myself, my heart was broken without him.

But then, the days came and the days went. And I met Adam. And life blossomed again. I felt joy. And for the first time in almost a year, I laughed—like really laughed, until my stomach hurt. And it felt good. And after that, I never called Berlin again.

But I was still angry at him for a long time. I hated him. I loved him, but I hated him. I hated him because life wasn't fair to us. I hated him because I was here and he was still there. I hated him because he had done what I had done—he had chosen the one thing that he knew he could count on. For him, racing put life into his bones. For me, art allowed my soul to breathe. And neither one of those things had ever let us down, had ever made us cry ... had ever broken our hearts. And the thing is, we can't say that about each other. When I didn't have Berlin and he didn't have me, we both had those things. And I think that made all the difference.

It's messed up, I know.

But it is the story of Berlin and I.

So close. Nearly. Almost.

We *almost* were.

After the day he re-signed his contract, I heard from him one more time. It was on his birthday, and I was working. I could hardly make out his words on the voicemail. He was somewhere with loud music and loud voices. And his own voice was cracking. The only thing I could make out were the words: *I love you.*

And even though I secretly tucked those words away in my heart for safekeeping, I knew they carried no weight. Nothing had changed. I was here. And he was still there. And I never heard from him again.

And maybe we got it all wrong. Hell, we probably did. But that's where it gets tricky. It's not easy going back. It's not easy rewinding time. I mean, maybe when you're younger, it's easier. But the more life you live, the harder it is to say: *Let's just start over again. Let's forget the past and all the hurts, and let's set aside our lives and just ... love each other.*

God knows I wanted to do just that so many times in the last two years. But again, the more time that passes, the less sense that makes.

The Life We Almost Had

Berlin and I made our choices.
We chose our paths.
And we hurt each other along the way.
But the wounds do heal.

They don't heal completely. I can still see them—in the blues in my eyes—every time I look in the mirror. And some days, I can feel them, too. But they do heal enough to breathe again. They heal enough, I suppose.

I clear my throat and sit back in my chair, just staring at the computer's screen. I'm wondering all the usual things, I guess. I'm wondering how he's doing. I'm wondering if he ever thinks of me. I'm wondering if *he* still believes we made the right decisions.

And then, in a rush, I type his name into the search box. And I stop. And I stare at that name. I stare at the name that was almost mine. And I take a deep breath in, and then I quickly force it out. And without another thought, I hit *enter*.

The first thing that comes up is an article about a bed and breakfast. I think the article doesn't have anything to do with him, until I see his name under the title. I click on the link. It's a feature written in a paper from back home that talks about the new draw in the little town of Sweet Home: *The Lighthouse Inn.*

There are two photos. My eyes roam over the images of a couple of newly renovated, turn-of-the-20th-century homes.

I recognize both.

I read further down the page, and eventually, I get to the part about the owner. It says they were recently purchased by a local celebrity—the NASCAR driver by the name of Berlin Elliot.

I sit back in my chair and just stare at his name.
He bought them.

He literally brought life back to Sweet Home.

I study the photos. Everything looks the same—just the same as we had left it the first time, even down to those navy curtains hanging in his bedroom window and those yellow roses lining that old iron fence in my front yard.

I feel a small smile tug at my lips. I almost can't believe what I'm seeing. And yet, I'm not surprised at all.

After a few more moments of just staring at those two, little houses, I hit the back button. And immediately, I see the old photos of Berlin and I at the track on several race days. I stop and look at each one; I can't help myself. And I know I probably shouldn't, but I still love these photos. I love how happy we looked, how happy we were.

I scroll down the page, and I come to another photo. It's one of him ... with his arm around a tall brunette in front of a banner on some red carpet somewhere.

I had seen her before with him—in photos, of course, on the internet. But what I see next makes me fall back into my chair.

NASCAR star Berlin Elliot engaged.
Engaged?

At once, my body goes numb. The thought of him loving someone else is suddenly unimaginable. I thought I had prepared myself for this. But I don't feel prepared at all.

Tears overwhelm my eyes, so much so, that I can't even clearly make out his photo any longer.

Why is this such a shock? Why is this so hard? I've moved on. Of course, it was only a matter of time before he did, too.

The Life We Almost Had

I bring my fingers to my lips to try and hold in the pain. I've done this before. I've let him go twice before. And it broke my heart in half each time. Though each time, the two halves somehow fused back together. This time, however, I fear they won't.

Tonight, it's real to me. Out of all the days in these last two years since I left that little town in Kansas, tonight is the night it really feels true.

I've lost my first love—the love of my life.

Tonight, I lost him.

And it hurts like hell.

For two weeks, I only saw the world in black and white. And I cried. I cried out loud by myself in the kitchen. I cried secretly behind the bathroom door. I cried for me. I cried for the little girl and the little boy who loved with everything they had in a little town that nobody cared about but them. I cried because I felt as if no one else would cry for them.

But then, I stopped crying.

I stopped crying because I ran out of tears. And when my eyes cleared, I slowly started to see things in color again. And for the first time in a long time, I saw the brilliant man I'm marrying. I saw a man who loves me. And I felt how much I adore him. He's patient and kind. And most of all, he dreams his dreams on my side of the hemisphere. And in spite of everything, I'm happy to be here with him. If I had to choose all over again, I would be tempted to choose Channing, Kansas and the man who lives there, and I'm not altogether sure I wouldn't. But I love this man from Denver,

Colorado, who I met in a little coffee house on the shore of Christchurch, New Zealand. This life suits me, and I've grown to like it.

In the end, Berlin and I just lost too much time, I think. In the end, there was just too much time to make up. And I think I'll always wonder what might have been. But then, that's life, I guess. It ends how it intended to end. It's only the *in between* part that seems unwritten, at times. That's the part we get to make our own. It's that little part in between—in between the beginning and the end—where we get to go off-road for a little while and scribble down our own adventures. That's the part where we get to make our own mistakes—where we get to drive too fast and love too hard. It's the part that, later, we might begin to think it was all just a dream, if it weren't for the scratches and scars on our hearts, whispering to our souls that it was real.

It was all real.

And Berlin and I made the most of it. We made the most of our *in between*. And I'll forever hold onto that—my happiest ... and saddest memories.

Chapter Twenty-Four
You Have a Tattoo

Present

Berlin

I see a guy who looks a little lost in this big, old barn full of people. He keeps alternating glances between the floor and the crowd.

We're celebrating Isaac and Natalie's engagement tonight. Nearly the whole town is here. And I vaguely remember Isaac telling me he had a friend he used to work with coming into town.

I take one more swig of my beer. Then, I set the bottle down and walk toward the guy.

"Hey, man, you must be Isaac's friend."

"Um, well, I ..."

"Come on," I say, gesturing toward the door, "I've got something to show you." I briefly glance back at him. "He said you were into classics."

I walk swiftly to the shed, and he follows close behind. Then when I get to the door, I push it open and go to the front of the Chevelle.

"It's a *'72 SS 454*, but you probably guessed that already," I say.

"I, um ...," he stutters.

"Adam."

I hear her voice, and for a second, I'm stunned into silence.

"Hey, babe," I hear the guy beside me say.

I slowly close the hood of the Chevelle.

"Berlin!" Iva says, in a surprised voice.

And we just stand there, staring at each other. I don't think either of us knows what to do.

God, she's beautiful.

"Um," the man beside me mouths. He looks as if he doesn't know what to do, either. But then again, I'm hardly paying attention to him anymore. "I'm just going to go find Natalie and Isaac," he says. "You want a drink?" he asks Iva.

This is the first time I really look at him. He's tall and dark. He looks ... smart and successful. He looks like the type of guy I always thought she should be with, all the while I was thanking the good Lord that she had picked me.

I notice Iva shake her head, and then the guy gives me a not-so-subtle once-over. I can tell he rethinks leaving her alone in here with me.

"I'll just meet you back in the barn," Iva says, smiling at the guy.

He takes the cue and then reluctantly disappears.

The Life We Almost Had

"I was looking for you," she says. Her eyes are on me now. "They said you were here."

I refit my cap over my head. "Well, you found me."

I watch her pink lips slowly edge up her face. "Hi."
I bob my head. "Hi."

Soundless seconds dance between us, before her gaze slips to the floor.

"I didn't know you were back in the States," I say.

Gradually, her eyes level off. "I'm not. ... Well, I'm not for long. Just for tonight."

I nod. "So, it must be pretty nice there."

"I like it." She looks almost starry-eyed as she says the words, and I know she's made the right choice, even though just the thought sends a blunt knife straight through my chest.

"And, uh ... You," I start, only to lose my words. "You ... met him there, I'm guessing?"

She rakes her fingers through her hair. It's longer than it was the last time I saw her.

"I did," she says. "That's, um ... Adam."

She gestures toward the barn, and I catch, for the first time, the ring on her finger. It's not the one I gave her. A lump forms in the back of my throat, and I try my best to swallow it down.

"Is he, uh ... your ..."

I know she notices me struggling.

"Fiancé," she softly says, looking down again at the little shed's floor.

I suck in a sharp breath. Then I lean up against the Chevelle to steady myself a little better.

"We came to see Natalie and Isaac. I haven't seen either of them since they got engaged." Her gaze falters momentarily. "But I wanted to stop by and say *hi* to you, too."

I lower my head, as the quiet takes over.

"Well, they finally did it," I say. "They finally made it official."

A beautiful smile lights up her face. "They did."

And with that, I get stuck in her eyes. "I'm glad you did—stop and say *hi*, that is," I say.

There's an awkward pause.

"Well, how have you been?" she asks.

I hear her words, but her eyes tell a different story. That's not quite the question she wanted to ask.

I answer it, all the same.

"Uh, good. I've been good."

I'm pretty sure that's a lie, but I don't even really know what I'm saying. I'm on autopilot, still trying to find my bearings.

"Good," she says. Her facial expressions are delicate, cautious.

"Are you, um, getting marr-ied?" she asks, glancing at my left hand.

It's hard for her to get the word out. I understand.

"No, I, uh ... I know there are rumors, but ... No, we're just ... seeing each other, for now, I guess."

I try to clear my throat because it feels as if something is stuck in it. Meanwhile, she distracts me with her voice again.

"I see you're still driving. And doing well."

"Yeah," I say, sounding surprised. For a moment, I'm shocked that she knows anything about me anymore.

"We do have internet in New Zealand," she says, catching me off guard.

"Yeah." I lower my head and laugh to myself. "I see."

After a second, I look up, and I just so happen to meet her sweeping gaze. "And you, the famous painter."

She studies me, curiously.

"We have internet, too," I say.

Instantly, her eyes go to her shoes. "It's a work in progress," she says. "But I've been fortunate, so far. Sinclair has a lot of connections."

"That's good," I say. "That's really good."

There's a moment of silence, where all I can hear is the echo of my heart pounding in my chest, as the sounds from the party ever fade into the background.

"I also saw you brought life back to Sweet Home."

I look at her. Her eyes are glassy, all of a sudden.

"Somebody had to," I say.

She slowly nods. She doesn't have to tell me she approves of what I did. I can see it on her face.

And then she takes a breath.

"Well," she says, "I probably should get going. I just wanted to make sure I saw you."

I nod because I don't know what else to do.

"Iva, I'm sorry." I just blurt it out. "I'm sorry about the contract ..."

She stops me. "I understand."

I let go of a sigh. I hate that she understands. She shouldn't. What I did is unforgivable. The day just came to sign it, and I panicked. I didn't know what else I'd do, if I didn't race. Hell, I feared I wouldn't even know who I was anymore.

"I do," she assures me. "I do understand."

Her lips turn up ever so slightly, but she doesn't move. Neither of us does. And I know this is just me and her, trying to do something we were never really good at doing—saying goodbye.

Finally, she starts to turn but then stops and slowly pivots back around.

"You have a tattoo ... on your arm," she says, pointing to her own forearm but looking at mine.

I look down at my arm. The tattoo is covered by my shirt sleeve.

"I saw it," she quickly explains, "a while ago, in a photo ... online."

I look at her and smile. I don't even try to hide the fact that I like that she's been stalking me. In turn, she just shakes her head in that playful, scolding way of hers.

I roll up my sleeve, so that we both can see the word *saudade* in swirling, cursive letters on my forearm.

"What does it mean?" she asks.

I take a long look at the word. "It's a longing for something that cannot be ... and the love that remains."

She stares at it for a few moments, and then her eyes lock in mine. There's a sober look on her face. And I know that she knows. I know that she knows it's for her.

She nods once, and then I watch her start to leave for the second time.

"Iva?"

She turns back. And I try to ask her the question with my eyes that I don't have the courage to ask her with my voice.

Do you long for me?

She answers with a soft smile. "I brought back a few of my favorite pieces from my collection," she says. "I left them on your porch. They're yours to keep."

She leaves her gaze in mine for longer than she should.

"When I lived in Sweet Home," she says, letting

The Life We Almost Had

her eyes trail off to a spot in the corner of the shed, "I painted the ocean. When I got to the ocean, I painted Sweet Home."

Her eyes finally stumble back on mine, but only for a brief moment. And then she turns. And this time, she slips through the door and disappears.

I practically treat the back roads as a racetrack trying to get home as fast as I can. After hearing that Iva's life's work was just sitting on my front porch, all the people and the glow from the barn suddenly lost its charm.

I pull up to my house, and immediately, I see several large boxes on the porch. I hurry out of my truck and jog up the steps.

It takes me a minute to get all the boxes inside. There are four—total. Four large, slender cardboard boxes lean up against the den wall in front of me now.

I take a seat in my desk chair and just stare at them for a good minute. I've waited a long time to see this Sweet Home girl's famous works of art. Whatever she's done, I know it's a part of her, and that means a great deal to me. So, I'm a little nervous to even touch them.

Finally, though, I take a deep breath and stand up.

Each box has a number on it. Carefully, with a pocket knife, I cut the cardboard of the box labeled *1* and gently pull out the first frame and hold it up in front of me.

It's a black and white drawing of a little house on an empty street. It's my house in Sweet Home—the way you'd see it, if you were looking at it through a window—her window across the street. I examine the picture. Even though the drawing is in black and white, it's summer there; I can tell. Every detail, even down to those little, red anthills in the cracks on the sidewalk, is there. I run my fingers over the drawing, without touching it, remembering the life we shared there. Then, I catch some words in the bottom right corner of the drawing, just above her signature, and I read over them: *When I Close My Eyes*.

I look into the drawing a little bit longer. There's something in me that aches to be inside this frame. Suddenly, I want to be the little boy staring back at that little girl again. I want this day—that she's captured on this page. I want *this* day back.

I don't know how long I'm lost in the drawing, when I finally find the courage to carefully set the frame down. And then I go to the next box, labeled *2*. I'm gentle with the knife and the tape. I don't want to damage anything inside the cardboard.

After a few, tedious moments, I get the second box open, and I slide out the frame inside. It's another black and white drawing. But this time, it's of a tree house in a big oak. And in the right corner of the drawing is the word: *Kiss*.

I trace every black line, before my eyes stop on the place in the tree house where her initials are carved. I run my fingers over the *I* and the *S*. And I try not to remember the taste of her lips, but I can't stop my mind from going there.

I force out a long breath, and then I set that frame down next to the first one. And I stare at both of them. I stare at both of them, until that grandfather clock in the hall chimes me out of my trance, urging me toward the third box.

The next frame easily slides out of the cardboard, and I take it and hold it out in front of me. This one is in color. It's a painting of a bright red Chevelle, with a license plate that reads: *NASCAR*. And in the bottom right corner of the painting above her name is the title. It simply says: *She Was Red*.

I smile.

Then, I let my eyes wander around the painting. Even the scuffs on the dashboard are there. I close my eyes and try to feel the wind on my arm that first day I got my license—the same day I went back home to get her. I was so happy.

I hold onto the memory for as long as I can. Then, it slowly fades away, and I'm just left staring at the box labeled *4*.

I sigh, and then I gently set the painting of the Chevelle on the floor against the wall. And I pull the last frame out of its box and turn it so that it's facing right-side-up. And instantly, I walk backwards and fall into the chair behind me.

It's a painting. And for a second, I think it's a photo. But it can't be. There's a man, who looks an awful lot like me. But I can only see his profile. I can't see his full face. So, I can't know that it's me, for sure.

The painting is in color. And the man is standing on a shore. His body is toward the ocean, but his face is turned back toward the beach. It looks as if he's looking at something or someone that isn't in the painting. He looks happy. My eyes quickly go to the bottom right corner of the frame and to the title. And in her black handwriting, I read over the words: *My Dream*.

I slowly force a breath out, as my heart speeds up in my chest. And I don't know why—I don't know if I'm looking for something more, something that might confirm my suspicions, anything—but I turn the frame over. And I notice a few words written on the back.

In her handwriting, in black ink, this time, it reads: *That little boy from Sweet Home will always have my heart.*

I read it.

And then, I read it again.

And then, I put my hand to my heart as it, at once, both aches and soars.

I love this girl.
And I'll love her until my heart stops beating.

Chapter Twenty-Five

Did You Love Her?

Present
Berlin

"Uncle Berlin, who drew this picture?"
"Which one, baby?"
"This one." Madeline points to a spot up on the wall above her. "The one with the ocean."

My chest expands with a breath. "The artist's name is Iva Scott."

"Iva Scott," she repeats in her little voice.

"Mm-hmm," I say, rocking back on my heels. "Iva Sophia Scott."

I watch her stare at the painting. It's the one of the man on the shore. I can't quite tell what she's thinking based on the puzzled look on her face, but I know she's thinking.

"It's you, Uncle Berlin."

I smile. "You think?"

She gives me a hard nod. "I know."

"Well, if *you* say it is, then it is."

"You look happy," she says.

I glance at her and then at the painting, and then I feel my smile start to fade.

"It's because I am happy, baby."

"But why are you so happy?"

I let go of a lungful of air and then put my hand to my mouth. "Because Uncle Berlin is looking at a very special person he used to know."

"Who? Who are you looking at?"

"Well, she was a girl who Uncle Berlin grew up with—a girl who made me smile."

She looks back at me.

"Did you love her?"

I meet her pretty, blue, curious eyes. "I did," I breathe out.

"Like you love Mommy and me and Oliver?"

I shake my head. "No, not like I love your mommy and you and Oliver." I reach down and wrap my arms around her and whisper into her ear. "No, I love all of you each differently. See, when you grow up, you'll find out that your heart is pretty big, which means you can give different pieces of it to people who are very special to you along the way. And along the way, I gave a really big piece of my heart to you and to your brother and to your mommy ... and also to the girl you can't see in the picture."

She looks back at the frame. And for a good while, she doesn't say anything. Together, we just stare at it in silence.

"What was she like—the girl you're smiling at?"

I laugh to myself. "Well, she was ... a banana Popsicle."

She giggles, and her little body falls back into my arms. "A Popsicle, Uncle Berlin? People can't be Popsicles."

"Well," I hum. "She was. And she was an orange with extra sugar in a mason jar. And she was tractor oil and paint and chocolate milk and red and blue lights. And she was beautiful and different. But best of all, for some reason, her heart wanted me."

She keeps her eyes trained on the painting.

"See, Madeline Bear," I go on, "me and her, we got lucky as friends. We were lucky enough to find each other sooner than most, so that we could have a lifetime of friendship. And it didn't matter that we lived far, far away from each other at times. Because you know why?"

She rests her finger on her chin, as if she's thinking really hard about it, and then suddenly, her eyes come to rest on me. "Because she had a piece of your heart, too," she finally says.

Instantly, there's an ache in my throat.

"How did you get so smart, munchkin?" I ask, trying not to choke up.

"Mommy," she says.

I laugh. "Yeah, that's definitely true." *It sure wasn't her daddy.*

"And yes," I say, once my laughter grows faint, "it was because she had my heart. So, it didn't matter how far the waves took her away from me, she was always right here." I put my hand over my heart, and I watch as her eyes trail to my chest.

She's quiet after that, while I just stare into the blue and white waves in Iva's painting.

"Does she still have it—your heart, Uncle Berlin?"

I know she looks at me, but it's hard for me to tear my stare away from the painting.

"Yes," I say, eventually meeting her bright blue eyes. "She still does."

Suddenly, the screen door slams, and the dog dashes into the hallway.

"McMarbles!" she yells, leaving my arms for the German shepherd.

I watch her through the doorway wrap her little arms around the dog that's at least twice her size.

I love that little girl.

I notice Elin next. She bends down and kisses Madeline on her head, as she walks past her.

"Hey," Elin says, stopping when she gets just inside the room.

"Hey," I say, standing up.

"Thanks for watching her."

"It's no problem," I say.

She looks at me and then at the painting on the wall, and then back at me. She's putting two and two together; I can see it on her face.

"I'm sorry things didn't work out with you and Vanessa." She stops and shifts her weight to her other leg. "But no one's ever gonna work out if you don't let Iva go." Her tone is patient but stern.

I follow her eyes to the painting. "For all we know, she's married," she adds.

Her gaze eventually wanders back to me, and then she gives me that look she likes to give me. It's a mom look. I know it too well.

"She's not."

"What?"

I shake my head. "She's not married. I talked to her mom."

"You talked to her mom?"

"Yeah," I say, shrugging a shoulder.

She scrunches up her brow. "When would you have talked to her mom?"

"I, uh ... still had some of her things at the house." I pause and refit my cap over my head. "I just didn't know what to do with it all."

She keeps her stare on me for several, long seconds. "O-kay," she finally says. But her eyes are still narrowed, and now she's giving me a look—as if she doesn't really buy anything I'm saying.

I don't react to it.

"Dad says you're going on a trip on Monday," she says then, thankfully giving up on the last subject.

"Yeah."

"You don't have a race next weekend, right?"

"Right," I say.

"Then where are you going?"

I don't say anything at first, as I hook my thumb into my back pocket. "The coast. Just to get away, clear my head. That's all."

Her eyes bore a hole into mine. I know she's trying every which way she can to read my mind.

"Are you going with anyone?"

"No," I say.

"So, you're just going by yourself, then?"

"Yep."

Several more silent seconds drop to the floor. Meanwhile, she just keeps staring and studying.

"All right, then," she eventually says.

It looks as if she wants to say something else on the

topic, but she doesn't.

"Well, thanks again for watching Madeline."

"Anytime," I say.

She softly smiles, and then she disappears back into the hallway, leaving me alone again.

I start to turn, too, but my eye catches on the painting one, last time. And this time, I just get lost inside of it.

For a little while, we had each other. For a little while, we got to hold each other's hand and make out and make up and live fast. And best of all, we got to fall in love. And we got to fall in love twice. So, all in all, it was a pretty darn good run we had. And it doesn't matter that we didn't get sixty years or even twenty. In the end, we didn't need them. Someone smarter than us knew that our love, despite the little time we had together, was enough to last a lifetime.

Iva, you always said that a memory was enough to get us through the rest of our lives. You were right.

And you were wrong.

I needed more.

And that's why I think God gave me that one week in April. I would have loved to have more. But the thing is, I'm not so certain that one week, much less the weeks that followed, was ever originally written in the books for us. I think it was a gift. It's as if God himself brought you to me and said: Here's one more day.

One more day.

Here's one more day to get you through the rest of your life.

Because while I have no doubt a single memory can get some through life, it couldn't get me through mine. My soul ached for just one more.

And it still does.

And today, those memories float through my mind like a string of white lights. I remember you in the little things.

The Life We Almost Had

I remember you in the big things, too. Sometimes, I think about who we would be or where we would have gone. And other times, I see your smile or I hear your laugh. In those moments that pass between consciousness, like that split second before I cross the finish line or that pause just before the next song clicks over on the radio, I think about you. I think about that little house in Sweet Home and that first day I caught you in the window. I knew I had caught a glimpse of my future, right then and there. At the time, I just pictured a different kind of future—the one with you in it. But you still are—my future. I can't pluck you out of my pending thoughts no more than I can pluck you out of my prior ones.

And you'll always be that dream just out of reach— that one daydream I'll have every so often, and then just before it dissolves into the fog of the day, I'll catch myself thinking: What if?

My favorite what-if.

Iva, my heart still wants you. And I'm a little lost because of it, but no matter what happens in this life, I know we'll meet again. I have no doubt that we'll meet again, eventually. Someday, I'll see you in that window of that little brick house across the street, and you'll look up from your desk, with your hands full of color and oil, and you'll notice me. And you'll smile. And without saying a word, we'll both promise each other that this time ...

I briefly look at the floor and swallow down the ache in my throat before returning my eyes to the painting.

We'll promise each other that this time, we'll dream our dreams in Sweet Home. And with my cherry-red Chevelle and your little charcoal drawings tacked to the walls, we'll build the life we painted in our minds while in that little tree house that Angel's daddy built. And this time, we won't look back. This time, we won't look back on the life we almost had.

I reach into my back pocket and pull out the plane ticket I bought a couple days ago. And I look at the date and time stamped onto the piece of paper. And then my eyes wander to that final destination.

It's a coast, all right. It's just not a coast in the United States.

Iva, you might be my favorite what-if, but I was never really a fan of what-ifs.

Chapter Twenty-Six

Saturday

Present
Berlin

"**E**lliot, what do those kids have you working on now?"

I laugh and shove the last piece of lumber onto the bed of my truck.

"Tree house," I say.

Doug takes out his handkerchief from his back pocket, wipes his forehead and then bites down on the corner. "Spoiled rotten," he says, shaking his head.

"Yeah, well, don't get too jealous. I can build you one next."

He laughs. "Be careful, I just might take you up on

that offer." He shoves the handkerchief back into his pocket. "Can you rig up a TV into one of those things? And then can you camouflage the whole thing, so the wife and kids can't find me?"

I smile to myself and close the tailgate.

"So, when can I get that ride in your car?" he asks.

"When I know you can keep your lunch down at 200 miles an hour."

He gives me a long, thoughtful look.

"I'll work on that," he eventually says, nodding his head to the words.

I laugh, just as he's disappearing back into the lumberyard. Then I climb back into my truck. And right before I turn the key, I flip down the visor. Clipped to the edge is a photo of Iva and me. Nobody drives my truck, so nobody knows it's here. We took it the day she moved in—the day we got engaged. It's my favorite picture of us.

I smile at the photo, and then I check to make sure the ticket is still safely tucked behind it.

I see that it is. So, I flip the visor back up and head to Elin's.

I pull up to the house, and then I back into the driveway, so I can get the lumber to the backyard easier.

"Hey."

Elin comes around the corner of the house, just as I'm getting out of my truck.

"Hey," I say. "You tell the kids we're building the tree house when they get home?"

She doesn't answer me at first, so I stop what I'm doing and look at her.

She's got a big smile plastered to her face.

"What's wrong with you?"

She flashes me a funny look. "Why does something have to be wrong with me just because I'm smiling?"

I don't answer her. I just watch her a little more closely now.

"And yes, I told the kids," she says. "They're excited."

"Good," I say.

"But before you unload that, just come inside for a second."

I quickly find her again. "Why?"

"Berlin," she scolds, before turning. "Quit asking so many questions."

I watch her walk back around the corner of the house.

What in the hell is wrong with her?

I shake my head and then make my way to the back door.

"Elin, this better be good. You're acting like you've got that guy you like in here—that one from that movie where he goes to war and then he comes back and builds that big, old house."

"Ryan Gosling."

I hear the voice, and immediately, I look up.

Iva's standing in the kitchen.

And just like that, all my words are lost.

"Were you hoping for Ryan Gosling?" she asks, with a sweet smile.

I feel my mouth turning up into an awkward grin.

"I'm sorry," she says. "It's just me."

I still don't have any words. I almost feel as if I'm

dreaming, so I'm scared to say anything and wake myself up. But I'm also nervous. And my heart is about ready to beat right out of my chest. *Why is she here? Had she somehow found out? Is she here to intercept, to let me down easy?*

I just stare back at her. Her eyes are mesmerizing. I've forgotten how much I missed them—her. And after several more seconds, I finally find a small word.

"Hi," I say.

Her gaze briefly falters.

"Hi," she says, looking back up.

Neither of us moves. And neither of us says another word. I know time must keep going, but I could swear it's stopped.

"Berlin ..."

Her word is somber, and I immediately cut her off. "Iva, I just had to give us one more shot. I just ... I had to." I realize I'm rambling, but I keep going anyway. "We deserved one more chance; that's all. I know you have your life there ... I wasn't trying to interfere, necessarily ..."

"What?"

I find her blue-gray eyes. They look lost.

"The ticket I bought to see you," I say.

Her expression doesn't change.

"I ... I'm supposed to fly out Monday. I thought that was why you were here. I called your mom to get your address. I thought maybe she had told you."

"You bought a ticket to New Zealand?"

I slowly nod. "Yeah."

"Why did you buy a ticket to New Zealand?"

I take off my cap and refit it over my head. I'm beginning to think it's a nervous habit.

"To see you," I say. "And to tell you that ... I might

not be the best at figuring out how to maneuver my way around this life, but I know what I want. I always have."

Her face turns downward. And when her gaze flickers back up, there are tears in her eyes.

I hate that there are tears in her eyes.

"Berlin, what are we doing?"

I swallow and then slowly shake my head. "I don't know," I say. "Going a hundred miles an hour and not thinking about the consequences."

She laughs despite her tears. And then her eyes stumble upon mine.

"I couldn't do it."

"What?" I ask.

"I couldn't marry him."

For the first time, I look down at her left hand. There's no ring on her finger.

My stare travels the short distance to the floor, while a long, steady breath tunnels past my lips.

"Why are you here, Iva?" I ask, carefully looking back up.

She runs her fingers through her hair and shifts her weight to her other leg. She's stalling—maybe to gather her words; I don't know. I brace myself for whatever she's about to say.

"I left here to chase my dreams." She looks straight into my eyes. "And one day," she says, pausing to take a breath, "I just realized I had caught them all."

She shrugs her shoulders and attempts to smile.

"All but one," she adds.

A tear slides down her cheek. And in the quiet that follows, I slowly walk over to her and wipe the tear away.

This girl has my heart. She's the only one that ever

has.

I reach for her hand. She lets me take it.

"Iva, which dream is that?" I whisper near her ear, just barely getting the words out.

She closes her eyes, sending more tears racing down her cheeks. I wipe those away, too. Then, finally, she smiles, and it's not long, and her lips part: "The one with you in it."

Epilogue

Iva

"You ready?"

I look at my momma and smile.

"Yes," I say.

We're in the Church of Christ, down the street from where Berlin and I first fell in love.

They came back. The people came back to Sweet Home. They pushed the ghosts out, and they filled up all those unloved houses and boarded-up buildings. They filled them up again with light and conversation and laughter and life.

They started trickling in after Berlin bought The

Lighthouse Inn. But if you ask Berlin today, he'll tell you that it was Mr. Keeper and his lighthouse in the woods that guided them all home.

Either way, there are no boards covering up God's doors or windows anymore. In fact, today, blues and reds and yellows pour through the stained glass, making little rainbow prisms, which dance on every pew.

My momma smiles at me and then gathers my veil and gently lays it over my face.

"You look beautiful, honey."

"Thank you, Momma."

She squeezes me tight and then finds her place in the front of the procession.

I force out a breath and then look over at my daddy.

"Your momma's right," he says.

I interlock my arm with his, being careful not to bump my rose bouquet. "Thanks, Daddy."

"She's always been right," he adds.

I look back up at him, but his stare remains straight ahead.

"Maybe I should have listened to her a long time ago," he says.

At that, I lower my head and smile to myself. "It's okay, Daddy."

The processional music starts, and then one by one, the couples make their way down the aisle, until it's me and Daddy's turn.

I hear the song from the old pipe organ change, and then the ushers open the doors one final time.

And then I see him—that little boy from Sweet Home—that same little boy in that ugly brown seat on that yellow school bus; that same little boy standing in that window in Angel's old house across the street; that same little boy, pushing one hundred, behind the wheel of that cherry-red Chevelle. I see that same little, long-haired, wild boy—dressed in black—for whom my heart has always longed.

I squeeze my daddy's arm, and together, we walk down the aisle toward the man that little boy became.

I can't take my eyes off him. And the closer I get to that alter, the more the people surrounding us dissolve into the white walls of this little church. And soon, it's as if we're the only two souls left in this great, big world. Of course, it was always like that with me and him.

A big smile lights up Berlin's face, and immediately, I feel the tears welling up in my eyes.

I love this man from Channing, Kansas, just as much as I love that boy from Sweet Home. And I love all of him—every last, wild and crazy piece.

Daddy lifts my veil and kisses me on the cheek when we reach the alter. And then he turns to Berlin.

Berlin extends his hand, and for a long second, Daddy just looks at it. And in that moment, you could have heard a pin drop to these old floors. But then, just like that, Daddy reaches out and firmly grasps Berlin's hand.

I can see that Daddy's eyes are red. In all my years, I've never seen him cry.

They stay just like that, until a slow-moving smile gradually reaches Daddy's eyes. And then he nods. And Berlin nods, too. And then Daddy turns and finds his seat next to Momma in the front pew.

And then it's just Berlin and me.

He takes my hand and gently caresses the tops of my fingers, grazing the yellow diamond.

"You look so beautiful," he says.

I press my lips together, before letting go of a happy smile. Then, carefully, he leans into me and breathes a soft whisper into my ear: *Our greatest dreams are born under the stars.*

And with that, he looks up.

I follow his gaze to the ceiling, and I immediately see them.

High above us are my neon stars. I know they're mine because I recognize the ones with the blue stripes.

I try not to let the tears fall, as I find his eyes again. There's a look on his face now.

I know that look.

That look is love. That look is home.

I'm home.

It took nearly a decade, but I'm finally home. I'm finally where I belong.

And suddenly, I remember that little firefly that I sent up to heaven once upon a time. And I thank God for answered prayers.

For how close had we come?

How close had we come to going through this life with only half of our hearts?

I feel a tear slide down my cheek. Berlin wipes it away. And with his gentle touch, I hear my soul whisper to my heart: *We're free.*

We were spared.

Our souls will never again be forced to wander.

Our hearts will never again feel ache for the other.

And from now until forever, we will never have to look back and long for the life we almost had.

I am where my soul has always been—with this wild boy from Sweet Home. And today, my heart is full—and finally, at rest.

The End

I don't believe in endings, when it comes to you.

ACKNOWLEDGMENTS

Creating these characters and stories is a dream come true. So, as always, I thank God, first, for giving me the desires of my heart. Seriously, never stop dreaming! And never stop believing that God answers prayer! He can do more than we could ever imagine, and because He lives in us, we can, too! So, dream big.

And thank you to my amazing editors, beta readers and sources for all your time and contributions. Thank you especially to Donna, Calvin, Kathy, April, Sharon, Jon, Jesse and Mike. Thank you from the bottom of my heart. None of my stories would be what they are today without you!

And thank YOU, for reading. Through these stories I have had the wonderful privilege of getting to know so many of you. I feel truly blessed to have had that opportunity to meet you, talk with you and become amazing friends with so many of you. I know there are so many stories out there. Thank you for taking a chance on my small-town characters. Thank you for taking the ride with them—for pulling for them, for cheering them on. And as always, thank you for cheering me on! I am forever grateful.

Also, I would like to say a special thank you to all the amazing bloggers all over the world for their enthusiasm and loyal support and love of fairy tales. Many readers know my stories because of you. So, please know that we, as writers, are ever grateful for your commitment to literature.

I would like to thank my family as well, including Jack, Aurora, Levi and Augustus, who continue to be my biggest fans and greatest supporters. And thank you also to my friends and mentors, who are ever inspiring me along the way.

And because it always comes back to you, lastly, I would like to thank my best friend and husband, Neville. This has been an adventure from Day One, and you have been with me every step of the way. I can't imagine taking this journey with anyone else. I have heard it said that the sexiest thing someone can do for you is inspire you to think a thought you never thought possible. And honey, you do that for me every day. Thank you for encouraging me to dream. Thank you for believing in me. I love you—as sure as the sky is blue.

BONUS
A letter to Julia from Will
from the best-selling novel,
BUTTERFLY WEEDS

Jules,

I'm watching you stare out the window. Your hair is down. It falls over your shoulder as you lay your head against the sill. I'm sure you're dreaming. I swear, your mind never stops.

As your eyes follow the world outside that window, you think I'm writing another song.

And I am.

With every curve in your smile and every designful shift in your stare, I'm writing. In fact, in every word I've ever written, and in every word I will ever write, you'll be there—hidden in the letters scratched in ink on this lined paper, immortalized in the lyrics scrolling down the page and woven into the melody that plays in my heart. You'll be there, and yet, you won't ... because I could never personify you fully in words. Words will never be able to capture the smooth beauty of your whisper or the potency of your touch or even the way your eyes read my secret thoughts—even from afar off.

So, you think I'm over here, writing a song.
And I am.
You are my song, Jules.

I love you, my butterfly. A million times a million. And to the moon and back.

Love,
Will

Photo by Neville Miller

LAURA MILLER is the national best-selling author of the novels: *Butterfly Weeds, My Butterfly, For All You Have Left, By Way of Accident, When Cicadas Cry, A Bird on a Windowsill, The Life We Almost Had* and *The Dream*. She grew up in Missouri, graduated from the University of Missouri-Columbia and worked as a newspaper reporter prior to writing fiction. Laura currently lives in the Midwest with her husband. Visit her and learn more about her books at LauraMillerBooks.com.

ALSO BY LAURA MILLER
Butterfly Weeds
My Butterfly
For All You Have Left
By Way of Accident
When Cicadas Cry
A Bird on a Windowsill
The Dream
Love Story
Pay It Forward

"BEAUTIFUL."
~Aestas Book Blog on *Butterfly Weeds*

"THIS IS PURE ROMANCE AT ITS BEST."
~Kathy Reads Fiction on *My Butterfly*

"ONE OF MY FAVORITE LOVE STORIES EVER."
~A Novel Review on *For All You Have Left*

"Newcomers will have their faith in good literature restored."
~Books to Breathe on *By Way of Accident*

"Filled with small-town charm."
~2 Book Lovers Reviews on *When Cicadas Cry*

"SO GOOD."
~BF Bookies on *A Bird on a Windowsill*

★★★★★
~Southern Belle Book Blog on *By Way of Accident*

"Young love at its finest."
~Jesus Freak Reader on *A Bird on a Windowsill*

"A beautiful and charming love story."
~Cinco Garotas Exemplares on *When Cicadas Cry*

★★★★★
~Nancy's Romance Reads on *For All You Have Left*

"A STUNNING READ."
~Pretty Little Book Reviews on *A Bird on a Windowsill*

★★★★★
~Back Porch Romance Book Reviews on *My Butterfly*

"A BEAUTIFUL STORY."
~Livros Minha Terapia on *A Bird on a Windowsill*

"DEEPLY HEART-TOUCHING."
~*InkedPages* on *The Dream*